# THE CORNISH CAMPSITE MURDER

A Nosey Parker Cozy Mystery

FIONA LEITCH

One More Chapter
a division of HarperCollins*Publishers* Ltd
1 London Bridge Street
London SE1 9GF
www.harpercollins.co.uk
HarperCollins*Publishers*
Macken House, 39/40 Mayor Street Upper,
Dublin 1, Ireland, D01 C9W8

This paperback edition 2024
2
First published in Great Britain in ebook format
by HarperCollins*Publishers* 2024

A catalogue record of this book is available from the British Library

ISBN: 978-0-00-864726-1



Printed and bound in the UK using 100% Renewable Electricity
by CPI Group (UK) Ltd

This book contains FSC™ certified paper and other controlled sources to ensure responsible forest management.

For more information visit: www.harpercollins.co.uk/green

# Chapter One

I've never liked festivals. Don't get me wrong: I love music, and I love going to concerts, but I love going home afterwards even more.

The worst thing about festivals is the weather. Festival weather is predictable only in its unpredictability. It's either scorching hot, turning festivalgoers lobster pink and making them half crazed with dehydration; or the heavens open and the showground turns into a recreation of that bit in *The Never Ending Story* where the pony gets sucked into a bog (a scene that traumatised a generation of young moviegoers), only with Crocs rather than ponies, and mud instead of quicksand.

The other worst thing about festivals is having to listen to a load of bands you have no desire to see, because you only came to watch the headliners and of course they're on so late in the day that it's almost next week. I was persuaded (against my better judgement, but I was young and naive) to go and see Radiohead at Glastonbury in 1997. And of course there was a monsoon and I ended up getting trench foot, but worse was to come. We sought refuge from the downpour in the World Music tent, which was probably a mistake. I discovered that I wasn't really interested in Portuguese folk singing, although I have to admit I *was* fascinated by one song, a traditional ballad sung by the women of a small fishing village on the beautiful Mediterranean coast while their fishermen husbands were out at sea. Entitled 'Meu Marido Continua Olhando Para os Banhistas de Topless (e não se Concentrando nos Peixes)', which roughly translated into 'My Husband Keeps Looking at Topless Sunbathers (and not Concentrating on the Fish)', there was much wailing and gnashing of teeth, and a fair bit of tearing at their hair, but it was at least authentic and strangely catchy. I found myself singing 'Ignore as vadias de seios nus e leve suas sardinhas para casa' ('Ignore the bare-breasted floozies, and bring your sardines home') for a whole week afterwards. It was certainly better than the display of Inuit throat singing, performed by a bohemian-looking woman from Huddersfield, that came on after.

But actually, no, the *worst* worst thing about festivals is being forced to camp in close proximity to other people. Some festivalgoers are determined to wring every last drop of fun out of the experience, and while in theory I think, *Good for them!*, in real life I hate them. *It's 5am, when do you plan on going to sleep? You don't? Okay, then. I'll stay awake all night too. Don't mind* me, *I'm sure…*

So it was with a feeling of mild surprise and a fair bit of trepidation that I found myself heading to Wave Masters, a music, arts and surfing festival just along the coast from my home town of Penstowan. Wave Masters had started back in the 90s, and had primarily been a surfing contest. It had proved popular enough to grow from a one-day event to two, then three; a market had sprung up, offering the surfers fast food, handcrafted jewellery and clothing. And then buskers had turned up and started playing, even though nobody had asked them to; which had led to stages being erected and bands being invited, until now it was really all about the music, and the surfing was almost a second thought. And once you'd driven through the gates onto the campsite and parked your car, entry wristband fastened on tightly, there was no way out of the maze of vehicles and tents until the end of the festival…

'Cheers, mate.' Nathan thanked the steward on the gate and turned the van in the direction the hi-vis-clad man had indicated. He looked over at me. 'You all right, babe?'

'Yeah,' I said, watching out of the window as we passed the labyrinth of parked cars, bewildered festivalgoers weaving in out of them. If they were bewildered now, wait until later. 'Yeah,' I said. 'Only I was looking forward to this weekend being just you and me, not – LOOK OUT FOR THAT PLONKER ON THE UNICYCLE!'

The plonker on the unicycle, who had veered dangerously in front of the van, steered himself out of our path, where he stopped and glared at me. And then I remembered that I had the window open, and that he'd heard me call him a plonker. I stood by it, though. Germaine, my inherited Pomeranian and quite possibly the cutest dog in the entire universe (although I might be biased), obviously agreed with me, as she barked loudly at him and then snuggled back down on the seat between me and Nathan.

'I saw him,' said Nathan, mildly. 'He's wearing a red and blue jester's hat. I could hardly miss him.'

'It's even got bells on,' I said, unable to contain my disgust, but the jester hat-wearing, unicycling plonker had moved on. That was the *other* worst worst thing about festivals. They were full of people wearing ridiculous trousers, waistcoats (over bare chests) and stupid hats, riding unicycles or walking on stilts, and if you were unwise enough to catch their eye and not look away again in time, chances were they would come and juggle at you.

Nathan laughed and changed gear, easing the van up an incline and parking it in a spot marked by a couple of flags. We got out and stood admiring the view as Germaine, never one to let an opportunity pass her by, relieved herself. We'd certainly got the best spot, perched on top of the hill which looked out across the whole festival site. From here we could see the campsite to the right, and to the left, the field that was normally home to a herd of sheep but now – for this weekend, anyway – housed the main stage, with a couple of other big tents scattered around. And in front of us, down the hill and across the sand dunes, the sea, sparkling turquoise in the sun. I couldn't deny it was beautiful. I sighed. Nathan reached over and pulled me in for a hug.

'Come on, it's not *that* bad,' he said. I snuggled into him.

'I know it's not, it's just that this weekend was supposed to be you and me in Paris, wasn't it? Not you and me running a food truck in a muddy field.' Germaine yapped and I corrected myself. 'All right, you, me and the dog running a food truck in a muddy field.'

'It was you that said yes,' he pointed out, and I

couldn't deny that, either. A friend of mine from catering college, Sean, owned the food truck, and he made a good living going around all the festivals in the summer. He'd already booked his spot at Wave Masters, which was one of his best earners, when his daughter had told him she was getting married on a beach in Halkidiki and that she (of course) wanted him there. Sean had offered me the chance to take over the food truck for the weekend, in return for a share of the profits. I got the impression he'd already asked a few other people and was getting desperate. Besides, the extra money would be welcome.

'I know…'

'And it means you can keep an eye on Daisy and her mates,' he said. My almost sixteen-year-old daughter had been pestering me for the last six months about coming to the festival with her friend Jade, and Jade's older cousin Ellie. There was no way on God's green earth I was going to let them come without a responsible adult – Ellie had just turned eighteen and *seemed* sensible, but that was in front of the grown-ups; who knew what shenanigans she would encourage my sweet and innocent daughter to engage in once they were free of the parental shackles? But of course, the last thing any of them wanted was a responsible adult tagging along and cramping their style, plus all the responsible adults I knew could think of much better ways to spend the weekend than in a muddy field with a bunch of teenage girls.

'Yeah,' I said, knowing that he was right and that the weekend would probably be more fun than I was expecting, but slightly unwilling to let my grumpy mood go, 'if I ever manage to find her in amongst all this—'

'There you are!'

I turned to see Daisy standing behind me. Honestly, was *no one* going to let me carry on being moody?

'Where have you been? We got here ages ago.'

'We had to pick up some stock before we left,' I said. 'Where are you camped?'

'Down there,' said Daisy vaguely, waving her arm over at the campsite, which was already starting to resemble a Brazilian favela constructed of brightly coloured but poorly erected tents. A few campers swayed in amongst them, clutching bottles. I narrowed my eyes. There was already someone juggling.

'Rather you than me. We'll be all nice and cosy in the truck,' I said, although I actually had a few reservations about that.

'You wouldn't catch me dead sleeping in that,' she said firmly.

'What's the matter with it?'

Daisy looked at me like I was a bit simple. 'Mum, it's

called Pie Hard. It's got pictures of pies painted all over it.'

'And? We're selling pies, what should it have painted all over it? Noodles? Hot dogs?'

'Now you're just being silly,' said Daisy. 'I'll stick with Jade and Ellie in the tent, thank you very much.'

'All right,' I said. 'But no bringing boys back to the tent.'

Daisy rolled her eyes. 'Not much likelihood of that happening. Ellie prefers girls and Jade's asexual, although her mum reckons she's going through a phase and she'll change her mind when she meets the right bloke. But if you're straight, no one ever says it's just a phase you're going through, do they?' She had a point.

'No, that's true,' I said. 'Anyway, if you do change your mind and you want to sleep here instead, there's room for you – all of you.' Nathan cleared his throat and looked at me with an alarmed expression. I put up a placatory hand. 'Not inside the truck, obviously. But we've got an awning we can put up next to it. If there's heavy rain, or you're just scared…'

'Why would I be scared?'

'You never know. I mean, you can take the dog with you for protection if you like.' Daisy snorted. 'Okay, she's not much of a guard dog. But there are some weird people around…'

'Cooee!' We all whirled round to see my mum standing behind us.

'I see what you mean,' muttered Daisy.

'This is exciting, innit? I never been to a festival before. Not one like this, I mean. I've been to the harvest festival at the church—'

'I think that might be a bit different, Shirley,' said Nathan. 'Did you find your tent?'

'Jocasta says it's a yurt,' said Mum.

'She does, does she?' I said. I wasn't entirely sure I approved of Mum's new friend, who had moved to Penstowan almost a year ago. She was a retired lawyer who had left London to 'find herself', a process which seemed to involve crystals, scarves and metre upon metre of tie-dyed cheesecloth. She'd also found my mum, who had taken her under her wing and introduced her to the regulars at the Wednesday coffee morning (ten till twelve, Penstowan Methodist church hall and community centre, entry fee of £2, which entitled you to one cup of tea or instant coffee and two biscuits). In return Jocasta had introduced Mum to reiki and CBD oil. 'And where is Jocasta? Off scoring some patchouli?' Daisy and Nathan both snorted, but Mum either ignored the jibe or didn't hear it.

'She's setting up her foot massage stall,' she said. I shuddered. Having been in a tent full of fellow trench foot sufferers all those years ago at Glastonbury, the last thing I'd be doing at a festival would be going anywhere near people's toes. Mum noticed my look of disgust. 'Jodie, love, you're so narrow-minded.'

'I am NOT narrow-minded!' I spluttered, mildly outraged.

'Yes you are. You should let Jocasta have a go at your feet. I feel twenty years younger since I let her loose on my bunions,' said Mum. She sighed, and her face took on a dreamy expression. 'I never realised another woman's touch could bring me such relief,' she said. Nathan choked back a laugh, while I snorted like a hysterical pig.

'Is there something you want to tell us, Nana?' asked Daisy, completely straight-faced. 'I promise we won't judge you.'

But my elderly mother missed her chance to come out and was forced to stay in the closet (or the yurt), as we were interrupted by one of the festival marshals coming to check that we were set up okay. Mum tottered off to the glamping area, which was set back from the rest of the festival, away from us workers and plebs. Daisy wandered back to the rather less salubrious tent where Jade and Ellie were waiting, Germaine trotting beside her, sniffing at all the exciting smells coming from all the exciting people, her little doggy nostrils flaring as she passed a group of festivalgoers smoking suspiciously scented cigarettes.

The festival was very proud of its green credentials. There were solar panels and wind turbines all around the site, although with the great British summertime being as unpredictable as it was, I was betting there were probably some back-up generators hidden away under the main stage just in case. Here in the food stall area, a dedicated row of solar panels had been erected, along with a complex array of tubes which piped clean water to each cooking site; a godsend, as it meant we didn't have to keep the engine or a petrol-powered generator running to keep the fridge on, or rely on bottled water. There were three food trucks, including ours, and four or five stalls were also being set up to serve food. It looked like festivalgoers would have plenty of choice. As well as our pies and pasties, one of the trucks would be serving burgers and hotdogs, while the other dished up organic ice cream and homemade fruity ice lollies. I already had my eye on the Cornish clotted cream vanilla and strawberry sundae. It was too early to tell yet what food the stalls would be selling – they were still setting up – but one of them had already started cooking, and the smell of cumin, coriander, onion and garlic wafted across to us. Oh dear. It was still fairly early in the day and I was already feeling hungry. Good job I'd given up diets years ago.

The rest of the morning (not that there was much of it left by now) flew by as we set to work. I was used to working with Nathan, of course, but not in a kitchen; I'd helped him (or 'stuck my nose in', as some people might uncharitably – and more accurately – call it) with several murder investigations since moving back to Cornwall. I'd even been given a trial as an auxiliary detective a year earlier, as I'd served as a sergeant in the Metropolitan Police for almost twenty years, and I wasn't exactly an amateur. That had been a weird but ultimately very useful experience. Weird because Nathan, the love of my life (after Daisy), had been my boss, which was difficult for both of us; and useful, because it had confirmed in my own mind that I had been absolutely right to leave the police force in the first place. Daisy had begged me to quit after a nasty terrorist incident when she was ten, and I'd remembered how I used to worry about my dad when I was her age. Eddie Parker had been Chief Inspector of the police at Penstowan, which in those days had been a pretty sleepy place with very little serious crime. My own daughter had had far more to worry about than I had, so how could I put her through that? She'd been so relieved when I quit, and so angry with me when I'd put myself in harm's way again by rejoining.

I'd handed my notice in at the end of the trial period, and I'd kept my word and not done any investigating since. Admittedly it helped that there had only been two suspicious deaths since then, and both guilty parties had done such a lousy job of covering their tracks that they were practically wandering around with flashing neon signs above their heads saying 'I DID IT!' I'd let Nathan handle them on his own.

And now he was helping me in the kitchen, or rather the tiny work area of the truck. We were cooking with gas (literally, rather than motivationally), so after hauling the heavy gas bottle into place I turned on the oven; Sean had pre-made all the pies, which were now residing in the fridge, and all we had to do was cook them.

'Do you think we've got enough?' asked Nathan sardonically, holding the fridge door open. It was crammed with pies, plus there was an emergency stash of ready-made pastry and fillings in the freezer section in case we ran out. I laughed.

'Touch and go, I reckon,' I said. 'The oven's nearly warmed up. Let's get out that first tray and egg wash them.'

'What on earth is "egg wash"?'

'Er, egg. Beaten. You brush it on the pastry to stop it burning and make it go a nice golden colour.' I looked at him. 'Seriously? You didn't know that?'

'I have never made a pie in my life,' said Nathan. 'Eaten a few, though.' He patted his annoyingly flat stomach. I scoffed.

'Oh *please*. They're never going to sing, "Who ate all the pies" at you, are they? Even after living with a chef for two years you're still fit as a butcher's dog.'

'I'm just trying to keep in trim for the wedding,' he said.

'That's not for another year,' I pointed out. We'd been engaged now for about ten months, which was already longer than I'd expected. We'd originally talked about just having a nice, quiet wedding, which would've only have taken a couple of months to organise, but it had somehow snowballed into something massive. I was half-excited about getting to wear a fancy frock and have all eyes on me as I wafted down the aisle, and half-terrified that I would trip over in front of everybody, or fart while I said my vows, or have spinach in my teeth in the photos. But then my first (ill-fated) marriage had taken place in a grotty registry office with just my parents and my mother-in-law as witnesses, so I was taking it as a good sign that *this* marriage would start in nicer surroundings.

But this was not a time to be thinking about weddings. There were pies to be sold! We got the first lot in the oven, and soon the delicious smell of buttery pastry filled the truck. It was divine torture, and from the moans Nathan made every time he opened the oven door to check on them he obviously felt the same.

'Stop opening the door!' I told him off. 'I know they smell amazing. Just remember we will have to check one of each flavour for quality control purposes...' He grinned at me and shut the oven door again.

The side of the food truck folded down to make a counter, and once the pies were out, they were placed on display in a heated cabinet, where hungry passersby would be able to see them and, more importantly, smell them. I went outside to check how they looked (fabulous), and then took a piece of chalk and started to write up the menu on the blackboard on the side of the truck.

'Jodie? Is that you?'

I turned round and came face-to-face with Carol, a lady in her fifties who I'd done a dinner party for a few months ago. She'd just moved into Hilltop Farm with her husband, lan, although the name (Hilltop Farm, not Ian) was a bit of a misnomer, because there wasn't much of the farm left other than the beautiful house, which stood on a hill (obviously) overlooking Penstowan and the sea beyond. From what I could gather, neither Carol nor her husband worked anymore, but they seemed very well off. I'd been given a pretty big budget for their housewarming dinner party for eight, which had made a nice change. So much of my work was catering for parties, and all most people wanted was a buffet. They weren't usually very adventurous, and sausage rolls, sandwiches and quiches tended to feature heavily. Even weddings with sit-down meals were quite 'safe', as the guests usually covered several generations, which meant I had to cook food that would appeal to all of them.

Carol and Ian wanted something 'a bit posh'. I did beef carpaccio and teriyaki-glazed scallops for starters, crispy-skinned duck breast with fondant potatoes for the main, and a decadent dessert platter of berries, meringues, biscotti and cubes of sponge cake, with a massive bowl of chocolate fondue to dip it all in. Carol had asked me to cook nine portions of everything, which I assumed was in case of disaster (dropping a plate, burning a scallop), but it actually turned out that she wanted to make sure I got to eat too, although of course I stayed in the kitchen. That had really surprised me, as I knew another catering college alumna who had taken a job as a private chef, and the stories she told me would make your hair curl. She hadn't been allowed to eat any of the family's food, even when she'd gone away on holiday with them and it had been very difficult to buy her own. She wasn't allowed to eat until they'd finished their dinner either, and as they didn't tend to eat until at least 8pm it was often midnight before she sat down to eat her own meagre plate of beans on toast.

'I didn't know you had a food truck,' said Carol, squinting at the menu I'd just written. I noticed she was wearing a faded Nirvana T-shirt; I hadn't had her down as a rock chick. 'Or that you were such a diehard Bruce Willis fan. No pun intended.'

I laughed. 'It's not mine, I'm doing a friend a favour. He told me his dream was to have a whole fleet of these. So truck number one is Pie Hard, number two would be Pie Harder…'

'And then Pie Hard With a Vengeance, and A Good Day to Pie Hard…' finished Carol. 'That's brilliant! So cheesy. What are these flavours, though? What's a Bruce Willis pie?'

'Beefsteak,' I said. 'The Nakatomi Plaza is teriyaki chicken, and the Hans Gruber is bratwurst and sauerkraut.' Carol wrinkled her nose. 'Yeah, apparently he doesn't usually sell many of those, but it tastes nicer than it sounds. And of course we do steak and kidney, chicken and mushroom, we've got a vegan one with curried chickpeas in it…'

'They smell amazing.' Her phone buzzed, and she pulled a face but didn't look at it. 'That'll be Ian saying, "Hurry up, Caz!" I'll have to come back later and try a Nakatomi Plaza. Good to see you again.'

'And you,' I said. As she left I became aware of Nathan standing behind me. I turned round to see him staring at me in amazement. 'What?'

'Do you know who that was?' he asked. I rolled my eyes.

'Er, yeah. I did that dinner party for her and her husband.'

'You mean *that's* the Carol you cooked for? Why didn't you say?'

'I did! I told you, I cooked for that nice new couple that had moved in, Carol and Ian—'

'Carol Harper!'

'No, Carol and Ian Holt.'

'That's her married name.' Nathan looked at me like I should know what he was talking about, until suddenly the penny dropped.

'Wait – Carol *Harper*? As in, Caz Harper, bass player with The Burners and girl power idol before girl power was even a thing?'

'Yup.'

'And that means her hubby is Ian the keyboard player? Oh my God, I had *such* a crush on both of them when I was a teenager!' I turned and stared in the direction Carol – *THE Caz Harper!!!* – had gone, but I couldn't see her. 'Holy cow, to think I didn't know who they were – I mean, they do look a lot different now – but I was in their *house*!'

'Yeah, I think it's probably just as well you didn't,' said Nathan, grinning. 'I've never seen you fan girl over anyone before. It's pretty funny…'

# Chapter Two

By about half past three we'd run out of pies. We hadn't baked a full day's worth, as we hadn't been properly set up and open to the public until eleven-thirty, but still, we'd sold out earlier than I'd expected. There wasn't even a Hans Gruber pie left. I *could* have put another load in the oven when we started to run low on Bruce Willises, but to be honest we were both already starting to get sick of the sight of pies, which didn't bode well for the fact that we had another two full days of the festival to get through yet.

As well as that, although our vantage point overlooking the rest of the festival meant we were at lower risk of potential jugglers and plonkers on unicycles, we were also further away from all the fun everyone else seemed to be having. I kept hearing snatches of music, wafting over to us on the breeze, and I was starting to feel left out despite my deep dislike of festivals.

Nathan handed over the last pie and turned to me with a pleading look on his face. I laughed.

'All right,' I said, 'let's yippee-pie-yay out of here…'

We cleaned down the surfaces (although there wasn't much to do, as I always try to clean as I go and I'd instilled the same ethos into Nathan), then had a quick wash in a bucket of cold water and changed into fresh T-shirts that didn't have a whiff of sauerkraut or teriyaki chicken about them. We wandered hand in hand past the other food stalls and then down into the festival site proper.

It was good-natured mayhem. There was a fair smattering of family groups, hippie-looking parents smiling indulgently at their anarchic toddlers, who ran around completely out of control and got in everyone's way, but no one minded because they were cute or drunk (I mean the toddlers were cute, not drunk – the people who didn't mind were the ones who were drunk, not Little Timmy with home brew in his sippy cup or anything). There was a surprising (to me) number of middle-aged ravers and stoners, with Happy Mondays T-shirts and decent camping set-ups, because they were old hands at this and knew that it was worth spending a lot of money on a really good inflatable mattress to ensure you were in a fit state to dance the next day. And then there were the youngsters, the ones who had thrown off the parental yoke (for a few days, at least) and were going to do (and take) *everything*. I realised with a shudder of horror that this group included my own daughter.

We watched a young man in his early twenties dancing by himself to God only knew what tune, because it obviously wasn't the same one the band currently onstage were playing. He was totally away with the Cornish piskies, but at least he looked happy.

'Don't worry,' said Nathan, reading my mind. 'Daisy and her mates are sensible. They won't end up like that.'

'No,' I said. I hoped he was right. Daisy and I had had both 'the sex talk' and 'the drug talk' recently. I'd learnt a lot. 'I told her that it was natural to want to experiment, but you have to be careful. I said if she was going to take any drugs, let someone else take them first and see how they are after an hour…'

Nathan laughed. 'That's a very pragmatic approach.'

'If she really wants to try them, I can't stop her,' I said.

'No. I more or less told her the same thing.' Nathan nodded across the field, to where two large tents had been erected off to one side, slightly away from the madness. 'I told her if her friends bought anything, they should take it to the drug-testing tent first so they can see what's in it.'

'Only she might not do that, because Debbie's one of the volunteers.' My friend Debbie, a nurse from Manchester, had moved to Penstowan with her husband Callum, an old school chum of mine, not long after I had. We'd hit it off immediately.

'And she thinks that if she took some drugs in to be tested, Debbie would tell you?'

'Yes. Which, to be fair, she might…'

We walked on, heading away from the campsite and towards the stage. A sea of music lovers stood between us and the band, who I didn't recognise, but then they could've been having number one hit singles (were they even a thing these days?) every week for the last three years and I still wouldn't have known who they were. I quite liked their music, though.

'They're good, aren't they?' said Nathan, nodding towards the stage.

'Yeah, who are they?'

'No idea.' He grinned at me. 'At least they don't look like they're about to break into some hardcore Inuit throat singing at any moment.'

'Praise the Lord for that!'

'Don't let Carmen hear you say that,' said a voice behind us. We turned to see a sweaty but happy-looking man in a Foo Fighters T-shirt. Tony Penhaligon was my oldest friend in the world. We'd sat next to each other on our first day of school, and I'd not managed to get rid of him since. Not that I wanted to. He'd obviously been dancing and having a whale of a time, although to be fair 'dancing' was probably pushing it a bit. Jigging about with more enthusiasm than skill was probably a more accurate way to describe Tony's gyrations. 'If Carmen hears you saying stuff like that she'll have you baptised and helping her out in the peace tent before you can say, "I'm an atheist". Shirley was in there earlier.'

'Mum was?' I was concerned. 'Is she all right?'

'Yeah, yeah, she was just a bit lost.'

'Spiritually or physically?' asked Nathan. Tony laughed.

'Bit of both, I reckon... Nah, she just couldn't find her mate. That weird middle-class hippie woman? I think she was a bit overwhelmed by all the noise and the people, but Carmen sat her down and got her a cup of tea.'

'Is she still in there?'

'No, her friend came and found her. I think they'd agreed to meet up there if they got split up.'

'Oh right. I told Daisy to do that, too – to go and see Aunty Carmen if she needed any help or if it all got too much and she wanted somewhere to chill out for a bit.' I grinned. 'I think she's a bit freaked out that there are so many of her "aunties" all over the festival, isn't she, Nath?'

'Yeah…' said Nathan, vacantly. He was watching a couple of nervous, geeky teenage boys across the field. I followed his gaze and saw them furtively hand some money over to a taller, older bloke, who was dressed in a hoodie despite the temperature being in the mid-twenties. He handed something back to one of them, looking around first to make sure they weren't being watched. He obviously didn't look hard enough, though, as he didn't spot me and Nathan.

'Nath…don't get involved…' I said. 'You're not on duty.'

'Don't worry,' he said. 'I'm on leave. I'm not ruining my holiday for them.' And then he set off towards them. I exchanged glances with Tony and then hurried after him.

The bloke in the hoodie had already sauntered off, but the two younger boys were excitedly (and not very discreetly) checking their purchase. Nathan approached without them even noticing. He slapped a hand on each of the boys' shoulders.

'All right, lads?' he said, his Liverpudlian accent sounding stronger than usual. He always seemed to exaggerate it – or maybe stop suppressing it – when he was trying to relax people. It didn't work though, as both boys leapt about a foot off the ground. 'What you got there, then?'

'Nothing!' said the first boy, who had a terrible case of acne, although by the smell of him it was nothing a good wash with a bar of soap and some Clearasil wouldn't have cured.

'What's it to you? You filth?' asked the other, who was slightly braver. Nathan grinned.

'I am actually, as it goes.' Both boys shrank, obviously hoping to sink into the rough grass beneath their feet. 'Now, I *should* arrest you for possession, and I should get you to grass your drug dealer mate up, too. But you're in luck. I'm on me holidays and I don't want to be bothering with scallies like you. What's your names?'

'Spencer,' said the spotty one quickly. The other boy shot him an angry look. 'What?'

'You shouldn't have told him your real name, you muppet!'

Behind them, Tony and I looked at each other and suppressed sniggers. I had seen this sort of conversation so many times during my time on the beat in London, and it felt weird to see it again here, but also sort of reassuring. Teenagers, it seemed, were the same wherever they lived.

'All right Spencer, see that tent over there?' Nathan pointed to the drug-testing marquee. 'I want you to go over there and tell them that DCI Withers sent you to get your pills tested. I want you to tell the nice people in there your name. And then once you know what's in there, and they've told you whether it's safe to take them, the rest is up to you.'

'You're not going to arrest us?' The slightly more streetwise boy, despite his bravado, looked relieved. 'Or confiscate them?'

'What do I want with what appears to be—' Nathan peered into the other boy's hand at the tablets he was holding '—a couple of aspirin and some indigestion tablets?'

'Indigestion tablets? But we paid—'

'Shut up, Spencer!' hissed the other boy.

'Off you go then, lads,' said Nathan, standing back to let them pass. They started to shuffle off, but he put out a warning hand to stop them. 'The lady who runs the tent is a friend of mine, and I will be asking her later if she saw you. And if she didn't…' He didn't finish the sentence, letting it trail off menacingly. I looked down at the ground so the boys wouldn't see me laugh.

'Bloody hell, mate!' said Tony admiringly, as they left. 'That was brilliant! You proper put the wind up them! Have they really just bought indigestion tablets?'

'Probably not,' I said. 'But they'll definitely go and get

them tested now, won't they?' We all laughed. 'What about the dealer, though?'

Nathan shrugged. 'I told you, I'm on holiday.'

'Who are you and what have you done with the real Nathan Withers?'

He grinned. 'I'm not *completely* on holiday. I'll pass his description on to the security guards and they can keep an eye on him. Although to be fair, it feels a bit pointless, doesn't it? If they arrest him, people will just buy their drugs off another dealer. He won't be the only one here.' He furrowed his brow. 'I didn't actually get that much of a look at him, did you?'

'Mid-thirties, about six foot, tanned, dark blond hair, I think – it was a bit hard to see with his hood up—' I stopped as I realised Tony and Nathan were both looking at me. 'What? It was my job for twenty years. You don't just turn it off, you know.'

'Obviously not! Did you get a look at his hoodie? It had a pattern or something running down one sleeve, but I didn't see it properly.' Nathan ran a hand up and down his right arm, demonstrating.

'It was a snake,' said Tony. 'A curly green and yellow snake. The head was up by his shoulder, and it had something in its mouth…'

'A rose!' I said. 'A red rose.'

'Okay,' said Nathan, 'I'll pop over to the security

point and tell them, then it's up to them what they want to do about it. I'm a civilian this weekend.'

Nathan left me and Tony to dance while he went to find a security guard. Tony headed through the crowd towards the stage, but I grabbed his arm to stop him.

'There's too many people,' I said. I'd never been fond of crowds, but my time in the Metropolitan Police force had made me really hate them. Bad things can happen in large crowds. 'Let's head over that way instead.' I pointed to an area at the side of the stage, where there were fewer people and the leaping around was rather less frenetic.

'Lightweight,' said Tony, but he let me lead him into a comparatively quiet spot, where we wouldn't get jostled and where it would be easier for Nathan to find us again.

A safety barrier ran along the front of the stage, to discourage over-enthusiastic fans clambering up to join the bands or start crowd surfing. The barrier curved past us and then stopped, joining onto a tall, temporary white fence, which cordoned off the backstage area. There was a gate into it, guarded by a security officer with a very serious set of muscles and a facial expression to match, with a sign on it saying, 'Artists and Crew Only'. Next to it, plastered onto the fence, was a billboard with the weekend's acts on it. Tony hooked a thumb towards it.

'So who do you reckon that lot are?' he asked.

'Who? What lot?'

'This lot here…' He tapped the billboard and read it aloud. '"Special Guests, The Burnouts". I hope they're not some dodgy Burners tribute band.'

I looked at him, the ghost of teenage Jodie beginning to jump up and down inside me. 'Oh my God, Tone, that's not a tribute band, that's them!'

'The Burners? What, playing here?' He shook his head. 'Doubt it.'

'No, no, it's true! It must be. You know that couple who bought Hilltop Farm…'

'My mum's met them. She reckoned they're bankers or something that made a load of money, retired early and moved down here.' He had the slightly disapproving tone of someone who had lived in the same town all his life and couldn't understand why anyone would do differently. He'd never really even got why I'd moved to London as soon as I was old enough.

'Well, she's wrong. It's Caz Harper and Ian Holt! From The Burners! I did their catering!'

He looked at me, astonished. 'What? Why didn't you tell me?'

'Because I only just realised it was them myself. Nathan recognised her this morning.'

'You mean *CAZ HARPER* is actually here?' He looked around wildly as if he'd be able to spot her lurking in the crowd, but of course she was nowhere to be seen. 'Caz Harper! Bloody hell. I had some special times with that poster of her on my bedroom wall, I can tell you.'

I grimaced. 'Anyway, she came by the food truck earlier. She didn't say why she was here, I assumed she was just having fun, you know, but – The Burnouts? It's gotta be them, hasn't it? But why the name change?'

'I dunno. But they split up years ago, didn't they? Maybe it were all very acrimonious and they're not allowed to use the name.'

'Acrimonious?' I laughed. 'Blimey, someone's swallowed a dictionary.'

'That's what going out with a woman who speaks Latin for her job does to you,' grinned Tony. 'I've had to up me game and learn big words and everything…'

Nathan found us, and he brought a friend: Debbie, fresh from her stint in the drug-testing tent. I opened my mouth to greet her, but she stopped me.

'Before you ask,' she said, 'I haven't seen Daisy or her mates, and I wouldn't tell you if I had. Patient confidentiality.'

'I wasn't going to ask!' I said, indignantly, but not as indignantly as I might have done, because I had indeed had it in mind to bring up, casually, in conversation later. Something like, 'Yeah, this band are great, aren't they? By the way, have you come across my daughter snorting anything yet?'

We had a bit of a dance and a few drinks, until the jigging about began to cause warning twinges in my bladder.

'Where's the loo?' I asked Debbie, looking around. She grimaced.

'The nearest ones are over there, but they're disgusting.' She pointed to the far side of the field, where a row of blue plastic Portaloos stood like a smelly Tardis army. 'The ones near your food truck are probably better, there are fewer people around there.'

'I might not make it that far,' I said, hopping about. I looked at the fence behind me, and the gate with its 'Artists and Crew Only' sign on it. The gate was open, and the serious-looking security guard was nowhere to be seen. An idea formed in my mind. 'I bet the toilets back there are nicer,' I said, nodding over to the backstage area.

'You can't go in there!' said Tony, shocked. Nathan rolled his eyes.

'Nice one, mate. Now she's definitely going in.'

I glanced around surreptitiously but no one official was looking in our direction. 'Right, I'm off to pee with the stars.'

'Hell yeah,' said Debbie. 'Wait for me.'

We scuttled through the gate and then headed around behind the stage, where we stopped and looked at each other before bursting into laughter. It was surprisingly quiet back there – or at least nowhere near as noisy as I'd expected it – but then the massive stack of speakers front of stage was pointing in the opposite direction, towards the crowd. A passing stagehand looked at us, eyebrows raised, but I flashed my festival vendor's lanyard at him and muttered something vague about delivering pies. He shrugged and carried on with his task.

There was another tall, white fence to one side, sectioning off part of the backstage. On it was one sign saying, 'VIP Area', and another saying, 'Toilets'. Both had arrows underneath them, pointing the same way. Debbie and I exchanged glances.

'I'm a VIP,' I said. 'It's Very Important that I Pee, and soon.' We followed the arrows and there, praise your deity of choice, was a row of toilets. We both nipped inside a cubicle and enjoyed a brief moment of relative peace while we relieved ourselves. The peace didn't last, however, as I could hear a kerfuffle begin outside.

'Get your bloody hands off me!' A man's voice, furious but strangely muffled. I opened the toilet door a crack – I'd pulled my pants up by now, so there was no danger of me flashing anyone – and peered out to see a couple of security guards bundling a struggling man away. He looked vaguely familiar; in his fifties or sixties, a bit grizzled and in need of a shave. He was wriggling around, trying to get away from the security guards, but they had a firm grip on him – one of them had him in a half-nelson – and were managing to drag him out of the VIP area despite his best efforts. Another man followed, an exasperated expression on his otherwise rather good-looking face.

'You're just making it worse for yourself,' he said. 'How did you *think* they'd react? This is not the way to do it. Give them time to calm down and let me talk to them, smooth things over...'

Suddenly Caz Harper burst round the corner of the VIP area, storming along in a foul mood.

'I don't bloody believe you, Lee!' she spat, ferociously. I was quite taken aback and shrank back inside the toilet cubicle. I still left enough of a crack to see out, though; I wasn't *that* shocked. 'As if the court order wasn't bad enough, you rock up here and start on us! We're not playing any of your bloody songs!'

'Caz – it's not like that!' said the struggling man – Lee. The lead singer all those years ago had been called Lee, I remembered. He'd left the band, and that had been the catalyst for that acrimonious split Tony had mentioned earlier. But he'd been young and cool and the epitome of rock 'n' roll; *this* man looked like a hobo. They couldn't be the same person, could they?

'No? Then what *is* it like?' Caz folded her arms and tapped her foot in the traditional come-on-then-I'm-waiting pose. Lee opened his mouth to speak again, but the good-looking-but-exasperated man held up his hands in the equally traditional everyone-calm-the-hell-down manner. Caz rolled her eyes. 'What? Let him speak, Dougie. I want to hear this.'

'No, this isn't the time or the place for this. I don't want any of you saying something you might regret later on.' The other man, who I assumed was Dougie, was trying to be the voice of calm and reason but I wasn't sure it was working.

Another man appeared, this time someone I recognised: Ian Holt, keyboard player and Carol's – I mean, Caz's – husband. He reached out and grabbed his wife, firmly but with care, and held her still. 'Leave it, Caz, he ain't worth it.' He looked at his former bandmate and shook his head, an expression of contempt on his face. 'State of you, mate.'

'That's enough! Go away and take a moment, all of you,' said Dougie. But that was a bit of a redundant suggestion as Ian was already leading his wife away, and the security guards had redoubled their grip on Lee's arms, dragging him unceremoniously out of the VIP area.

I quietly let out a breath, not wanting anyone to realise I was there.

Dougie stayed where he was, watching the still struggling ex-rock star's undignified exit. He took a deep breath, clenching and unclenching his fists, and it looked to me like he was forcing himself to relax. And then in the cubicle next to me, Debbie sneezed. He turned towards the toilets as the two of us left our hiding places. I nodded to him in greeting.

'All right, mate?' said Debbie casually, as if we hadn't just witnessed all that drama. Dougie looked at us in surprise, obviously wondering how much of that we'd heard (all of it).

'Who are you? This area is for the performers only,' he said.

I held out my official lanyard, covering the bit that said 'Food Vendor'. 'We're just testing the toilets, guv. Gotta make sure they're fit for purpose.'

'Or poopose,' said Debbie. We both snorted.

He opened his mouth and I waited for him to tell us off or call the security guards back. But after a brief hesitation he relaxed and laughed.

'Go on. I've not seen you,' he said. 'Just for your sheer cheek.'

'Cheers, guv,' said Debbie. She peered round him, trying to get a look into the VIP area. 'Any free beers back there? Or bowls of M&Ms with all the blue ones taken out?'

'Sorry about her,' I said, grabbing her arm. 'She's been in the drugs tent all morning and I think the fumes have got to her.'

'Oi!'

Dougie smiled, showing us a row of perfect white teeth. *He* certainly didn't look like a hobo, or an ageing rock star for that matter. 'I'd love to invite you ladies backstage, but things are a bit fraught at the moment.' He gave a little self-deprecating shrug. 'Artistic temperaments and nerves.'

'No worries, we were only here for the soft loo paper,' I said, and then dragged Debbie away before she could talk us into trouble.

## Chapter Three

'You'll never guess what we just saw!' said Debbie, excitedly, and proceeded to launch into a blow-by-blow account of the fracas by the VIP toilets.

'Lee Roskill was here?' asked Nathan. 'I thought he died of a drug overdose years ago.'

'If he did, he's pretty lively for a corpse,' I said. 'It looked like it was going to descend into fisticuffs at any moment. Caz said something about a court order.'

'That must be why they're playing under a different name,' said Nathan. 'He must own the rights to The Burners or something. But didn't he write all their songs?'

I shrugged. 'I thought he and Caz wrote them together. She said they weren't going to play any of his, so there must be a few she wrote on her own, or the others wrote.'

'We'll find out soon enough,' said Tony. 'It looks like they're on next.'

'Brilliant!' I said, pulling out my phone and holding it up high. 'But I'd better check up on Daisy first, if I can get a signal…'

'No need,' said Debbie. 'Isn't that her over there?'

Daisy was indeed deep in the crowd, dancing next to Jade and Ellie. But there was one of their group missing.

'Where's the dog?' I cried, fighting my way over to her. Daisy turned to me with an exasperated look on her face.

'Oh hello, Mother, yes I'm fine, thank you for asking…'

'Of course you're fine, it's only been six hours since I last saw you. But you're supposed to be looking after the dog.'

'Calm the farm, Mum, I left her with Nana.'

'And how does Nana feel about that?'

'Well, I know she's always demanding food and needing a wee, but…'

'That's no way to talk about your grandmother.' We laughed. 'No, the dog can be a bit high maintenance around crowds. Nana's all right having her, yeah? I didn't want to bring her, but it was too short notice to get a kennel booked.'

'You can't leave Nana in a kennel!'

'Funny girl. But she doesn't mind being lumbered with the dog, does she?'

'Nana said she's happy to have her until eight o'clock, because her and Jocasta are going to a twilight primal scream circle and she thinks the wailing might set Germaine off howling.'

'Fair enough. Am I allowed to dance with you and your mates for a bit, or am I cramping your style?'

'I was cramping her style,' I said two minutes later, when I returned to where Nathan and Debbie were waiting. Tony had gone to meet Carmen, who had done enough vicar-ing for the day and was going to take off her dog collar and let her hair down.

There was a roar from some of the older members of the crowd – and bemusement from the younger ones – as Caz, Ian, and the rest of their band appeared onstage. I'd seen them once, years ago, and they'd bounded around with so much energy then; I wondered if they'd be quite so lively now.

'Hello Cornwall, we're The Burnouts!' Caz grabbed the microphone and peered at the audience. 'I'd like to dedicate this song to my old friend Lee…'

The band launched into one of their hits – obviously

not one written by their ex-lead singer. Caz, who had previously only sung backing vocals, had a much better voice than I remembered; not exactly a diva, but a proper rock and roll growl.

'Woah, she is *not* happy with him,' said Nathan, mildly. 'Listen to the words…'

*'When I first met you, baby, it was loathing at first sight.*
*You asked me for my number, I asked you for a fight.*
*When hate comes knocking at your door there's nowhere you can hide,*
*So save the last dance just for me and I'll meet you outside.'*

'I wouldn't want to be Lee Roskill right now,' said Debbie, and we all nodded in agreement as, onstage, Caz reached the chorus with a snarl:

*'I got this feeling running round my brain.*
*These thoughts of you are driving me insane.*
*So please, may God forgive me, but it's true –*
*I don't know why I hate you, but I do!'*

The band played for almost two hours. There weren't many of their other hit songs, presumably because Lee had written or co-written most of them, but the crowd still seemed to enjoy their set. There were a few new original songs, which weren't bad, but the playlist was mostly made up of cover versions of the songs the band had grown up listening to – they did a cracking version of 'Just Like Heaven' by The Cure – and newer stuff that fit the same kind of vibe as their own music did. Ian howled his way through 'Tick Tick Boom' by The Hives, while the rest of the band leapt around as if it were still the 90s, although I did notice the drummer grimace at one point; none of them were quite as fit in their fifties as they had been in their twenties, but then who was? They looked to be having a whale of a time, though, the upset of the earlier confrontation forgotten.

They finished to loud applause and the vibration of my phone in my shorts pocket as a text came in (not that the band would've felt it). I looked at the screen; Mum had sent me a text, some time ago by the looks of it, but the signal here was so rubbish it had only just come through.

'Uh oh,' I said, looking at the time. 'It's almost eight o'clock. I'd better go and get the dog. Do you want to come back to the truck with me or stay and see the next band?' I asked Nathan and Debbie.

'I've had enough,' said Nathan. 'I want something to eat, a cup of tea, and a nice sit down.'

'All right, Grandad,' said Debbie, grinning. 'But actually I like the sound of that, too.'

We headed up the hill to the posh camping area, where the yurts stood overlooking the sea. The view from here was even better than from our truck.

'Oh thank God you're here,' said Mum, gratefully. 'Jocasta has been fussing around like an old woman, worrying about getting to the scream circle in time.' She rolled her eyes. 'I wasn't too fussed about going meself, but I could definitely do with a good scream now…'

'Oh dear,' I said. 'Are you going to be all right sharing a tent with her, or is she winding you up too much?'

'Of course I'll be all right, she's my friend,' she said, passing me Germaine's lead. 'I said I'd go with her and I didn't want to let her down. This New Age stuff is fascinating, innit?' Germaine gave a little bark and reared up on her hind legs, resting her front paws on Mum's shins. Mum immediately melted. 'Aww, bless you, sweetheart. Granny's got to go and release her inner dream child. You go off with your mum.'

Debbie watched, shaking her head. 'Blimey, what are you lot like with that dog?'

'I don't know what you could possibly mean,' I said haughtily, although I couldn't deny that Germaine was basically our fur baby, a phrase I had always hated until I'd found myself using it un-ironically not long after inheriting her. Mum scurried off with Jocasta, and I watched them go.

'You don't like her, do you?' said Nathan, quietly.

'Who, my mum?' I said, although I knew exactly who he meant. 'She's all right. A bit irritating, sometimes, but, you know – family.'

'I meant Jocasta, and you know it,' said Nathan.

'She seems nice,' said Debbie. 'The tie dye and that's a bit much, but Shirley likes her. They seem to have fun.'

'Yeah…' I said, darkly. Nathan shook his head.

'You sure you're not jealous?'

'Jealous? Me? Of what?' I scoffed. 'What makes you think I want to float about like a patchouli-scented explosion in a scarf factory?' Nathan and Debbie exchanged a look, but didn't say anything, for which I was truly thankful as I was starting to feel like I was being an idiot. Which I should've been used to.

We had a lovely evening sitting outside the truck, chatting and enjoying a drink (mostly tea for me and Nathan, because we had more pie selling to do the next day, although Debbie had no such qualms about hitting the beer). I set about making dinner for the three of us, and allowed myself to wonder if Daisy was getting something to eat before reminding myself that I was letting her have some freedom this weekend, and it wouldn't kill her if she missed dinner for one night. Plus

I could always find her the next day and force-feed her a Bruce Willis.

On my previous (and, until now, only) festival experience I'd had a gas burner, with one tiny ring, and an ice box that had been next to useless by the second morning. I'd existed on two tins of baked beans, a loaf of bread, and a lot of unhealthy fast food. This time round, it couldn't have been more different. Not only did I have a proper stove top with four burners, I had an oven and a fridge packed full of goodies (as well as pies, of course). I set Nathan and Debbie to work, her in the kitchen with me and him giving the dog a quick walk round the site, as he'd had enough cooking for one day (not that I considered heating up ready-made pies and then selling them 'cooking'). Debbie boiled the kettle and crumbled a vegetable stock cube into a bowl of couscous, before pouring the hot water over and covering it. I chopped a red onion and fried it until it was soft in a little olive oil, then added some skinned and diced chicken breast, browning it on all sides. I added a couple of tablespoons of tagine spice paste and a good glug of pomegranate juice. I brought the pan to a simmer and, while we waited for the chicken to cook through and the sauce to thicken, I started on some flatbreads to go with it. I combined self-raising flour, baking powder and natural yogurt, mixing it into a dough and then kneading it until it was smooth. As Debbie fluffed up the couscous, which had now absorbed the vegetable stock, I heated a griddle pan and rolled out the dough into thin rounds, and then cooked them for a minute or two on each side. The final touch was adding a few pomegranate seeds and almonds to the couscous, and brushing each cooked flatbread with melted butter, before piling everything onto a big plate. I'd made far too much for just three of us, but it could be eaten cold the next day if we had any left.

'Smells like I timed it just right,' said Nathan, peering into the truck. He grabbed some plates and cutlery, and we sat on a picnic blanket next to the truck and tucked in. A few of our food truck neighbours were doing the same, and somehow we ended up all having a big communal feast, sharing food and swapping stories about past festivals. The sun went down and it started to get chilly, but between all of us we managed to pull together enough blankets and hoodies to keep everyone warm. I leant against Nathan and he put his arm around me.

'Enjoying yourself?' he asked. I nodded.

'Surprisingly, yes,' I admitted. 'This is lovely, isn't it?'

He smiled. 'Yeah, who needs Paris anyway?'

'Hmm… as long as no one gets out an acoustic guitar and starts playing "Wonderwall"…'

Debbie yawned and stretched out on the picnic

blanket. 'I think I should head back to the tent, otherwise I'm going to fall asleep right here.'

'Busy day, keeping our youth safe from the scourge of drugs?' I asked. She nodded.

'I very much doubt I stopped anyone taking anything,' she said ruefully, 'but at least they know *what* they're taking now. Can't say we didn't warn them.' She sat up and looked at Nathan. 'Oh, that reminds me! I met two friends of yours today. Two daft kids who got sent to see me by some "Scouse dickhead", as one of them called you.'

Nathan laughed. 'Good to know I haven't lost my people skills since I joined CID.'

'They weren't happy when I told them what they'd bought.'

'What, they hadn't really bought indigestion tablets, had they?' I asked, swapping a surprised look with Nathan. Debbie shook her head.

'No, of course not. There *was* MDMA present, along with the usual stuff they tend to cut it with, like glucose, but there was also a surprising amount of ascorbic acid.' She saw the let's-pretend-I-don't-know-what-that-is expression on my face. 'Vitamin C. Less "disco biscuit" and more "nutritional supplement".'

'So they won't get that high, but they won't catch a

cold either?' Nathan laughed. 'Oh my God, that's brilliant.'

'Yeah, that's what I thought. They didn't catch on at first, but I heard them talking to some older guys who were in getting their own stuff tested, and they were the ones who told them they'd just handed over their pocket money for a couple of vitamin pills.'

We all laughed. 'Bless 'em,' I said, hoping that my own daughter wasn't currently doing the same thing, although if she was, hopefully she'd end up just getting a dose of vitamin C too.

'But the interesting thing was,' continued Debbie, 'the older blokes told them about the dealer they'd bought their stuff off – which was a lot stronger – and it was the same bloke!'

'That is weird,' said Nathan. 'He must've bought a dodgy batch of drugs. You can't get the consistency these days...'

'Yeah,' I said. 'Or he's done it on purpose.' Nathan looked doubtful. 'There's a lot of kids at this festival, aren't there? It's probably the first time a lot of them have done anything like this. If I was a dealer I wouldn't want some spotty teenager buying stuff off me and ending up OD'ing because they didn't know what they were doing. Not because I cared about them particularly, but because I wouldn't want the police sniffing around. They turn a bit of a blind eye to the drugs as long as no one's getting hurt, don't they?'

'So a weak batch for the newbies, and a stronger one for the old hands,' mused Nathan. 'I suppose it does make sense.'

'Works fine until the newbies and the old hands start talking to each other and comparing drugs,' said Debbie. 'The last thing I heard, the kids were talking about confronting the dealer about it, and the older ones were egging them on, laughing at them.' She smothered a huge yawn and got to her feet. 'I've really got to go, I'm knackered.'

'Where are you camped?' asked Nathan, also getting to his feet. Germaine, who had been snoozing with her head on his lap, jumped up indignantly. 'You might not be getting a lot of sleep tonight.'

'I know… I'm right down the back of the campsite though, near the beach, so hopefully all I'll hear is the sound of the waves.' She smiled. 'If I wasn't sharing with Madeleine it might even be romantic.' Debbie worked part time as a district nurse, visiting mostly elderly people in their homes, and Madeleine was her boss. It was Madeleine who had persuaded Debbie to volunteer in the drug-testing tent all weekend.

*The sound of the waves, or the sound of people partying on the beach until four in the morning,* I thought, but I didn't say anything. Maybe Madeleine snored and would drown out any other noise.

'You want us to walk you back?' I asked. 'It's pretty dark over by the tents, and Germaine could do with another walk. I want to wear her out before we go to bed.'

'Good idea,' said Nathan. 'The truck still smells of pies, and that might make her want to chew things.'

'You'd better wear Jodie out as well, in that case,' said Debbie.

Despite the fact that she didn't deserve an escort after that remark, the three of us (four if you counted Germaine) soon found ourselves wandering through the labyrinth of tents. To say that they'd been thrown up in a haphazard fashion was understating it. Before we'd arrived I'd imagined orderly rows of canvas, like the time my parents had taken me camping in France to one of those sites where the tents are already up and waiting for you, but I was soon disabused of that notion. Here people seemed to have set up camp wherever they fancied. Some of the tents had enough space around them for us to walk through easily, but others (probably where a group of friends were camping together) were cheek by jowl, with little or no space between them. Add guy ropes, tent pegs, and random rubbish left outside, and the fact that it was properly dark by now, even with the light from our torch, and getting from one side of the festival site to the other had become a test of nerve, manual dexterity and mental problem-solving worthy of *The Krypton Factor*. It really *was* dark here, too, as most of the tents were unlit, the occupants currently engaged in leaping around in the mosh pit in front of the stage where the headliners – a dance music act whose generic take on 90s techno and happy house was inexplicably (in my humble opinion) popular with the under-thirty crowd – were now performing.

We were chatting and bitching amiably about the state of the campsite (all three of us had already tripped over at least one set of guy ropes), Germaine nosing around and in a couple of cases *inside* the tents, when a hooded figure appeared apparently out of nowhere and rushed towards us. Debbie leapt to one side as he (or she) shot past us, careering into me and knocking us both to the ground. I narrowly avoided falling onto the tent next to us, visions of me crushing it and getting tangled up in the ropes running through my head until I realised I'd missed it. The figure turned slightly to look at us as we tumbled to the ground, but they didn't stop.

'Oi, you bloody idiot!' shouted Nathan. The figure kept moving. I reached out a hand to stop Nathan giving chase. Germaine growled, not sure what was happening but knowing that she needed to step up and be the guard dog she was born to be.

'Leave it,' I said, scrambling up. 'No harm done. They're probably drunk or high and didn't even notice us until they were on top of us.'

'Yeah, I'm fine,' agreed Debbie, brushing herself down. Germaine stood down, visibly relieved to *not* have to step up and be a guard dog after all.

'You know who that was?' asked Nathan, still annoyed. 'That dealer, from earlier.'

'You sure?' I said. 'I didn't get a look at him this time.'

'He had that hoodie on, the one with the snakes up the arm. The yellow and green pattern glows in the dark.'

'There's probably other people here with the same hoodie,' I said, but Debbie shook her head.

'No! You remember I said those kids were talking to some others about him, in the tent? They said they'd been told to look out for the bloke in the snake hoodie but they were worried about approaching the wrong person, but he told them that he's an artist as well as a dealer and he designed it himself.'

'He needs to watch where he's going,' grumbled Nathan. I patted his arm.

'DCI Withers, may I remind you that you're off duty,

and on holiday, and we're not going to let some clumsy petty drug dealer ruin it, are we?'

He grinned in spite of himself. 'You've changed your tune,' he said. 'I thought we were doomed to have a terrible time?'

'As long as we avoid anyone carrying an acoustic guitar or juggling, we'll be fine.'

'There's a scantily clad woman fire-dancing over there,' said Debbie, pointing. I rolled my eyes.

'Of course there is…'

I slept well that night, despite the fact that the truck did still smell of pies (the admittedly pleasant fragrance of pastry seemed to be ingrained in the very fabric of the vehicle). I'd also been concerned that I'd find the sleeping quarters, which was basically a double mattress suspended over the driver's cab, terribly claustrophobic, but Nathan let me sleep on the side that opened out into the rest of the truck, so I was fine. Even with Germaine twitching in her sleep on the end of the bed, I still nodded off quickly and slept deeply until six-thirty, when we were woken by someone pounding on the door of the truck.

'Who the hell is that, at this time of the morning?' grumbled Nathan, sleepily. I swung my legs over the edge of the bed, remembering just in time not to sit up and smack my head against the ceiling, and wriggled out sideways.

'Bugger off!' I called out. 'We're not open for breakfast, not this early, anyway.'

'DCI Withers?' said a voice outside, loudly. 'Are you in there?'

Nathan groaned. 'There's no DCI, it's just Nathan this weekend,' he said. 'I'm on holiday. Sort of.'

'DCI Withers – Nathan – we need your help,' said the voice – female, and one that we both recognised. There was a hint of panic in it. Nathan frowned.

'Chrissie? Is that you?' He crawled out of the sleeping space and pulled on a T-shirt to protect his modesty as I opened the door, and sure enough there stood PC Chrissie Cardew, a grim look on her face. 'I'm not on duty. If you need more hands to help round up drunks or whatever, call the station.'

'It's not drunks, sir,' said Chrissie, glancing around to make sure no one was paying us any attention, which was completely unnecessary because anyone who wasn't asleep at this time of morning probably hadn't been to bed yet, and they weren't in any state to notice *anything*. 'It's a bit more serious than that…'

# Chapter Four

A small crowd had already gathered, clustering around the footpath down onto the beach. A couple of festival security guards stood in front of them, arms crossed over their chests in the pose beloved of nightclub bouncers everywhere, trying hard not to look too thrilled that their jobs had just become a bit more exciting with this completely unexpected turn of events. Beyond them, two more uniformed police officers did their best to secure the scene and shelter it from prying eyes and, worse still, mobile phone cameras.

'Down there?' said Nathan, nodding towards the rocks. Chrissie nodded.

'Yes, sir. Looks like he was out after dark, probably a bit worse for wear, and fell over and banged his head.

Doesn't look like anything more than that, but I thought I should come and find you.'

'Yeah, fair enough. You called it in?' Chrissie nodded again. 'All right, I'll have a quick look but then you're probably okay to wait for CID to come and take over. I told you, I'm officially on holiday, so if it's just some poor sod who's had an accident someone else can do the paperwork.'

'Thank you, sir.' Chrissie smiled as Nathan raised his eyebrows at her. 'Sorry, *Nathan*. You're on holiday.'

'Now you're getting it.' Nathan gestured towards Germaine, because no, there'd been absolutely no reason for me to go with him and Chrissie, but yes, of course I absolutely had. And I'd taken the dog because I didn't trust her in the truck alone with a load of pies, let alone the hygiene issues that would bring up... 'Can you take the dog while we go and have a look?'

Chrissie looked surprised, but took the lead from me. I smiled my thanks and followed him past the security guards and onto the sand.

Nathan turned to me and grinned. 'Just like old times, eh?'

'*Recent* old times, yeah. If this was like *real* old times you'd be threatening to arrest me, just so you'd have an excuse to spend more time with me.'

'It was easier than trying to find a chat-up line to impress you with.'

The uniformed officers turned to look at us, and I was surprised to realise that I didn't know either of them. I was out of the Penstowan Police loop nowadays, and they'd been recruiting as some of the older officers – men my late father had signed up during his time in charge – began to retire. Nathan nodded at them in greeting.

'All right, lads? Let's have a look at what we've got, then. She's with me.'

The victim was sprawled across the rocks, his bottom half on the sand, his body and face twisted and smashed wickedly against the jagged boulders. He'd been there since high tide, judging by the dampness of his trouser legs, but the water had long since receded. It looked as Chrissie had said: he'd probably had a few drinks, or taken something else, and had for whatever reason decided to head down to the beach the night before, but had lost his footing somehow and tripped heavily.

'Looks like an accident to me,' said Nathan. 'He's obviously been here overnight, so…'

'Yeah,' I said, but suddenly I wasn't so sure. I recognised the mussed-up hair, and the scruffy clothing.

'Brett, have we got an ID for him?' asked Nathan. One of the officers shook their head.

'No, Guv. Chrissie went through his pockets to see if he had a wallet on him, but there was nothing.'

'Nothing? No driving licence, phone, no money or anything?'

'No, Guv.'

'Hmm…'

'We don't need a driving licence,' I said, squatting down and taking a closer look at the dead man's face, taking care not to touch anything. 'I know who that is. That's Lee Roskill.'

'Who?' asked PC Brett, and I immediately and unfairly disliked him for being too young to know who The Burners' late front man was.

'Lee Roskill? Are you sure?' Nathan squatted down next to me. 'Doesn't look like the Lee Roskill I remember.'

'No, I know. But I only saw him yesterday, and that's definitely him. This is definitely the man who was screaming and shouting the odds with Caz Harper yesterday, before Security dragged him away.'

'And before Caz dedicated a song to him about how much she hated him.' Nathan looked at me, tight-lipped, and I knew what he was thinking. Abruptly he stood up, and I followed suit.

'Good job it's still too early for most people to be up,'

I said. 'Nothing gets a crowd going like a celebrity death.'

'Yeah…' Nathan turned back to Brett and the other officer. 'Make sure no one gets wind of our victim's identity just yet. And get DS Turner to call me when he gets here.'

'Yes, Guv.'

We headed back up the beach and relieved Chrissie of the dog.

'So, we all good?' asked Chrissie. 'You reckon it was an accident?'

Nathan and I exchanged looks. 'I don't know at this stage,' he said. 'I don't think we should rule anything out yet. Keep everyone off this bit of the beach and if anyone asks, just tell them that the police always respond to unexpected deaths as a matter of routine.' She nodded, and we left her looking thoughtful.

'Okay, just because the deceased was last seen having a furious argument with someone, it doesn't mean it *wasn't* an accident,' I said.

'I know.'

'But it also doesn't mean it was.'

'I know that, too,' said Nathan. He glanced at me. 'What are you thinking?'

I stopped and let Germaine sniff at the feet of an

unconscious (hopefully sleeping) festivalgoer, which were sticking out from beneath a tent flap. 'I'm thinking, easiest thing in the world to get lost amongst the tents in the dark after a few drinks or pills, and end up on the beach. And the second easiest thing in the world would be to not see the rocks and trip over them and knock yourself out.'

'Go on.'

'Not so easy to go anywhere these days with absolutely nothing in your pockets, though. Not even money, or a phone? How likely is that?'

'Someone could've robbed him.'

'Before or after he was dead?'

'Well – yeah. Was it a robbery that went wrong, or was it made to look like that?' Nathan turned to look further up the hill, scattered with higgledy-piggledy tents. 'And let's not forget who we literally bumped into last night.'

'The drug dealer?' I replayed the incident in my head. 'He was in a tearing hurry… But why would he have anything to do with Roskill?'

'You mean apart from the fact that our victim famously had a massive drug problem, and the dealer is a dealer?'

'Okay, yes, but as someone who was potentially a customer wouldn't he want Roskill to stay alive and able to buy drugs off him?' I sighed wearily. 'A "drug deal gone wrong" is *such* a cliché, and it wouldn't normally apply to someone buying or selling a bit of weed or a few disco biscuits. We're in Cornwall, not Colombia.'

'We can't rule him out, though,' said Nathan. 'He was definitely coming from the beach. There weren't many people around, because they were all watching the band, and it was dark, so…'

'Perfect murdery conditions. Yeah.' I tugged at Germaine's lead and pulled her away as she began to lick a motionless big toe. The unconscious feet twitched and a moan escaped through the tent flap. 'It just feels a bit *convenient* to pin it all on the drug dealer.'

Nathan laughed. 'Not Sherlock Holmes enough for ya? You know as well as I do, murderers aren't always that bright, and the most obvious solution is normally the right one.'

'Yeah, I know…'

'I do think we should go and have a chat with Caz Harper, though,' said Nathan, and I looked at him in surprise.

'You do? I thought you were on holiday, and not getting involved?' I looked down at my watch and groaned. 'Dammit, I need to get some pies in the oven. We're not really on holiday at all, are we?'

'No. Come on, I'll give you a hand and then we'll see

if we can sneak off later and have a word with your teenage self's rock idol.'

But as it turned out we didn't need to sneak off, because in amongst our breakfast patrons a couple of hours later – a number of festivalgoers, it seemed, needed a stodgy, carb-laden pie to counteract the effects of whatever they'd imbibed the previous night – were Caz and Ian. They happily held hands and spoke to a couple of fans, even posing for a selfie with them. I looked at Nathan.

'They either don't know yet, or they *really* didn't like him,' I said.

There was still a bit of a queue, but we needed to keep the two of them nearby if we were to get a chance to talk to them. Nathan nipped out of the truck and dislodged Daisy and Jade, who I'd collected on our way back to the truck and who were now feeding Germaine bits of pie crust, from our two folding chairs round the back.

'VIP area behind the truck, if you need it,' I said lightly, handing over their pies and trying to tread a fine line between still being completely star-struck by them and accusing them of the murder of their old front man.

'Cheers, Jodie,' said Caz. She lifted the pie to her nose and sniffed it. 'Oh my God, that smells *amazing*. I'm starving after last night.' I raised an eyebrow and she laughed. 'It's been a long time since we played a festival and I'd forgotten that we were a lot younger last time.'

'Bloody remembered it when we woke up this morning,' grumbled Ian good-naturedly. 'This is just what we need. Good to see you again, Jodie.'

'And you,' I said, trying not to gush. *These people could be cold-blooded murderers,* I reminded myself, *they could be knackered because they spent last night knocking off Lee Roskill.* But I couldn't really believe they had. I watched as they headed around to the back of the van, and gave Nathan a thumbs-up as he rejoined me at the counter.

'What was all that about?' asked Daisy, appearing at the counter. 'I was just letting my Bruce Willis go down.'

'No plans for this morning?' asked Nathan. 'No decent bands on until after lunch...'

'We were just going to have a wander around.' She narrowed her eyes as I grinned at her. 'Oh no, what are you two getting into now?'

'I'll tell you all about it later,' I said, then stopped as Nathan shook his head, 'I mean – I won't tell you because I'm not allowed... But nothing dangerous, I promise. And you and Jade can have free pies for the rest of the day if you cover for us for half an hour.' I opened the door of the truck and stood back to let her in before she could refuse. Warily, she stepped up.

'Half an hour?'

'Yeah. Or an hour. No more than two, anyway.' I took off my apron and handed it to her. 'Three, tops. We'll just be outside for a minute.' Nathan looked at her bemused face and shrugged, then followed me out to the impromptu VIP (Various Indulgent Pies) area, where our middle-aged rock star idols were now seated. Ian wiped gravy from his chin and laughed as Germaine, who never let her pride or self-respect get in the way of a potential foodie titbit, sat at his feet and gazed hopefully at him.

'Look at this poor animal,' he said. 'She's obviously not eaten for *weeks*.'

'You can see how she's wasting away,' I said. Germaine ignored me and lay down, still trying very hard to look like some poor, unfed stray who really deserved a bit of pie. 'Germaine, what are you like? You're fooling no one.'

'Sorry Germaine, this pie is too good to share,' said Caz, swallowing a mouthful.

'Yeah, they're good, aren't they?' said Nathan, and then we all just sat or stood there, looking at each other awkwardly. How should we break the news that their old front man, who they'd presumably been close to in the past, was dead? If either of them had killed him they were doing a very good job of acting like nothing had happened. But if they genuinely didn't know, how would they react?

'So, look…' I started, looking helplessly at Nathan. I'd never been very good at breaking bad news, and it had been part of the job I'd hated when I'd been in the Met.

'You must be Nathan?' asked Caz. 'Jodie told me all about you. You're a copper, right?'

'Yeah, that's right,' said Nathan. He cleared his throat and I realised that he was a bit star-struck, too. 'Look, I'm sorry to have to tell you this, but a body was discovered down on the beach earlier this morning, and we have reason to believe it's Lee Roskill.'

Ian stopped with his pie halfway towards his mouth. 'What?'

'Lee? On the beach?' Caz looked shocked. Ian put his pie down and reached out to touch her arm. She turned to him with a look of disbelief on her face, then looked up at us. 'What do you mean, "a body"? You mean a dead body?'

'Yes,' I said.

'And you think it's Lee?' I nodded, but she shook her head furiously. 'No, no that can't be right, Lee hates the seaside, he's a city boy through and through…'

'Are you sure it's him?' asked Ian quietly.

'We'd need a next of kin, or someone who knows him

well like yourself to formally identify him—' said Nathan, but I interrupted.

'Yes. I saw him yesterday. I didn't recognise him at first, but you were arguing with him and you called him Lee, and then I knew who it was. And I'm sorry, but it's him, on the beach.'

'No, he can't…' Caz sounded bewildered. She looked at Ian. 'But that means I'll never – the last thing I said to him was horrible and I'll never…' Her voice trailed off, and she burst into tears.

Nathan and I looked at each other. He gestured to me to follow him around the van, and we left the two apparently grieving rock stars to it.

'Well, what do you think?' murmured Nathan.

'She seems genuinely upset. Ian less so, but still shocked.'

'Yeah…' Nathan was less convinced, I could tell.

'Yeah what?'

'They're performers, remember. They could be putting it on for us.' He risked a glance back at them. Ian was on his knees in front of her, arms around Caz as she clung onto him. He rubbed her back as she cried softly onto his shoulder.

'They're musicians, not actors,' I pointed out. 'If Caz is putting that on she deserves an Oscar.'

'Yeah, but if he *was* murdered – and I do think it looks

suspicious – who had motive?' He gave a small grin. 'You've already shot down my drug dealer theory.'

'It *could* have been random, a mugging gone wrong,' I said, but I couldn't deny that I had that tingling feeling, my detective sixth sense telling me there was more to it than that. I shook my head. 'I don't know, I don't really believe that either. But I can't believe that either of those two was involved.'

Nathan reached out and took my hands. 'Is that because the evidence isn't pointing towards them, or because they were your idols years ago and you don't *want* them to be guilty?' I sighed.

'Okay, there is a bit of that, I suppose. The only thing worse than meeting your heroes and them turning out to be dicks is them turning out to be murderers. The argument, and the song dedication – I know that doesn't look good, but if that's all we've got to go on at the moment it's hardly conclusive, is it?'

'No,' admitted Nathan. He was about to say more when his phone rang. 'That'll be Matt. I'm amazed I've got a signal…' He answered. 'Hey, Matt, you on the scene?… No worries, I'll come down.' He disconnected the call and turned to me. 'I'm going to have a word with him, tell him what we know – which is not much. You stay here, see if you can get them to talk about the argument.'

'I'm not a copper anymore,' I said, like that had ever stopped me in the past. And like I wasn't dying to get involved in this investigation.

'I know. Which is why you might get more out of them than me…'

## Chapter Five

I grabbed two bottles of water from the food truck and headed back to our grieving VIPs. I smiled sympathetically and handed Caz a bottle as she looked up at me, sniffling.

'How you doing?'

'All right,' she said, although she didn't really look it. She took a deep breath and visibly pulled herself together. 'How did he die?'

'It looks like he fell over on the rocks and banged his head,' I said.

'So it was an accident,' said Ian.

'The police are looking into it,' I said, in my best non-committal tone of voice. Caz looked at me sharply.

'So it *wasn't* an accident?' she said. 'Someone did this to him?'

'Like I said, the police are looking into it…' I dragged the chair Ian had vacated closer to Caz and put my hand on her arm. 'I'm not the police, not anymore, but I do know how this will go. They'll want to talk to you about your relationship with Lee, about the argument.'

'You mean we're suspects?' Ian sounded angry. I shook my head to placate him.

'No, of course not. No more than anyone else… But if they come to the conclusion that his death is suspicious, then of course they'll be trying to determine who had motive. Who would gain from his death, did anyone bear him ill will, that sort of thing.'

'None of us bore him "ill will", even when he was being an arsehole,' said Ian.

'No? That's all right, then. But I'm sure the police will be interested to hear about the song you dedicated to him last night, Caz. What was it called again?'

Caz went pale. '"I Don't Know Why I Hate You But I Do",' she said. 'But that wasn't – I didn't *mean* that. Yes, I was pissed off at him, but I didn't *hate* him. Half the reason I dedicated it to him was because Ian and I wrote it, so he couldn't stop us playing it even though it was a Burners song.'

'Yes, about that. Is that what the argument was about? There was another bloke there—'

'Dougie? That's our manager, Dougie McKay.'

'He said something about "how did you think they'd react?" React to what? And you mentioned a court order?'

Ian and Caz both looked at me, surprised.

'How did you know about the court order?' asked Ian. 'Or the argument, for that matter?'

'I was hiding in the toilets in the VIP area when all the shouting was going on,' I said. 'Not with the intention of eavesdropping or anything, you understand. I was only there for the soft toilet paper. The eavesdropping was just a bonus.'

Caz sighed.

'It's a long story,' she said.

'I have time,' I said, trying to ignore the large queue that was building outside the truck. Daisy and Jade were obviously struggling to keep up with orders, and I knew that I really didn't have long before I'd have to go and rescue my poor put-upon daughter and her friend.

'Well… we last played together about fifteen years ago,' said Ian. 'We were on tour in the States, and one night after a gig – something happened.' I raised my eyebrows.

'Lee's girlfriend died,' supplied Caz. I nodded.

'Ah, right. I vaguely remember that happening, it was all over the news…'

'Yeah. Emily usually came and watched us play, but

for some reason she didn't that night, and when we got back to the hotel Lee found her in their room,' said Caz. 'She'd fallen over and crashed through a glass coffee table. She must've bled to death.'

'Oh, God,' I said. 'And Lee found her?'

'Yeah. She'd been snorting coke off the table and was high as a kite, so it could've been worse. She probably didn't feel a thing,' said Ian. I looked at him, shocked; it seemed like a callous thing to say. 'That might sound harsh, but it's true.'

'You didn't like her?'

'Neither of us did,' said Caz, defiantly. 'She was no good for him.'

'No?'

'Lee had struggled for years with drug addiction, and before he met her he was at least trying to keep it under control, but she was just as bad as he was,' said Ian. 'Although touring isn't the best way to keep clean, to be fair.'

Caz shook her head. 'We managed to. Most of the time, anyway. It was her, she used to egg him on.'

'Yeah…' It looked like Ian was about to say something else, but he stopped himself and turned to me. 'We might not have liked her, but Lee was devastated. We cancelled the rest of the tour, and when we got back home he went on a bender.'

'We were really worried about him,' said Caz. 'He was just taking anything he could get his hands on. He disappeared and we didn't see him for about six weeks. And then we heard he was in rehab.'

'And that's the last time you played together,' I said.

'Yeah. Lee was in and out of rehab for the next two years,' said Caz. 'It became obvious that he wouldn't be fit to tour again, not for a long time, if ever. And we didn't want to do it without him. So we just stopped.'

'Did you keep in touch with him?' I asked.

'Caz spoke to him now and again. Dougie reckons he called him a few times, but…' Ian let the sentence trail off.

'You don't think he did? Didn't they get on?'

'Not really,' said Ian. Caz looked at him disapprovingly. 'What? They didn't. Lee could be a bit of a dick to him, and Dougie thought he was a liability. I think he was just sick of clearing up Lee's mess.'

'I spoke to him a couple of times a year, and we exchanged Christmas cards and that so I knew he was still alive,' said Caz, 'but that was about it, until about six months ago.'

'What happened six months ago?' I asked. 'Is that when he took out the court order?'

'No,' said Caz. 'Quite the opposite, actually. He rang me up and told me he felt better than he had done in years. He sounded really happy, for the first time since Emily died. He said he'd met someone – Rebecca – and it was serious, they were "in love".' She rolled her eyes, as if the thought of Lee actually being in love again was unlikely. 'He said she was really good for him. And he even mentioned getting the band back together.'

'Really?' I was surprised. The Lee Roskill I'd seen arguing the day before had not looked like he was there for a musical reunion.

'Yeah, I didn't believe it either,' said Ian, dryly. 'Caz was keen, weren't you? But the thought of touring again … well, I didn't really fancy it, and I didn't think it would be good for Lee. I thought we should just leave things as they were.'

'But you played here last night,' I pointed out. Ian laughed.

'Yeah, third on the bill on opening night, at a local music festival. It ain't Wembley Arena, is it? And it's just down the road. We could've gone home if we'd wanted to.'

'But you stayed on site? Why? Home's a hell of a lot more comfortable than a tent.'

Caz stretched out. 'Tell me about it. I'm too old for camping. But we thought it would be fun.' Her face clouded over. 'And it was, up until the moment you told us Lee was dead.'

'So how did you end up playing here? And how did Lee know about it?'

'Because originally he was going to play too,' said Caz. 'I was talking to Mark Draycock, one of the festival organisers, a couple of months ago down the pub. He was one of the few people who still recognised me.' She smiled ruefully at me. 'You didn't when you did our dinner party, did you? And you must be about the right age to have heard us in our prime.'

'Yeah… I even had a poster of you on my bedroom wall,' I admitted. 'But then none of us look the way we did when we were in our twenties, do we?'

'Some of us less than others,' said Caz, with a sigh. 'Anyway, Mark asked if we'd be interested in playing a one-off gig. He said they usually managed to get a few bigger bands in as headliners, but they also like to showcase local talent too. He said it would be great if we could play, as we'd be like a mixture of both. Not that I think anyone really sees us as locals yet.'

'How long have you lived here, about ten months? Yeah, you've got about another hundred years and four generations to go yet before you're even classed as residents, let alone locals,' I said. 'So you mentioned the festival to Lee?'

'Yeah, he was up for it. He seemed quite excited about it, too. Mark was really pleased, he thought having a

Burners comeback for one of the headline acts would be a real coup for the festival.'

'So what happened?'

'We invited Lee to come and stay, but he said he had stuff going on, so we ended up rehearsing a couple of times over Zoom,' said Ian. 'I thought we might be a bit rusty, but after a couple of songs it was like we'd never stopped playing.' He smiled sadly. 'It was just like old times, only better. Lee was sober, and happy. He hadn't been like that since our early days.'

'It was like we'd finally got the real Lee back,' said Caz with a sniffle, and Ian put his arm around her. 'I just wanted him to be happy,' she said, and Ian nodded.

'I know, hun.'

'When did he tell you he wasn't playing? When did he take out the court order?' I asked.

'About a month ago, he stopped taking my calls,' said Caz. 'I didn't think anything of it, really. I didn't think he was avoiding us or anything. Then he missed a Zoom rehearsal, but even then I didn't think there was anything to worry about, because he was meant to be coming to stay with us for a few days before the festival, so we could make sure we were really tight. But then he rang and said he'd changed his mind about playing.'

'How did you feel about that?'

'Worried,' said Caz, as Ian said, 'Pissed off.' He

shrugged. 'Pissed off *and* worried. I was annoyed that he'd left it so close to the festival, but also worried that we'd pushed him too much and he'd relapsed or something.'

'And of course Mark wasn't pleased,' said Caz. 'He said he might have to move the acts around a bit. We weren't really The Burners without Lee, so he didn't think we could headline Saturday night anymore.'

'That's a bit harsh,' I said.

'Yeah, but... Lee was our front man, wasn't he? If you said "The Burners" to someone back in the day, they'd think of him, not us.' Ian spoke calmly enough, but was there a hint of bitterness beneath it? 'It's just the way it is. If you say, I dunno, Coldplay, most people can name Chris Martin but none of the others. No one ever knows the keyboard player's name.'

'And the court order?' I prompted. Now Ian looked openly angry.

'Oh, *that* was the icing on the cake. That was the cherry on top. Three days ago Dougie gets hit with a court order saying the band can't use the name, because Lee came up with it, and we can't play any of the songs he wrote or even co-wrote with us. Dougie didn't go into details, but basically Lee didn't want us making any more money from "his" intellectual property. Never mind that we'd always been right there with him, making him famous. He wasn't a bloody one-man band.'

'So we went from the headline act on Saturday night to a bloody cover band playing the support slot on Friday,' said Caz. 'And we only got that because I told Mark we'd sue him if we didn't get to play.'

I opened my mouth to speak, but was interrupted by a crash from inside the food truck. Germaine, who had been sitting on my feet for most of the previous discussion, leapt up and ran to the door of the truck, doubtless to go and rescue her young mistress. But that was my job.

'I'd better go and check on that,' I said, standing up. 'I'm really sorry for your loss. The police will more than likely want to speak to you and the rest of the band about this, so you'd better tell the others not to leave the site for now.' I put a sympathetic hand on Caz's shoulder. 'Do let me know if there's anything I can do for you.'

Inside the food truck it was actually far less chaotic than I'd imagined. The loud crash had been an oven tray falling on the floor, but thankfully there hadn't been any pies on it. The queue had quietened down considerably, so I pulled both girls into a hug and thanked them.

'Yeah, all right…' said Daisy, squirming out of my embrace. Jade probably felt exactly the same, but was too polite to show it; I wasn't her mum, after all. 'You finished being all star-struck now, then?'

'Ooh, have you been talking to someone famous?' asked Jade, suddenly interested. Daisy shook her head.

'Nah, just some old fogey rock band from the seventies or something,' she said.

'The seventies?' I spluttered. 'Just how old do you think I am?'

Daisy grinned at me. 'Serves you right for taking liberties and making us slave away over your frowsy pies. I am *never* getting the smell of Hans Gruber out of this T-shirt.' She wrinkled her nose. 'And that sounds really wrong.'

I packed her and Jade off with a tenner each and instructions to keep hydrated, the unspoken implication being to spend it on soft drinks rather than drugs or alcohol. Daisy was very keen to take Germaine, which I thought was a little suspicious until I saw them across the other side of the food area, flirting with a couple of blokes who were playing with their own dog, a scruffy-looking mongrel on a piece of rope. But that suited me fine, because 1) having a dog in a catering van is far from ideal, and 2) dog owners are the salt of the earth and (hopefully) too busy being responsible pet owners to get completely off their trolley. Although now I came to think of it, I was sure I remembered reading somewhere that Adolf Hitler had had a German Shepherd. And a methamphetamine habit. Maybe he was the exception that proved the rule.

'Where's everyone gone?' said Nathan, appearing in front of me and (thankfully) derailing that train of thought. 'There was a massive queue of potential pie eaters when I left you.'

'I know, Daisy and Jade either served them all, or did something so publicly unhygienic that it put them all off,' I said. DS Matt Turner, who was standing behind him, laughed.

'As long as there's a steak and kidney pie left for the local constabulary,' he said, and I gave him a low bow.

'Of course, Officer. On the house.' I dished him up a pie. 'So, what tales from the crime scene?'

'You don't have to tell her anything,' said Nathan, grinning at me. 'She's not official anymore.'

'Oh yeah? And you're on holiday.'

'That don't mean anything,' said Matt. 'You know as well as I do, she has a way of finding things out.'

I stepped out from behind the food truck counter. '"She" is right here,' I said, pointing at myself. They both laughed.

'At the moment, we don't know any more than you and Nathan surmised yourselves,' said Matt. 'Could just as well have been an accident as something else.

Forensics are on the scene now, but if the cause of death is blunt force trauma from a rock to the head, then it ain't going to be easy to distinguish whether or not that rock was deliberately smashed onto his head, or if he fell on it.'

'What about blood on the rocks where he was found?' I asked Matt. He nodded.

'Yeah, there was a pool of blood on the rocks under and around his head, but that on its own don't prove or disprove anything. The way I see it is there's three possibilities. He could've tripped over something and fallen over, hitting his head; he could've been wrestled to the ground and had his head forcefully smacked against the rocks by an assailant; or that assailant could've picked up a smaller rock and bashed his head in, leaving him there to make it look like an accident. You reckon that's about the size of it?' Matt asked Nathan.

'Yeah, I think you're right. The last option, we wouldn't be able to prove that unless we found the rock used as the murder weapon.'

'Which is not going to happen,' I said. 'If I'd bashed someone's head in on the beach, I'd chuck the murder weapon in the sea as far as I could throw it.'

'Making it impossible to find, and on the off-chance it was, washing off any incriminating evidence,' said

Nathan. 'No blood, no fingerprints… We could pick it up and not even realise what we were holding.'

'What about being able to match the size and shape of the wound against the size and shape of the rocks?' I asked. Nathan shook his head.

'In theory, you should be able to match them up, as the shape would be unique, but in practice, something that irregular and organic would be hard to do with any degree of accuracy. If you look at things like knife wounds, it's much easier to tell how long the blade was and if it had a straight or serrated edge. But a messy wound like this one… It should have sand, fragments of rock and shells and all that, so Forensics will be able to confirm if it was a rock that caused the blow, but other than that…'

'Other than that, we're back to square one, not knowing whether it was an accident or murder,' said Matt. 'But that's all right, that's why we're here.' He grinned. 'And yes, I am including Jodie in that.'

'Talking of which – did you get anything useful from our rock stars?' asked Nathan.

'Possibly,' I said. I told them about the court order, and what the argument had been about.

'So the rest of the band would definitely have been pretty angry with him,' said Nathan.

'Yeah. And their manager, Dougie, and maybe even

the festival organiser, Mark,' I said. 'Caz reckoned he thought getting The Burners to stage their big comeback here would've been a real scoop for the festival, and then of course it didn't happen.'

'What happens to their old songs now?' asked Matt.

'What do you mean?'

'Well, when Roskill was alive, they weren't allowed to use the name, or play any of their old hits,' said Matt. 'But what happens now he's dead? Do they get the rights to the name and that back now?'

Nathan and I looked at each other. 'I don't suppose you asked that?' asked Nathan.

'It didn't even occur to me,' I admitted. 'It also felt a bit insensitive, because don't forget if they had nothing do with it, they just lost an old friend and are grieving. I didn't want to go blundering in there.'

'We need to find out,' said Nathan. 'Matt, call Sunil back at the station and get him to look into Roskill's legal affairs. I've heard of writers leaving their literary estates to family or even to charity, musicians must be able to do the same. See if he specified who was to get the rights to his songs after his death.'

'Will do, Guv.' Matt got onto his phone and dialled Sunil, the young and very keen detective constable who (bewilderingly, to me at least) seemed to prefer the intellectual, deskbound (boring) side of police work to actually physically chasing after criminals. It takes all sorts.

'There was something else that I found quite interesting,' I said quietly, watching Matt on the phone. I'd been reluctant to mention it in front of him, because it could've been me imagining it, it could've been completely unrelated, or it could've pointed to Caz as a more likely suspect than I wanted her to be. 'When Caz told me about Lee's girlfriend, she wasn't happy.'

'Which one? The one who died, or this mysterious new one?' asked Nathan.

'Both. She admitted she didn't like the one who died, and she looked completely unimpressed at Lee's claim that he was in love again.'

'You mean she was jealous?' Nathan lowered his voice. 'Do you think she was having an affair with Roskill?'

'No…no, I mean she and Ian seem very happy together. They were all loved up when I did their dinner party, and even this morning they were holding hands and cuddling, weren't they?' I shook my head. 'I really don't think she'd cheat on him. But she and Lee used to be an item, didn't they?'

'Did they?'

'Yeah, I'm sure they did,' I said, trying to remember. 'I'm sure they were boyfriend and girlfriend first, and then they started the band and decided to just be friends. And then Ian joined and she got together with him.'

'You think it was a case of, she didn't want him herself, but at the same time she didn't want him to be with anyone else?' asked Nathan. 'And she wouldn't like anyone who *did* get into a relationship with him?'

'I think it's a possibility,' I said, willing my cheeks not to go bright red, because it had just occurred to me that maybe that was how I felt about Tony. I hadn't liked his ex-fiancée Cheryl, and I'd been a bit snooty about other women he'd briefly been out with before getting together with Carmen. But then I had liked his first wife, and I was really fond of Carmen; in fact I'd been the one who had sounded her out and then told him to ask her to dinner. I wasn't one of those women, was I? I didn't want him – I loved Nathan, and I'd never been happier – but Tony had always been my back-up boyfriend, my Plan B. That's the problem with murder investigations. The stuff you dig up sometimes makes you confront unpleasant things about yourself.

Thankfully Nathan seemed completely unaware of my inner turmoil. 'Do you think that would be motive to kill him, though? I could see it more if she wasn't happily married herself, if she'd been harbouring hopes that they'd end up together and then he'd fallen for someone else.'

'Yeah… I think you're right, there's probably nothing in it. I just thought I should mention it,' I said. Matt finished his call and came back to us.

'Sunil's hitting the phone lines,' he said. 'God bless him, he loves ringing people up, combing through witness statements. Weirdo.'

'What next?' I asked.

'Get Uniform to canvas the people camping down near the beach,' said Nathan. 'Ask them if they heard or saw anything.'

'Chrissie's already on it,' said Matt. 'There's more Uniforms coming to help with that.'

'Depending on when the murder—' I started.

'Or accident,' said Nathan.

'Or accident happened, that's probably a long shot,' I said. 'We were down there with Debbie around twelve, twelve-thirty, and there was hardly anyone about, they were all watching the band. And later on anyone who was still awake was probably, shall we say, "chemically enhanced" and not necessarily the most reliable witness.'

'Still worth a try,' said Nathan. 'And get someone searching the beach, see if they can find the victim's phone and wallet. I might be wrong, but it doesn't feel like an opportunist mugging gone wrong to me, so where are his valuables?'

'In the sea, probably,' I said. 'But it would be good to

know if he called anyone before he went down to the beach, and it'll help Sunil track down this Rebecca woman. I got the impression Caz and Ian didn't know anything about her, other than her first name.'

'Will do,' said Matt. 'Sunil's trying to get his phone number and call log. We're also looking out for your drug dealer. Even if he wasn't involved, you reckon he was coming from the direction of the beach, so he might've seen something.'

'That might be why he was in such a hurry to get away,' I said. 'I hadn't thought of that.'

'Nice work,' said Nathan. 'Okay, you're in charge but remember I'm here if you need to run anything by me.'

'Thanks, Guv,' said Matt, and he strutted off to marshal the troops looking very pleased with himself. I sighed.

'Aww, they grow up so fast, don't they? Little man with a big job to do.'

Nathan roared with laughter. 'Don't let him hear you say that. But yes.'

'So now what do *we* do?' I asked, but I had the sinking feeling that I already knew. Nathan nodded to the food truck.

'Sell pies…'

# Chapter Six

And sell pies (and bake more pies) we did, even though I was itching to go off and poke around at the crime scene, which I wouldn't have been allowed to do anyway. I could tell Nathan wanted to as well, but he'd promised to help me with the food truck and he wasn't a man to go back on his word. Plus he hadn't had a proper holiday since he'd moved to Penstowan (not that this had turned out to be a proper holiday), and we were using it as a test run to see how the station would cope with an emergency, were we to actually leave the country at some time in the future. I was hoping we'd manage to go somewhere hot for our honeymoon next year, somewhere with a nice beach, although I had to admit that England had been absolutely boiling over the last couple of summers (thank you, climate change, although not really), and that Cornwall had some of the most beautiful beaches in the world. It would be nice to go somewhere though where the local food delicacy wasn't wrapped in shortcrust pastry, and the local tipple wasn't made from apples and strong enough to strip paint, power a lawn mower, or cause temporary blindness.

'I didn't expect to see you two here,' said Debbie, appearing at the counter.

I wiped my sweaty forehead with a floury hand. 'Where did you expect to see us?' I asked.

'Down by the beach, by whatever it is that's going on.' She waved her hand in the direction of the sea. 'What's happened? There's a ton of Old Bill down there. That PC Chrissie asked me if I'd seen anything suspicious last night, as well. I told her about that dealer bloke running into us, but she wouldn't tell me why she was asking.'

I looked at Nathan, asking permission, and he shrugged. 'It'll be all over the news soon enough,' he said, making Debbie even more excited.

'They found a body on the beach,' I said. 'Down on the rocks.'

Debbie deflated slightly. 'Is that it? An accident? I thought maybe someone had been bumped off.' I raised my eyebrows. 'Oh my God, they were? Really? Who?'

'A certain person we last saw being dragged away by security yesterday,' I said. Debbie furrowed her brow. 'Arguing,' I prompted her. She still looked puzzled. 'Bloody hell, Deb, how much did you have to drink after we left you last night? Lee Roskill. Lee Roskill was found on the beach, his head bashed in, on the rocks.'

'Wow, a celebrity murder! Even if it's a washed-up celebrity murder.'

'He wasn't washed up, I told you – he had his head bashed in.'

'No, I meant "washed-up" like – you know what I mean. So, who did it?' She looked at us expectantly.

'How would we know? We've been here all morning,' I said. 'You'd have more luck asking us who ate all the pies.' I lowered my voice and nodded over to a wiry man standing on the opposite side of the food area. 'He did. Look at him! He's had three already. How is he so skinny?'

'I can't believe you're not investigating,' said Debbie. Nathan grinned.

'We didn't say that, did we?' He fanned himself with a napkin; it really was hot inside the truck. 'We might not be out there doing all the donkey work, but we've given Matt a few pointers.'

'Like finding that dealer,' I said. 'I wonder if they've picked him up yet?'

'Well they hadn't half an hour ago,' said Debbie, 'because we were still getting kids in with pills to test that they'd bought off him.' She looked at me and hesitated.

'Go on,' I said. She took a deep breath.

'Okay, patient confidentiality means I shouldn't be telling you this,' she said, and I thought, *Oh no, it was Daisy, wasn't it?* 'In fact I shouldn't really have told you about the pills we tested yesterday, but as I didn't tell you any names I think it was okay.'

'Was it Daisy?' I asked her, not really wanting to hear the answer.

Nathan reached out and touched my arm. 'At least she's being sensible and getting it tested first,' he said. But Debbie shook her head.

'No no no, what are you two like? Of course it wasn't Daisy, she's got a flipping ex-copper for a mum and a DCI for a stepdad. That's enough to make anybody think twice about breaking the law.' She grinned. 'Or at least make sure that if they *did* break the law they made it worthwhile, like a massive diamond heist and not some daft drug offence.'

'Then who…?'

'It was her mate, Ellie. Daisy and Jade were lurking in the background when she brought the pills in to be tested, but she only had a couple, so I reckon if Daisy *does* take anything she'll only get a cheeky half.' She looked at my face, obviously registering that I didn't care if it *was* 'only' a cheeky half, I didn't want my daughter taking anything. 'Half of a pill that's mostly vitamin C, remember. She'd probably get more of a high from a cappuccino.'

'Yeah, okay…' I said. 'If they haven't been able to find him, maybe that means he's lying low today. And why would he do that?'

'Because he's got something to hide,' said Nathan.

'Or he's run out of pills. Or he's sold enough and he just wants to enjoy the rest of the festival,' said Debbie. 'But if Ellie was telling the truth about how she got hold of the drugs, then she might know where he is.'

'Why, what did she say?' asked Nathan.

'She said her sister's boyfriend gave them to her…' Debbie looked from me to Nathan and back again. 'And now you're going to ask me to cover for you, aren't you?'

'You know me so well.'

I was all for going to find Daisy and her friends, but I had no idea where they were. We headed down towards the stage area, but just as we were about to lose the tenuous mobile phone signal we'd had at our vantage point on higher ground, Nathan's phone rang.

'Yeah…? I can't hear you, Matt… You have? Brilliant, where are you…?…Yeah, we're coming now…' He hung up and looked at my amused face. 'What? Yes, I know we're on sort-of holiday, but my troops need me.'

'Yeah, right… Did Matt actually say that?'

'Well, the line was pretty bad…'

'Uh huh.'

'But yeah, I'm almost certainly definite that he said those exact words…' Nathan grinned. 'Or something like that, anyway.'

We headed to the security tent, which Matt had annexed and turned into a mobile crime investigation unit, much to the initial absolute joy of the festival security guards; initial joy, because they were starting to realise that other than stand around and stop people going onto the beach, there wasn't that much for them to do. Just like being a Uniform, as I recalled. Murder investigations were nowhere near as much fun when you weren't in CID. Or catering.

The erstwhile drug dealer was sitting in the corner of the tent, closely watched by PC Brett whatever-his-name-was. Matt looked up and saw us as we entered through the tent flap. He looked slightly surprised.

'Oh. All right, Guv? There was no need for you to rush over,' he said. I rolled my eyes.

'"My troops need me",' I muttered. Nathan ignored me.

'I just thought I should check that you had everything

in hand,' he said. Matt looked at me and rolled *his* eyes too.

'Yeah, that's what I thought,' I said.

'You're meant to be on holiday,' said Matt. 'I can handle this.'

'I know you can. I just thought…' Nathan stopped. 'Okay, full disclosure, I hate being out of the loop when I'm right here on site.'

Matt laughed. 'It's all right, I had twenty quid on you being here within ten minutes of my phone call. Sunil thought you'd hold out longer.'

He led us outside, where the security guards had set up a table and a few chairs round the back of the tent; somewhere to have a crafty smoke, by the smell of it. We really had ruined their fun. We sat down.

'So have you talked to him yet? What have you got?' asked Nathan.

Matt took out his notebook and referred to it. 'Name's Paul Dyer. He's got previous for possession, possession with intent to supply, all the usual stuff. One spell inside, but he only served six months as he was a model prisoner.'

'Nothing for violent crime? No assaults, or mugging or anything?' I asked. Matt shook his head.

'Nope. He told Chrissie he's a lover, not a fighter.' Matt didn't look very impressed. If anyone was going to do any loving around Chrissie, it would be Matt and nobody else.

'What does he say about last night?' asked Nathan. 'Where was he coming from when he bashed into Jodie?'

'He didn't know what I was talking about,' said Matt. 'Or he said he didn't, anyway. Swears he was in his tent all night. He said he was tired, and he didn't like the band headlining, so he went back to his tent at nine o'clock-ish and other than going for a pee at around one, he stayed there until this morning.'

'Where did he go for a pee? Near where we saw him?'

'No, nowhere near. His tent's much further up the hill, and there's a toilet block close by. There was no need for him to be anywhere near the beach.'

'Okay…' said Nathan. 'But the person we saw was wearing a hoodie with a snake pattern up the arm. A pattern that he apparently designed, and which only he has got. How does he explain that?'

'He said somebody nicked his hoodie,' said Matt. I scoffed.

'What's he wearing right now?'

Despite the day being just as hot as the previous one, the suspect was indeed still wearing his hoodie. Nathan and Matt sat down opposite him, while I lurked in the background. Maybe I'd been a bit hasty, quitting the police force again. I was pretty sure that, having resigned twice now from two different forces, I wouldn't be top of the candidate list when it came to recruiting again.

'Mr Dyer,' said Nathan pleasantly. 'Nice hoodie. Where did you get it from?'

'I already told yer mate,' said Dyer.

'Really?' Nathan sighed and shook his head. 'He never tells me anything. At the risk of you repeating yourself, tell me.'

Dyer looked belligerent for a moment, and I thought he was going to refuse to speak or ask for a lawyer, but instead he just laughed.

'Oh I get it, you're supposed to be the bad cop,' he said. Nathan smiled.

'Oh no, Mr Dyer. There's only good cops here. If there's been some misunderstanding over the events of last night then all we're doing is giving you the opportunity to tell us your side of it. Would a bad cop do that?'

Dyer looked exasperated. '*What* events of last night? I told him—' he nodded at Matt '—I never left the tent! I dunno what someone's said, but I was in the tent all night from about nine until this morning. I only left to go for a piss.'

'Which brings us back to your hoodie,' said Nathan. 'Popular design, is it?'

'You know it isn't,' said Dyer. 'I'm a tattoo artist by

trade. I designed it for a client. He went with a different one, but I liked it so I decided to put it on a sweatshirt.'

'Not on your own arm?' asked Matt. Dyer stared at him and rolled up his sleeve. Underneath, his skin was already covered in ink.

'No room for it, mate.'

'So the drug dealing is more of a sideline?' asked Nathan, casually. Dyer was unfazed.

'This isn't about me selling a few pills,' he said, leaning back in his chair. 'This is about whatever happened on the beach. Has some daft kid OD'd, is that it? Because I don't know if you've had any of my stuff tested, but I reserve anything stronger than an aspirin for seasoned festivalgoers who aren't going to neck it all in one go, washed down with eight cans of Strongbow. If someone's carked it on MDMA and cider, they ain't got it from me.'

'No? How about if someone was beaten to death, and a person matching your description was seen by several witnesses fleeing the area?' Nathan sat back, mirroring Dyer's casualness. Only now he didn't look quite as relaxed.

'I *told* you, I didn't leave the tent. I left my hoodie out there, hanging over one of the tent ropes, and when I went out for a wee it was gone, which really pissed me off. But then I got up this morning and looked outside, and it was back, hanging in exactly the same place.' He looked from Nathan to Matt, and then over to me. 'Why would I beat someone to death, anyway? Who was it?'

'Lee Roskill.'

'Who the bloody hell is Lee Roskill?'

'Former lead singer and guitarist with The Burners, who played here last night,' I said, forgetting that officially I wasn't there. He frowned.

'That lot who did all the cover versions? They might have murdered a few songs, but that's not enough to make me bludgeon their singer to death.' *Interesting,* I thought. If he genuinely thought Roskill had been onstage last night, then he didn't know who he was. And that would make it tricky to kill him. Deliberately, anyway. 'Oh, I get it,' he continued. 'Let me guess: it was a "drug deal gone wrong", yeah? You do know this is Cornwall, yeah, not Colombia? You're more likely to get into a fight about the proper way to eat a cream tea than over a drug deal round here. I'm not exactly Pablo Escobar's cousin. And anyway, I prefer my customers to be alive, so they can pay me.'

I had to admit he had a point, especially about the cream teas.

'The problem is, though, there doesn't seem to be anyone who can corroborate your story,' said Matt.

'You were on your own,' said Nathan, looking at the notes Matt had taken. 'That's a bit of an issue for you.'

Dyer shifted uncomfortably and I thought, *There's definitely something he's not telling us.* 'When I said I was on my own, I didn't mean on my *own* own,' he said. I snorted.

'There's another type of "on your own", is there?' I said. He looked at me, then back at Nathan.

'No, I mean, I *was* with some other people some of that time, but I didn't get their names,' he said.

'Customers?'

'No. I mean…' He sighed. 'Look, I'll level with you. The hoodie's my calling card, all right? People know to look out for the bloke with the snake hoodie. If they see me wearing it, it means I've got stuff to sell. If I've run out, or I just want to enjoy myself without some sweaty teenager coming up and asking—' he put on a squeaky urchin voice '—"got any pills, mister?" then I leave my hoodie in the tent.'

'What about last night?' I asked, stepping forward. 'What does it mean when you leave it *outside* your tent?'

Dyer looked at me, then back at Nathan. 'Are you allowed to bring your bird along on investigations?'

Matt and I both found other things to look at, because of course, no, he wasn't supposed to "bring his bird" along.

'She's a consultant,' said Nathan. 'Answer her question.'

'It means you're open for business, doesn't it?' I said. 'It's so people can still find you, so they know which one's your tent.'

Dyer nodded. 'Yeah.'

'So you had customers with you, for at least some of the night. And when your hoodie went missing, you were annoyed because it meant potential customers wouldn't be able to find you.'

'Yeah.'

'So when did your last lot of customers turn up?' asked Nathan. Dyer looked puzzled.

'Why?'

'Because it'll give us a rough time for when your hoodie was supposedly stolen.'

Dyer bristled at the 'supposedly', but didn't argue. 'About half ten. I didn't notice it was gone until around midnight.'

'So it was stolen some time after ten? And our witnesses saw someone wearing it around twelve-thirty.'

'Might've been stolen a bit earlier,' admitted Dyer. 'I wasn't really looking at the time.'

'So how long did your last customers stay with you?' asked Matt, taking notes. 'Do you normally socialise with them?'

'No…' Again, there was that hesitation.

'So, how long? How long does it take to sell some pills? Five minutes?' Matt's pen was poised over his notebook. Dyer looked like he was fighting, and losing, some internal battle, before he slumped in his seat.

'All right. My last customers left just after ten, they didn't stay long. But I did have some other visitors about an hour later.'

'So the hoodie must've still been there?' said Nathan.

'Not if the visitors already knew you, and knew where you'd pitched your tent,' I said. Dyer looked up at me but didn't say anything. 'Look, just because you sell a few drugs, it doesn't automatically make you a bad person, does it?' I said. Matt opened his mouth to speak but Nathan gestured for him to stay quiet. 'Maybe the person – or people – visiting you were underage, or maybe they're related to you in some way, and you're looking out for them. You don't want to get them into trouble.' Dyer still watched me, but still he didn't speak. I knew I was right. 'Maybe one of them was related to someone in law enforcement, and neither you nor they would want their mum to find out.'

Dyer's mouth dropped open. 'Bugger. You're Mrs Parker, aren't you?'

'Nope,' I said firmly. 'Mrs Parker's my mum. Can

your visitors corroborate your story? Were you with them all night?'

'Until about three a.m.'

I turned to Nathan and Matt. 'There's his alibi…'

We found Daisy and her friends (and the dog) with, of all people, Mum's friend Jocasta. The scarf-laden New Age retiree was forcefully pummelling Ellie's shoulders as the others looked on, somewhat bemused. Daisy looked up as we approached, and I swear she let out a silent sigh of relief.

'Mum, Nathan! Am I glad you're here,' she said.

'I dunno, are you?'

'Yes, I am. Ellie was having a bit of a panic, and Jocasta is—' she looked at me, as if daring me not to laugh '—helping her relax.'

'Yeah, that looks very relaxing… Why is Ellie panicking?' I asked.

'Because her sister just WhatsApp'd her and told her the police have arrested her boyfriend,' said Jade. Daisy rolled her eyes and gave her a *why did you tell them THAT?* look.

'That would be the drug dealing boyfriend, yeah?' I said, and Daisy and Jade both paled. Ellie might have turned pale too, but she was quite red in the face from Jocasta's therapeutic onslaught, so it was hard to tell.

Mum turned up, just to add even more confusion to proceedings. 'Here you all are!' she said. She turned to Jocasta. 'I thought you'd gone to check out the Tibetan singing bowls. It took me half an hour to fight me way through the scrying and fortune-telling trance space—' she paused and absent-mindedly rummaged in her cleavage, pulling out a tarot card and frowning at it before continuing '—and then you weren't even there!' She stopped and looked around at all of us. 'What's going on here, then?'

'Young Ellie here was upset,' said Jocasta. 'I was trying to be of assistance, or at least take her mind off it.'

'Yeah, you did that,' said Daisy.

Ellie took advantage of Jocasta's momentary distraction and wrenched herself out of the woman's grip.

'Oh, Mrs Parker—'

'Miss,' I said, 'or Jodie. Mrs Parker's my mum.'

'They found a body on the beach, and now they've arrested Paul and we don't know why!' Ellie was indeed panicking somewhat. I went to put my arm around her, then stopped. She was a good few inches taller than me, and her shoulders were probably a bit tender after Jocasta's brutal (but well-intentioned) ministrations.

'We know all about it,' I said, soothingly. 'He's not in trouble.' I paused, making sure that I had Daisy's attention too. 'You're not in trouble, either.' *But we know what you've been up to…*

'We do need the three of you to come to the security tent and have a chat with DS Turner,' said Nathan, doing his best 'stern but still approachable' voice. 'We just need you to corroborate his story.'

'Corro what?' asked Mum, looking bewildered. It was nothing to do with her age – she was only in her mid-seventies – she just tended to lose concentration in the middle of conversations and then realise she had no idea what was going on.

'Give someone an alibi,' I said. 'I need to go and rescue Debbie. Come with me and I'll fill you in on the way back to the food truck.'

## Chapter Seven

So Daisy and her friends went with Nathan, and I took Mum and Germaine back to the food truck, leaving Jocasta to bravely attend to the feet of festivalgoers at her reiki stall. Debbie was sitting outside, eating a pie and flirting with the (rather handsome) West Indian bloke running the soul food stall opposite. I was impressed, as it's quite hard to be alluring while eating a gravy-laden steak and kidney pie, but Debbie was a multi-tasker.

She looked up at us as we approached. 'It's my first one,' she said, holding up the pie, much to Germaine's interest. 'I put the money in the till.'

'Don't be daft,' I said, 'the least I can do is give you a freebie after you helped us out.' Although to be honest, what with bribing Daisy and Jade with pies earlier, I suspected my friend Sean would be slightly disappointed with this year's festival takings.

'Just as well, because I haven't really paid…' She jumped up as a customer approached, but I waved her back into her seat.

'It's all right, I've got it.' I *was* there to sell pies, after all. Plus I'd always found that doing something that didn't require too much exertion of the 'little grey cells' often helped when I was puzzling over an investigation. I'd be peeling spuds or cooking a roux or (in this case) handing over a teriyaki chicken pie, and suddenly my brain would go 'ping!' and the answer to the whole case – the Who, How, and Why – would appear as if by magic.

That was the theory, anyway, and occasionally it actually worked. Not today, though. I waited for the customer to walk off and then brought Mum and Debbie up to speed on things. I wasn't too worried about telling Mum the identity of the dead body, as she had absolutely no idea who Lee Roskill was, although she did vaguely remember me raving about The Burners when I was younger.

'Never meet your heroes,' she said, nodding sagely. 'Especially when they're dead.'

'So if that wasn't the dealer who ran into us last night,

who was it?' asked Debbie.

'I don't know,' I admitted. 'I don't think Nathan or Matt do, either. I was never entirely happy with it being the dealer. Selling drugs might make you morally a bit grey, but it doesn't make you a murderer.'

'Not a deliberate one, anyway,' said Debbie.

'Exactly.' I wiped down the kitchen counter, trying not to make it too obvious that I wasn't as impressed with Debbie's kitchen hygiene as I was with her flirting skills, but luckily she was still standing outside and giggling coquettishly at the soul food stall holder. 'For goodness sake, woman, behave yourself! You're a happily married woman.' Germaine barked at Debbie to show her own doggy disapproval.

'Don't you get all judgemental on me,' said Debbie, reaching down to make a fuss of Germaine. 'I'm not the one who goes around sniffing other dogs' bums.'

'I should hope not!' I said. She laughed.

'You know I'd never cheat on Callum, he's my big chunk of love. But just because you're on a diet it don't mean you can't look at the menu.'

Mum laughed. 'Ooh I like that! And he is a bit of a dish…'

'Yeah, but you think any bloke between the age of twenty and seventy with a pulse and all their own teeth is a dish,' I said. I rinsed out the cloth and put it to one side. 'Debs, what can you remember about last night? About the hoodie wearer?'

'I don't know, it was pretty dark...' Debbie screwed up her face, thinking. 'I didn't even notice him until he was right on top of us.'

'No,' I said, but I was thinking, *him?* Why were we assuming it had been a man? 'How tall do you reckon they were?'

'How tall? I dunno. My height, maybe? Probably a bit taller. Taller than you, anyway.'

'Yeah, I think so. How tall are you?'

'Five foot six.' She threw a pose, much to the amusement of Soul Food Man, who laughed and wolf whistled. She gave him a curtsy. 'The only thing stopping me having a modelling career was being too short.'

'The *only* thing? Surely not...'

'Oi!'

'So between five six and, what, five eight? Five nine?'

'Yeah. No taller than that, I reckon.'

'You're looking for a short bloke, then,' said Mum. 'Like Tom Cruise.'

'I doubt Tom Cruise is in Cornwall murdering ex-rock stars, Shirley,' said Debbie.

'You never know. Maybe this Lee fella was caught up in something to do with that weird cult all the stars are in. The Scientolologololists.'

'You've got about a hundred too many "lol"s in there, Shirley.'

'You know what they're like, though. They don't like it when one of 'em leaves the cult.'

I gritted my teeth. 'We are NOT looking for Tom Cruise, Mum,' I said. 'Or a Scientologist. We might not even be looking for a man.' Because it had just occurred to me that Caz Harper must be five foot six in her high-heeled boots. 'I should've known all along it wasn't the dealer, because he's at least six foot. Our mystery man is too short. We just immediately assumed it was the dealer because of the hoodie. And now we're assuming it's a man, when it could just as well be a woman.'

'So what do we do now?' asked Debbie.

'Apart from getting more pies in the oven? What we should've done in the first place. Find out who had motive.'

'Who had motive?' That was (or should be) always the first question in a murder investigation. 'Who had opportunity?' was usually next, followed by an often frustrated 'Can we prove it?' Most murders are relatively easy to solve, but not so easy to prove beyond reasonable doubt; most victims know their killer, and nine times out of ten it's a partner – normally romantic, but sometimes business. Or more usually an *ex*-partner, one who refuses to accept that it's over, the 'If I can't have you, no one else can' type. I thought uneasily of Caz, and her obvious dislike of Lee's late girlfriend. She hadn't even tried to deny it. And of course that girlfriend had died of unnatural causes… Had there been anything at the time to suggest it hadn't been an accident?

But that was ridiculous. Caz had just felt a bit possessive of Lee, surely, like I did with Tony; it didn't mean anything. She'd been with Ian for years, they had a grown-up child at university, they were happily married. She had no call to be jealous, certainly not jealous enough to murder anyone. And presumably she'd been with Ian all night, so she had an alibi. Although we hadn't checked yet. I meant, *the police* hadn't checked yet.

*Oh my God,* I thought, as it suddenly struck me that maybe that was why I wasn't keen on Jocasta. Maybe Nathan was right and *I* was being jealous? I'd had Mum to myself for the last four years, and I was used to her relying on me. As much as I moaned about her (not *that* much, honestly), and as much as I hadn't expected to have her living with me full-time, not until she was older, anyway – I loved my mum, and I was used to being her best friend, more so than Tony's mum was, or any of the others at the Wednesday coffee morning. And now this Jocasta-come-lately had turned up and it was all 'Jocasta says this' and 'Jocasta can do that', and… Oh my God, I was being a complete dick.

Mum passed me a tray of pies and I unthinkingly put them in the oven. She tutted and took them out again.

'They're already cooked,' she said, shaking her head. 'Honestly, when you're in the middle of an investigation your head's away with the fairies.'

'I thought they might need warming through before we put them out,' I lied. I wasn't going to tell her that I hadn't actually been pondering the investigation at that point, or what I'd really been thinking about.

'They've just come out of the oven,' she said, exchanging a what-is-she-like look with Debbie. 'I literally just put them on a cool tray so it wouldn't scorch the counter. Or burn your hands!' She turned to Debbie. 'Health and safety nightmare, this one.'

'Oi, do you mind? Who's the one who still insists on using the same spoon to taste everything? You remember that batch of mayonnaise I got you to make for the Rotary Club buffet? Three times I had to get you to make it, because you kept sticking your finger in to test the seasoning.'

'That's hygiene, not health and safety,' said Mum, with completely misplaced smugness. 'And me fingers were perfectly clean. I used a different one each time.'

'Really not the point…' I looked at my watch and was surprised to see it was almost three o'clock. I wasn't sure if it was later or earlier than I'd thought it was; festival time seemed to work in a different way to real time. The steady stream of festivalgoers coming into the food area was starting to increase as all the revellers who had stayed up late last night woke up and started to think about breakfast. As a wise man once said, time is an illusion, lunchtime doubly so. I needed to get my mind back on the job in hand.

Debbie went off to do a shift in the drug-testing tent, leaving me and Mum to serve the hungry hordes and Germaine to lie lazily in the shade of the truck. Soul Food Man opposite was cooking up a storm, and it smelt amazing. I was tempted by the aroma of the Jamaican jerk chicken, but having lived and worked in South London for almost twenty years, I knew it wasn't for me. A West Indian colleague had brought some into work one day and I'd tucked into it enthusiastically, only to have my mouth spontaneously combust from the heat of the chilli peppers. 'Oh, is it too hot?' my colleague had asked, innocently. 'I made it milder than usual, because I knew you lot would be having some.' The American hot dogs and the gourmet burgers also smelt delicious – it was the fried onions that did it – but I was more of a curry fan, and I was definitely going for an aloo palak with basmati rice and a paratha from the Indian vegetarian food stall when we had a quiet moment. I'd been too engrossed with the death of Lee Roskill and keeping a steady supply of pies going that I'd completely forgotten to eat lunch, which really wasn't like me at all.

'Is she daydreaming about food or the investigation?' said Nathan. I looked up from the counter and saw him and Daisy standing in front of me, grinning.

'Both,' said Daisy. 'She'll be thinking, "I could murder a hot dog."' Germaine whined in alarm. 'That's not a *dog*, Germaine, it's a sausage in a bun.' The dog pricked up her ears at the word 'sausage'.

'No,' I corrected Daisy, with as much dignity as I could muster. 'I was thinking I could murder a curry.' I smiled tentatively. 'Everything okay, is it?'

'Yeah, we're letting her go with a warning,' said Nathan. 'I've warned her not to spend the evening with a drug dealer again, unless she wants her mum to go ballistic.'

'Oh ha ha,' said Daisy, but there was a hint of forced bravado there; she was clearly worried that I *was* about to go ballistic. I smiled at her.

'I trust you to be sensible,' I said. 'You know my feelings on drugs.'

'You reckon they should all be legalised, so they can be properly controlled, taxed, and the revenue raised spent on rehabilitation and education,' she said. 'I overheard you and Nathan talking that time.'

'Yeah...' Bugger, my daughter had picked up my

talent for eavesdropping. 'Yes, well, be that as it may, and regardless of whether you think the odd pill or bit of weed is no more harmful than alcohol—'

'Which you do.'

'*Regardless* of that, taking drugs is still illegal, and if you get caught you'll get into trouble.'

'So the moral of the story is don't get caught,' cackled Mum over my shoulder.

'I give up.' I looked at Nathan. 'What about Dyer? Does this give him an alibi?'

'Looks like it. The ME came back with a rough time of death, although she reckoned that the tide coming in and covering some of the body makes it harder to pin down, with the water being cold. But she reckons between nine-thirty and one in the morning. Which is when this one—' he indicated Daisy '—and her friends were with him in the tent.'

'I don't suppose he was wearing a watch that happened to handily smash and stop as he hit the rocks?' I asked.

'That would've been nice. No fitness tracker either, to record when his heart stopped.'

'I don't think Lee Roskill was the sort of person who was into counting his daily steps,' I said. 'Were there any drugs in his system?'

'No idea, we won't get the results of any tox

screening back for at least twenty-four hours, probably more. I persuaded Dyer to voluntarily give up his hoodie for DNA testing as well, to see if the person who took it had anything to do with Roskill's death. I've told Matt to mark both of them as urgent, but at the moment we've not got anything to say for certain that it wasn't an accident.'

'It wasn't, though,' I said stubbornly.

'I don't think it was, either,' said Nathan, 'but we're just going on a hunch, aren't we? We can't say, "Please do this under extreme urgency as we just have this feeling", can we?'

'No, I suppose not…' I looked past him. The afternoon rush was coming to an end, not just for us but for all the other stalls too. They would all stay open, to pick off any hungry stragglers between them, and if Sean had been there he would no doubt have stayed open too. But Sean was on a beach in Halkidiki, watching his youngest say 'I do', and he didn't have a murder to investigate. 'I think we could probably shut for a bit,' I said casually. 'Mum and I could do with a break, and there's not so many people about now.'

'Good idea,' said Nathan, knowing full well that my 'break' would just be me switching into nosy detective mode.

I closed up the truck and got some cold drinks from

the fridge, then we sat out the back on folding chairs and a picnic rug eating our late lunch/early dinner. Jocasta joined us, fresh from her stint manhandling people's feet, contributing a loaf of heavily seeded bread from the nearby organic bakery stall to the feast. As I took it from her I thought, *I hope she's washed her hands,* but then I told myself off and thanked her. She looked at me slightly warily, and I felt awful, especially when the bread turned out to be probably the best I'd ever tasted. As we ate, the sound of music floated across the festival site on a very welcome breeze; a local band who did heavy metal versions of old disco classics were currently butchering 'I'm Every Woman'.

'Here you all are,' said Tony, coming round the side of the truck with Carmen. They both flopped onto the picnic rug.

'What a racket,' said Carmen, screwing up her face. 'We were hoping you wouldn't be able to hear it so much up here, but somehow it's worse for being a bit quieter. It's like you can almost *not* hear it, but it's just there, irritating your eardrums.'

I laughed. 'That's probably the most charitable review they've ever had.' Carmen assumed a serene expression and put her hands together as if in prayer.

'Well, I am a woman of God,' she said, and laughed. 'I think He'd forgive me for thinking a few less than

Christian thoughts about their version of "I Will Survive".'

'He should've sent a thunderbolt for that one,' agreed Jocasta, and we all laughed.

'So, Carmen's had an interesting morning,' said Tony. Carmen rolled her eyes and elbowed him. 'What?'

'What happens in the peace tent stays in the peace tent, remember?' she said, shaking her head.

'That's Confession,' said Tony. 'Your lot don't do Confession. I always thought that was a bit of a cop-out. You can do what you like, as long as you say you're sorry afterwards.'

'I don't think that's quite how it works,' said Carmen, raising her eyebrows at Nathan, who shook his head.

'Don't look at me, I'm a very bad Catholic. As a police officer though, I love confessions. I don't even care if they're sorry or not, as long as I get to bang them up.'

I sighed dreamily. 'Ooh, I love it when you talk like something out of *The Sweeney*…' I mopped up the last of my spinach and potato curry with my paratha bread and chomped on it. 'So anyway… What's been going on in the peace tent? Who's confessing to what?'

'No one's confessing to anything,' said Carmen. 'That's not what it's there for. We get people in who are just a bit overwhelmed with the festival experience—'

'Off their tits,' Tony translated. Carmen ignored him.

'—for whatever reason, whether that's because the music and all the people have got a bit too much, or, yes, maybe they've taken things they shouldn't have done, or if they're having a bit of a mental health crisis. We sit them down, give them a cup of tea and let them talk, if they want to. Or they can just sit quietly for a while. We don't hurry them.'

'So...?'

Carmen rolled her eyes, but she wasn't really annoyed. 'You won't let anything go, will you? I had your old rock idols in the tent for a couple of hours this morning.'

'Who? Caz and Ian?'

'Is that their names?' She looked at Tony, and he nodded. 'Yes, them. They seemed quite upset, especially her. They sat there for a long time, quietly at first, like they were a bit shell-shocked, and then they went into a little huddle, discussing something or other, and then they left.'

Tony looked at me. 'Is it to do with what's happened on the beach?'

'Why, what's happened on the beach?' asked Nathan, as if he didn't know.

'They found Lee Roskill's body on the rocks,' said Mum. Nathan looked surprised, then looked at me. I shrugged.

'You know what she's like… I had to tell her.'

'We heard it from Debbie, anyway,' said Tony. Nathan grunted.

'Is there anyone in the whole festival grounds who *doesn't* know what happened?'

'Now that Mum and Debbie know? And Tony? They probably know in Land's End by now.' I turned to Carmen. 'Did you hear what they were talking about?'

'No, and even if I did, I wouldn't be able to tell you. Because what happens in the peace tent—'

'Stays in the peace tent. Fair enough,' I said.

'So was it murder?' asked Tony, eagerly. 'Or are you just getting carried away as usual?' I flicked my curry-stained wooden fork at him.

'No I'm not! Bloody cheek!'

'We're not ruling out any possibilities,' said Nathan diplomatically. Jocasta nodded.

'So it *was* murder, then,' she said. Nathan rolled his eyes.

'Why do I bother denying it?' he asked. 'You lot immediately draw your own conclusions anyway. Yes, it *could* have been murder, but we're only really basing that on the fact that Jodie and Debbie witnessed that massive argument Roskill had earlier in the day.'

'I told you about that,' Tony said to Carmen. She laughed.

'Yes. You do like to pass on the gossip. You're worse than some of my parishioners.'

'But,' said Nathan, 'we do still need to consider the possibility that it could have been an accident.'

'But it wasn't,' I said. Nathan sighed.

'I'm glad you're still keeping an open mind…'

'So, hang on, does that mean Caz Harper's a suspect?' asked Tony, wide-eyed. 'After all, she was the one shouting at him.'

'Not just her,' I said. 'Ian was furious too. And I don't suppose their manager Dougie was best pleased.'

'Or the rest of the band,' said Daisy. 'It's not just the two of them, is it? They've got a bloke playing the drums and a guitarist.'

'Neil Hiller on the drums,' said Tony. 'He's part of the original line-up. I think the guitarist is a new bloke they brought in to take over from Lee.'

'That makes sense,' I said. 'Has Matt talked to either of them?'

Nathan shook his head. 'I don't know if he's had a chance to speak to any of the band yet. He's been concentrating on finding witnesses near the beach, and digging into Roskill's background.'

'Has he found the new girlfriend?' I asked.

'No. We only have her first name to go on. Sunil's running background checks to see who's listed as his next of kin but I haven't heard back yet.' He gave me a rueful smile. 'I know I'm not supposed to be on duty officially, but Matt's not senior enough to be SIO on this one, and if I don't step in he'll have to call in the new DCI over at Camelford to take charge.' The new DCI had transferred down from upcountry somewhere a few months previously, and already had a reputation for being a stickler for the rules. He definitely wouldn't have approved of me taking an interest in the investigation, despite my previous experience in the Met or my local knowledge.

'It's all right,' I said. 'I'm surprised you've resisted this long.'

Daisy looked at her watch. '"This long"? It's only been about ten hours since they found the body.' She shook her head. 'You two really are made for each other.'

'If we had Roskill's phone, that would help,' I said.

'Yeah, it would. No sign of it, though. Sunil's requested his phone and financial records, so hopefully we'll be able to trace her from that.' Nathan looked thoughtful. 'Caz and Ian didn't seem to know much about her, but maybe Dougie McKay does.' He stood up and brushed burger bun crumbs off his shorts. 'Fancy coming for a chat? You being friends with Caz might help.'

Was I really friends with my teenage rock star idol?

Probably not, but Nathan was right; it might be a way to ingratiate ourselves with the rest of the band and get more out of them. I wondered if we'd still be friends if I ended up getting her arrested for murder…

## Chapter Eight

'I wondered when you'd come and talk to me. Everyone always forgets about the drummer.'

We'd actually been looking for Dougie McKay, but Matt hadn't known if he was still on site, so we'd headed for the backstage area because it was as good a place as any to start. But instead of the band's manager we found their drummer, Neil, relaxing on a bean bag and drinking a bottle of beer.

'I think it's because you're normally tucked away at the back of the stage,' I said. 'And here you are, at the back again.' He shrugged and held up his bottle.

'Free beer back here. Want one? Although I suppose you can't if you're on duty.' He took another swig. 'Everyone always forgets the drummer, but we're the ones holding everything together.'

'Keeping everyone in time, you mean?' I asked, plopping myself down on the bean bag next to him and immediately regretting it, because there was no way I was getting up again without rolling off it in an undignified fashion.

'Yeah…and keeping everything together generally.' He grinned at our slightly puzzled expressions. 'Drummers are down to earth. We sit there and hit stuff while the others all ponce about at the front. If it wasn't for me, the band would've fallen apart years ago.'

'Yeah? Why's that?' asked Nathan. The drummer shrugged.

'The singers, the guitar players, they're just in it for the fame. I'm the one who had to keep reminding them what we were here for.'

'And that would be what?'

'Giving voice to our artistic muse, innit?' He laughed sardonically, and took another swig of beer. 'She's the only faithful mistress, at the end of the day. More so than any of the groupies Lee had flinging themselves at him.'

'Did he get a lot of that?' I asked, wondering to myself what Caz would've made of them. After all, she hadn't been impressed by any of his actual girlfriends, by the sounds of it.

'Lee could have his pick of the women when we were on tour,' he said. He looked like he was about to say more, but then covered his mouth to hide a burp. 'But then he always could, even before he was famous. You know how the band got started?'

'No,' said Nathan.

'I used to go out with a mate of Caz's. I already knew Lee from school. We'd been talking about getting a band together but there ain't much you can do with just a drummer and a guitarist.'

'White Stripes,' I murmured, and he laughed.

'Yeah, all right, but who wants to be in a band with their sister? Anyway, the three of us – me, Lee and my then girlfriend Abby – we were down the pub, when Abby points out this friend of hers.'

'Caz?'

'Yeah. Lee always fancied himself with the ladies, so he rocked over to her and said something cheesy like, "Wanna be in my band?" Only of course he didn't have one. And of course most of the time the girls would just giggle and look impressed. But this time, she said yeah, she would. She'd always wanted to be in a band.' He smiled, remembering. 'So unless he wanted to look like a complete muppet, he had to get a band together, and quickly.'

'He only started it up to impress Caz?'

'Pretty much. And then it turned out that she couldn't play any instruments, so he ended up showing her how to play the bass line to this song he'd been messing about with in his bedroom, and she was a natural.' He put down his empty beer bottle and leant back in the bean bag unsteadily, hands behind his head. 'Lee always was a jammy bugger. He was one of those people who could do just about anything he put his mind to. He had piano lessons during school lunch break, and one day I was taking the mickey out of him about it and he said, "All right then, I'll play the guitar instead," and he just picked one up and that was it, he was brilliant.'

'That would be annoying,' I said, but Neil shook his head.

'Nah, because he never showed off about it or thought he was anything special.' His face suddenly darkened. 'Not back then, anyway…'

'Him and Caz,' said Nathan. 'Why did they break up?'

'I don't know, I think they realised that the only time they really got on was when we were all onstage. There was no big falling out or anything, they seemed to just decide to be friends and bandmates, rather than anything else. And then Ian joined, and that was it. Caz and him were an item within days.'

'But Lee was all right with that?'

'Oh yeah. Truth be told, I reckon Lee was still picking up other women all the time he was supposedly dating

Caz.' He shook his head. 'He was a great songwriter, but a crappy boyfriend.'

'Still, must've been a bit awkward at first, especially all being on tour together,' said Nathan.

'What do you mean?'

'Him and Caz having been close – and then her being with Ian, and him being with different women, and then Emily...' Neil gave a slight start, but whether it was surprise or another burp I couldn't say.

'Lee might've been okay about it, but was Caz?' I asked.

'You know about Emily? The one who died?' We both nodded. 'Caz wasn't keen on her, but she wasn't jealous.' Was it me, or was there a slight emphasis on 'she'? 'I think she worried about Lee getting into trouble with the drugs again, that was all. Ian and Dougie, they were the ones who really didn't like her.'

'Why was that?' asked Nathan.

'I think Dougie felt like she made his life harder. Lee wasn't the same person when he was on drugs, and after we started to get famous... Well, he became a right nightmare, to be honest with you. He was a pain in the arse at times and Dougie had enough to do just making sure he was in the right place at the right time, and then she came along and he had to look after her, as well. She was all right on her own, it was just when her and Lee got together, they kind of…' He mimed an explosion with his hands.

'What about Ian?' I asked. 'You said he didn't like her either. It's probably not relevant,' I added, reassuringly, 'but it's good to have some background.'

'It's nothing, really,' he said dismissively. 'Ian's just really anti-drugs, and he didn't like the way Lee and Emily went on sometimes, that's all.' We waited for him to say more, and sure enough he did, to fill the awkward silence. 'Look, in the early days Caz used to take stuff when we were touring. Half the time she didn't even really want to, but Lee would moan and call her boring, and she'd kind of get sucked into it. At one point it looked like she might be getting a problem, but Ian made sure it didn't get that far. And Lee was starting to realise he couldn't go on like that, so he was trying to get clean. And then he and Emily got together, and she came to the States with us, and all the drug shite started up again. Ian and Caz were parents by then, and they brought their kid along for some of the tour. Ian didn't want his kid seeing his mum doing anything like that, which was fair enough. There were a few arguments, but they got past it. Why are you even asking me about Emily, anyway? It was years ago. It's got nothing to do with what's happened now.'

'Just background,' said Nathan, noncommittally, but I

could tell he was thinking the same as me: that there was more to the group dynamic than Neil was letting on. 'We need to build up a picture of Lee and what his life was like before he died. What about this new lady friend of his, Rebecca? Can you tell me anything about her?'

'No, not really. None of us ever met her. We didn't even hear about her until a few months ago. I got the feeling that Lee needed to compartmentalise things, you know what I mean?'

'He needed to keep his personal life and the band separate?' I said. Neil nodded.

'Yeah. I suppose because things went pear-shaped after Emily died, and it was all linked to touring and being with us lot. I suppose he wanted to keep the new one safe.' He smiled thinly. 'We were part of his old, bad life, and she was part of his new, better one. I can't blame him for trying to keep us separate.'

'I know you didn't meet her, but did he talk to you about her?' asked Nathan. 'We're still trying to track her down.'

'Sorry, I don't even know her last name. But I do know he was mad about her. I spoke to him a few weeks back, before he took out the court injunction, and he was talking about starting a family and everything.'

'Really? It was that serious?' Nathan made a note in his pad. 'You say you spoke to him – how was he? Did he say anything about taking out that court order, or anything that might've made you think he wasn't happy with you playing his songs?'

'No, quite the opposite.' Neil looked nonplussed. 'We spoke quite a bit, never for very long, but often. He was like the old Lee again, like the kid I knew from school, before he started believing all his own hype. He was actually really excited about playing here, so I was surprised when he pulled out, and then when we got the court injunction – I couldn't believe it.'

'He never gave you any indication he was planning to do that?' I asked.

'No, he didn't. Like I said, I was really surprised, because I was under the impression he needed the money.'

'Oh yes?' said Nathan, leaning forward.

'Yeah. Silly sod must've spaffed it all up the wall on drugs. I mean, I'm not rolling in it but I'm doing all right. So by rights he should've been loaded.'

'What makes you say that?' I asked. Neil looked at me like I was daft.

'He was the main songwriter, wasn't he? He did write a few with Caz, and some with Ian, but not many – that's why we ended up playing a load of cover versions on Friday night. You know how they split up song royalties?' Nathan and I shook our heads. 'It's pretty complicated – there's public performance rights, publishing rights, digital rights – I won't go into them all but basically, when you make a record, the money gets split fifty-fifty between the band and the publisher. The publisher pays for stuff like the recording studio and that. The other fifty per cent gets divvied up between the band. You get a share for performing on the song, then another share for composing. If someone composed most of the song but someone else wrote the chorus, say, they'd both get money for writing the song, but they might decide that the person who only wrote the chorus should get half a share and the one who did the rest gets a full share.' He looked at our confused faces and grinned. 'Are you still with me?'

'Just about. Can we cut to the chase?' asked Nathan. 'What you're saying is, Lee Roskill should've earned a lot more money than the rest of you, because he wrote most of your songs as well as playing on them?'

'In a nutshell, yes. I earnt royalties for playing the drums, but I didn't really have any other input in the songs themselves so that's fair enough. Ian sometimes wrote a keyboard riff or whatever, so he might get a little bit more than me as a co-composer as well as a performer. Caz wrote the lyrics on several songs, so she would get more money for that. But Lee wrote at least eighty per cent of our songs on his own, so he got the lion's share of royalties.' He sighed. 'I never resented him getting more than the rest of us, because he was a bona fide musical genius. If he'd been able to work out a way of playing more than one instrument at a time he wouldn't have needed the rest of us. He could play anything.'

'*You* never resented it,' I said. 'Does that mean the others did?'

'What? No, it was just a figure of speech.' Neil looked uncomfortable. 'Caz and Ian aren't exactly struggling themselves, are they? You should see their new house.'

'I have,' I said.

'Then you'll know they ain't short of a few bob. I think Caz misses the excitement of playing, but they don't need the money.'

There wasn't a lot more to be gleaned from Neil, especially when the local band who'd been performing finished and came backstage, keen to party. We said our goodbyes and left him holding court with the young wannabe rock stars, recounting tales of touring overseas to his eager little audience, but not before tipping us off about where we should look next.

We found Dougie McKay in the festival car park, although 'car park' seemed like an overly grand title for the heavily rutted field full of cars stuffed in cheek by jowl, or bonnet by trunk. I hoped that the weather wouldn't turn nasty and subject the deep muddy ruts to a downpour, because it would turn the whole thing into a quagmire which no one would be able to escape from; least of all McKay in his sleek, black and very new Audi TT, which in addition to being sleek and black was also very low to the ground.

McKay was sitting in the front seat of his car, door open as wide as possible to let in some air. He was talking animatedly to someone on his mobile phone. He saw us approach but continued his conversation. 'It's a bloody nightmare,' he said to the person on the other end of the phone. He covered the mouthpiece and looked up at us, and I hoped he wouldn't remember me hiding in the stars-only bogs the day before. 'Look, if you're from the press—'

Nathan pulled his wallet out of his pocket and flashed his warrant card at him. 'Douglas McKay? We'd like a quick chat, sir, if you have a moment.'

McKay paused, then quickly finished his telephone conversation. 'Gotta go. But you'll be there when we said, yeah?' He hung up and climbed out of the car. 'Sorry about that. Can I just see your ID again…?' He gestured to Nathan's warrant card. Nathan handed it to him and McKay studied it for a few seconds before handing it back. 'Sorry, Chief Inspector. I might be a bit paranoid but, as you can imagine, there's been a lot of fallout for me to deal with this morning. And of course the press have got hold of it now, so the vultures have started to descend. What can I do for you? I must say I am very glad to see the authorities investigating Lee's unfortunate death so thoroughly.'

'We investigate all sudden deaths where there's no obvious cause,' said Nathan.

'No obvious cause? I thought he fell over and hit his head?' said McKay.

'We are still establishing the cause of death,' I said.

'But it *was* an accident, yes?' he said, looking from me to Nathan and back again. 'Please don't tell me it was anything else, the last few days have been bad enough as it is.' He sighed. 'Shall we go somewhere more comfortable? Like I said, I had a few phone calls to make and my car was the only place I could find a bit of peace and quiet.'

'Of course,' said Nathan, stepping back and indicating to him to lead the way. McKay weaved between the cars and headed for a patch of grass at the side of the field. We all sat down under a tree. From here we could see the glamping area, where Mum had her yurt, and in the distance the stretch of beach where Lee Roskill had met his fate.

McKay leant back against the trunk of the tree and fanned himself ineffectually with his hand. He wasn't really dressed for the hot weather, or for a festival for that matter, in smart jeans and a designer polo shirt, but without his phone in his hand he seemed a bit more relaxed.

'I'm sorry, DCI Withers, I'm not sure what I can tell you but I'm happy to answer any questions you have. It's just been very stressful. I was led to believe that it was an accident, which is bad enough, but now are you telling me it was deliberate?'

'Do you think an accident would be more likely?' asked Nathan.

'Yes, probably. You obviously know that Lee had a drug problem?' McKay looked at us, and we both nodded.

'We heard that he had in the past, but that he'd been trying to get clean for a while now,' said Nathan. 'Do you think he was still taking drugs? Did it look like he was under the influence when he confronted the band on Friday afternoon?'

McKay looked mildly surprised. 'You know about the argument?' He glanced at me and gave a sudden start of amused recognition. 'Of course, you're the "toilet inspector", aren't you? You must've heard everything. You saw him. He didn't look like a man who was in a good place, did he? I'll be honest with you, when I heard about the accident I did just assume that he'd been high or drunk and hadn't looked where he was going. The way he confronted us... I wish I'd known how bad things were with him. I don't know that I could have helped him, but I could've tried.'

'What had the relationship between Mr Roskill and the rest of the band been like, before the court order and the argument?'

McKay pursed his lips, giving it some thought. 'I don't know. I don't really mix with them socially these days, but I know they all keep in touch with each other. I think things had been a bit strained over the last few years, but I was under the impression that they'd started talking more recently – him and Caz – and that they were on friendly terms. Caz and Ian seemed certain that he was happy about playing the festival, right up to the point where he told them he was pulling out.'

'What about the court injunction?' asked Nathan. 'What was that all about? We can get a copy, of course, but if you could tell us the gist of it…'

'No, no, of course I can tell you about it. That came as a complete surprise. It stated in no uncertain terms that the rest of the band were not allowed to perform any of the songs that he'd written or co-written, or use the name "The Burners" as he'd originally come up with it. If we'd had more time before the performance we probably could've contested it, particularly the use of songs the others had co-written, but I think he timed it to arrive that late so we couldn't do anything about it.'

'So did that just apply to performance rights?' I asked. I'd done a quick Google search on music royalties after we'd left Neil, but to be honest it had confused things more than clarified them. McKay looked surprised.

'Well, live performance, yes, because the main performance rights – the *public* performance rights, where royalties are paid every time a song's played on the radio, or used in a film or whatever – they apply to the *recordings* of the songs, which the band members all played on, rather than being able to perform them live. Those are totally different rights.'

'So the cover versions the band played in their set, they'll have to pay those songwriters royalties for performing them?' I asked.

'Yes. Well, not the band, the festival organisers should have a licence that covers all the songs being played,' said McKay. 'It's pretty complicated.'

'I'll say,' I said. 'And then there are publishing rights – that's when they record an album, isn't it? And loads of other weird ones. Mechanical rights or something…'

'Yes, yes, like I said, it's complicated,' said McKay vaguely. 'I could sit here all day trying to explain them to you, but I don't see how they'd be relevant.'

'What was *your* relationship with Mr Roskill like?' asked Nathan. 'Friendly? Just business?'

McKay sighed. 'It's not what it was,' he said, shaking his head. 'The band and I all started together. I was friends with them before they became successful.' He smiled ruefully. 'I'll be honest with you, I wasn't just a friend, I was a fan. I went to all their early gigs. I'd always dreamt of being a rock star myself but, as Lee was always only too happy to tell me, I didn't have an ounce of musical talent in me.' He snorted. 'Not that that's necessarily a prerequisite for a successful music career, but anyway… I'd never managed a band before but it was fairly obvious to me that they could be big, really big, if they had someone to steer them in the right direction, get them the right gigs, the right contacts. So I offered to help them out, and it just kind of grew into me being their manager. Which was great, but it affected our relationships because sometimes I had to make decisions they weren't happy about.'

'Like what?' asked Nathan.

'Things like tours. There were a few venues they weren't keen on playing but that always sold well, that kind of thing.'

'Still, must be fun, managing a band,' I said.

'Yes,' said McKay, but not terribly convincingly. He noticed my raised eyebrow. 'Yes, it was definitely more fun than an office job, and once they got successful I got to travel the world and everything, but – do you have kids?'

'Yeah, one. Teenager.'

'Imagine the logistics of taking four overgrown teenagers on a world tour,' he said, and I shuddered.

'Right. I get your point. You had to nanny them?'

'Some more than others. Sometimes they were overgrown teenagers, sometimes they were more like toddlers. I stopped just short of cutting up their food for them and wiping their arses.'

'How did you feel about Lee bringing his girlfriend on tour?' asked Nathan.

'You mean Emily?' said McKay, warily. 'I could hardly complain about him bringing someone. I met my wife when we were on the road in Europe, and she came on the first leg of that US tour with us. The two of them used to hang out together when we were busy doing band stuff. It would've been hypocritical of me to say that having Emily there was distracting him.' But that was clearly what he'd thought.

'What did you think of her?' I asked, watching him carefully. He shrugged.

'I didn't know her very well. She was Lee's girlfriend, I had no need to talk to her that much.'

'Not even when you were all on tour together for months?' I persisted. 'Staying at the same hotel?'

McKay stared at me, and for a moment I thought he was going to ignore the question, but he didn't.

'Okay,' he said eventually. 'I didn't like her. But I wasn't the only one. Caz was always funny about Lee's girlfriends – you know they used to go out together? I think she always felt a little bit possessive of him. Ian disapproved of her because she was a junkie, and a complete liability. Neil was sore about her coming along at first, and I did think it was insensitive of Lee to bring her—'

'Insensitive?' asked Nathan. 'Why?'

'Because he went out with her first. Not for long – only a couple of months – but then she dumped him for Lee.' Nathan and I exchanged glances. Neil hadn't told us about *that*. But then it had been a short-lived relationship, over fifteen years ago; time enough to get over it, one would think. 'I told Lee he should send her home – I even bought her a ticket, a couple of days before we reached New York – but she wouldn't leave him alone. And then of course she got completely wasted in her hotel room while the band were playing Madison Square Gardens, and when we got back she'd cut herself on the glass coffee table and bled to death.' He shook his head, a sad expression on his face. 'If only the silly girl had gone home when I told her to, things could've turned out very different for all of us.'

'How so?'

'Lee wouldn't have gone off the rails, the band would've carried on touring and they could've been global megastars. They were on the verge of conquering the States. They'd already been together ten years at that point. Ten years – that's how long I'd been working on getting them known in the US.'

'They were playing at Madison Square Garden,' Nathan pointed out. 'That must count as "conquering" the States, surely?'

'In front of twenty-four thousand people,' said McKay. 'That's more than U2 had at their first gig there. But it's still nowhere near capacity. We lost money on that venue, money we would've recouped if we hadn't had to refund all the tickets for the remaining gigs.'

'And you could've been driving a Ferrari instead of an Audi,' I said, and he smiled thinly.

'I'd have deserved it,' he said. 'I work hard.'

We left McKay heading back to his car to make more phone calls, and turned towards the glamping area. Apparently Caz and Ian were staying there in one of the yurts, while Neil was bunking in with the guitarist, a young guy called Danny who was a massive Burners fan; his mum had played their music non-stop when he was a kid, which Neil admitted had made him feel ancient. Danny had been found in a desperate last-minute internet search for a stand-in for Lee, and it seemed the fact that he had his own portable accommodation (an old VW camper van) had played almost as big a part in his recruitment as his guitar-playing ability. The camper van was parked behind the backstage area, so it didn't matter how much Neil drank, he could just roll out of his bean bag and over to his bed for the night. And it sounded like that's what had happened on the night of Lee's death. Neil, Ian, Caz and Danny had been backstage during most of the murder window, partying with a variety of different performers as they finished their sets. Ian and Caz had left them around ten-thirty, but Neil and Danny had carried on drinking with several members of the headline band and various hangers-on until well past three in the morning. By which time, Neil had gleefully told us, neither of them were even capable of speech, let alone of making their way to the beach and bashing someone's head in. We hadn't spoken to Danny, but we'd more or less discounted him; he hadn't known Lee, and it didn't sound like he wanted to join the band permanently – which *could* possibly have been a motive to get Lee out of the way for good – because he was planning to study abroad and had already booked his flights and paid for his course.

McKay hadn't joined in with the good-natured debauchery backstage, preferring to head back to the holiday cottage he was staying in a couple of miles down the road from the festival site. He'd laughed when we'd asked him if he was camping, claiming to be allergic to the great outdoors; not for him nights under canvas, not even the relatively glamorous canvas of the yurts. I wondered if it was more that he felt like an outsider. He wasn't one of the band, after all, just the poor bugger who sometimes had to make unpopular decisions and ensure everyone was onstage when they needed to be. He wasn't famous like the others were, or had been, despite his earlier dreams about being a rock star himself. I felt a bit sorry for him, and I could relate, in a way. Being a copper out for the night with a group of non-law enforcement friends had always felt a bit weird, a bit like people were watching what they said in front of you, making sure they didn't incriminate themselves. It was hard sometimes to watch everyone else being part of the gang, feeling like you were just hanging around on the periphery. I wondered how McKay had got back to his cottage; not in that shiny car of his, hemmed in as it was by about three thousand other vehicles. Maybe he'd walked? It would've been a bit of a trek, winding through the festival, out of the main entrance and then back along the road, plus it was pretty much all uphill.

Or maybe he'd got a lift from someone who'd had the foresight not to use the official car park.

'So what have we learnt?' asked Nathan.

'That everybody liked Lee, and then they didn't, and then they did again,' I said. 'Other than that, nothing helpful.'

Nathan laughed. 'No? Nothing at all? Nothing making your Spidey senses tingle?' He pulled me towards him and touched the palm of his hand to my forehead, as if feeling my temperature. 'Are you sickening for something?'

'Oh, very funny!' I said. 'What about you? What are you thinking?'

'I don't know, at this point I'm normally destroying some mad theory you've come up with.'

'Oi, you cheeky—'

Nathan's phone rang. 'Saved by the bell,' he said. 'Matt, how's it going? I'm going to put you on speakerphone…'

## Chapter Nine

'Now *that* was interesting,' said Nathan. Matt Turner had just given us the lowdown on Lee Roskill's finances, which could be summed up quite easily in the phrase 'nowhere near the amount of money you'd expect a bestselling rock star to have'. I shrugged.

'The Burners' heyday has been well and truly over for a while now. Neil already said he thought Lee needed the money.'

'Yeah, but this confirms it,' said Nathan. 'So the question is, what made him pull out of the festival, when it was a guaranteed payday? Matt spoke to the organisers and they confirmed that The Burners would have headlined if Lee had appeared, and they would've been paid accordingly.'

'Twenty-five grand for one night's work!' I said. 'Although when you break it down, split it between the four of them, give McKay his cut, pay any expenses getting here and that…'

'He still must've got at least five thousand,' said Nathan. 'I'm surprised they pay that much. It's not Glastonbury, is it?'

'You're joking,' said a cheerful voice beside us. We turned to see Ian, holding two hotdogs. 'You play Glastonbury for the kudos, not the money. You coming to see us?' He nodded towards a yurt set in the shade of a tree, obviously one of the better sites. Caz was sitting outside. She looked up and saw us, and gave a hesitant wave. Ian lowered his voice, although she was too far away to hear us. 'We've been lying low since you told us about Lee. It was a real shock. We're both upset, but Caz especially. They used to go out together, a long time ago, before she met me. But she'll be fine if you need to ask us any more questions.'

We followed him over to the yurt. He held up the hotdogs and smiled. 'We did fancy another pie, but our favourite food truck was shut.'

'Sorry, I needed a break from pastry,' I said. Caz smiled as she took the hotdog from Ian and tucked into it. Grief hadn't harmed her appetite then, I thought, but maybe I was being uncharitable. Maybe she'd had a good cry and it had exhausted her.

'Are you okay to answer a few more questions?' asked Nathan. 'I'm sorry to bother you again, but obviously this is an ongoing investigation.'

'No, it's fine,' she said, through a mouthful of fried onions.

'Where were you last night, after you came off stage?' asked Nathan. Caz looked surprised and hastily swallowed.

'Where were we? Is this you asking us for alibis?' She turned to me. 'Does this mean you think Lee was murdered, after all?'

'We still can't say for sure,' I said. 'Investigations are ongoing.'

'But there's something that makes you think it's suspicious?' she persisted.

'There are one or two things that are inconsistent with an accidental death,' I said carefully. Nathan nodded.

'We're covering all bases,' he said. 'So were you together for the rest of the night? Specifically between nine-thirty and one a.m.?'

Ian nodded. 'Yes, we were with the rest of the band until about ten-thirty, and then we went back to our tent to chill out for a bit and we didn't leave again for the whole night.'

Caz sighed and shook her head. 'Don't, Ian.'

'Don't what?' Ian tried to look innocent, but it was obvious he knew what she was talking about.

'I wasn't off murdering Lee, but if you lie about where I was at the time and they find out, it'll look worse, won't it?'

Nathan and I exchanged glances.

'So you *weren't* together at the time of the murder?' asked Nathan.

'No,' said Caz. 'Not for all of it, anyway. We were back at the tent by eleven, but I went for a walk about half an hour later.'

'Where did you go?' I asked.

'I don't know.' She looked at us both, then quickly continued. 'I don't mean I had a blackout or anything like that. It was just dark and I got a bit lost. I…'

'Go on.'

'Okay, in the past, when we were on tour, we sometimes used to, you know, "party"…'

'You used to take drugs,' said Nathan, careful to keep his voice non-judgemental.

'Yeah. I mean it was mostly Lee who did it, I only did now and again, if it had been a long tour and I was running out of energy. Well, even though we'd all been looking forward to playing again, on Friday we were all feeling a bit nervous. It'd been such a long time since we played in front of an audience…'

Ian smiled. 'We used to jump around onstage and that, but we're getting on a bit now. It's all right for me, I'm stuck behind the keyboard so I can't move about that much anyway, but Caz was worried she wouldn't have the energy to perform the way she used to.'

'And of course the argument didn't help,' said Caz.

'So you took something?' I asked.

'Yeah. I'm not sure what it was, just a bit of speed, I think. I was wide awake and all jittery, I couldn't sit still. In the old days Dougie would make sure there was stuff around to take the edge off the after-gig buzz, maybe a bit of weed or some sleeping pills or something—'

'Although *we* didn't normally do that,' said Ian. 'Normally Caz and I would go for a walk afterwards, get some fresh air and see a bit of the place we were playing.'

'So I thought I'd go and walk it off like we used to,' explained Caz. 'And I realised I'd left my phone backstage, so I decided to go and get it.'

'But you stayed in the tent?' I asked Ian. He looked a bit sheepish.

'Yeah. I was completely knackered. I did offer to go with her, but she was hyper and I was half asleep, so not a good combo.'

'So you went back to the stage to find your phone?' asked Nathan. There would definitely have been people around the backstage area, I thought, and they would be able to confirm her alibi.

'That was the plan,' said Caz. 'But I got completely lost. I don't know how, the stage was all lit up and I could see it in the distance, but I just seemed to keep walking around in circles. I think whatever I took was stronger than I thought. I think that's why I'm feeling so shady now, it's only just properly worn off and I'm hungry and knackered, as well a bit emotional, even without Lee… I'm annoyed that I didn't get back to the stage then, because my phone might still have been there.'

'It's not there now?'

'No. We went to have a look this morning, but someone must've picked it up.'

'Did you end up anywhere near the beach?' asked Nathan.

'I did find myself heading in that direction at one point,' said Caz, 'but I realised that I was going in the opposite direction to where I wanted to be, so I turned round. And then I ended up on top of the hill, not far from your food truck, actually. Totally wrong place. After that I started to feel a bit calmer, so I went back to the tent and, um, worked off some of my energy with Ian…'

Ian grinned. 'All these years together and she still fancies me.'

'I *was* on drugs, love,' said Caz.

'Thanks…' said Ian, pretending to be offended.

'Did you see anyone while you were wandering around?' asked Nathan. 'Anyone acting suspiciously, maybe, or even someone who can corroborate your story?'

Caz thought for a moment. 'No, not really… Obviously there were people about, but it was dark and I didn't see anyone I know.' She opened her mouth to say something else, then shook her head. 'No, he probably didn't see me, he was in a hurry.'

'Who?'

'This, er, bloke in a hoodie…' She was reluctant to say more.

'Do you mean our resident festival drug dealer?' I asked, and she looked surprised.

'You know about him?'

'We're aware,' said Nathan. 'How do you know him?'

'Oh, I don't. But I saw Dougie talking to him earlier. I assume that's who he got the speed or whatever it was from. I recognised the bloke's hoodie as he rushed past me.'

'Did you get a good look at him?' asked Nathan, glancing at me.

'No, I didn't, either time. I saw him in the distance talking to Dougie before we went onstage, and I only knew it was him in the dark by the hoodie. It had this day-glo snake pattern up the sleeve.'

'Do you think he had something to do with Lee's death?' asked Ian.

'Would Lee have known him?' I asked. Ian and Caz looked at each other, then shook their heads.

'Can't see how. I don't think Lee had ever even been to Cornwall before Friday,' said Ian. 'But he was always able to sniff out drugs, wherever he was.' The way he spoke made it clear that Ian didn't think that was a particularly admirable talent to have.

Caz shook her head. 'No, he wouldn't have done anything like that, not now. He was clean. He had been for over a year.'

'One more thing,' said Nathan. 'Did Lee ever talk about money with you?'

'No,' said Caz, but she looked uneasy.

'He never mentioned needing it?' I asked. 'Neil told us Lee was keen to play here because he needed the money. He couldn't understand why Lee pulled out.'

'He wrote all of our biggest hits,' said Ian firmly. 'He got paid more than the rest of us. If he decided to go off and waste it, that's not our fault.'

'That would be a lot of money to waste, though,

wouldn't it?' said Nathan. 'For someone who supposedly made the lion's share of royalties, he seems to have done rather less well than, say, Neil, or you two.'

'I don't like what you're getting at,' said Caz. 'What exactly *are* you getting at? You think we ripped him off or something?'

'You do have a very nice, very big house,' I said. She glared at me.

'Yes, one that we worked hard and saved up for,' she said. Ian put his hand out to silence her.

'Do you know where I worked before the band took off?' he asked. Nathan and I shared a glance, and shook our heads. 'I worked in the City, in investment banking. I wasn't a trader or anything like that, but I worked in Operations, doing all the back office stuff.' He grinned. 'Believe it or not, the City's not all Hooray Henries or Old Etonians, there's a fair few of us Essex wide boys working there, too. So I know a little bit about hedge funds and share accounts, about where to put your money if you suddenly find yourself with more than you know what to do with.'

'Right…' I said, thoughtfully. Tony's mum, Brenda, had been convinced they were retired City workers. I made a mental note to tell her that she was almost right.

'I gave Lee and Neil some advice about investing their money, after the second album took off. Neil took it, but Lee thought he knew better and asked me to help him invest in a few riskier schemes.' Ian shook his head. 'I did try to talk him out of it, but he insisted, and it was his money, after all.' He frowned. 'But he should've recouped those losses years ago, with all the ongoing royalty payments. Are you saying he was skint?'

'Pretty much,' I said. Nathan gave me a warning look that said, *Don't say anything else.*

'Ian felt bad when he lost that money, but it was Lee's choice,' said Caz defiantly. 'He didn't do anything wrong.'

'No, I understand that,' said Nathan, getting to his feet. 'Thank you for your explanation. I think that covers everything for now. Are you heading home today?'

'No,' said Ian. 'We always planned to stay for the whole weekend and relive our misspent youths, but Lee's death has put a bit of a dampener on that. We're quite keen to go home, but have you seen the car park? We can't get the car out.'

'You live near enough, you could always get a taxi to pick you up,' I suggested, although there was only one taxi service in Penstowan (and Bude wasn't much better), which meant you always had to book it well in advance. Caz shook her head.

'I'd rather stay til the end anyway,' she said. 'I know it sounds stupid, but it feels like Lee's still here somewhere, and any minute he's going to pop up and say he was just mucking about.' Her eyes filled with tears, but she blinked them back. 'Stupid.'

Ian put his arm around her. 'It's not stupid. I wish that would happen, too.' He looked at us. 'We'll probably be here until Monday morning, if you need to ask us anything else.'

'Thank you,' I smiled at Caz. 'You might even still find your phone if you're sticking around,' I said. 'If you can't get your car out, the thief probably can't get theirs out either. Have you got "Find my Phone" on it?'

Caz and Ian both groaned in exasperation. 'Of course,' said Caz. 'We linked our phones up, didn't we? Ian went through a phase of leaving his phone behind when we were on tour, so we set them up to share our location and we've just kept doing it.'

'We'll have to go further up the hill to find a strong enough signal, then we can try it,' said Ian. 'It is weird how it's only yours that's missing, though.'

'What do you mean?' asked Nathan.

'We never take our phones onstage,' explained Caz. 'I started it. I always used to jump around when we were playing, and you know what the pockets are like in women's clothes – tiny or non-existent. So I started leaving my phone with Dougie while we were playing, and after Neil dropped his and stood on it mid-gig the others started doing it too.'

'So Dougie had all of your phones on Friday night?' I asked.

'Not exactly. There was a plastic box backstage that we put all our stuff in – keys, phones, wallets and that,' said Ian. 'Theoretically Dougie was supposed to be keeping an eye on it, but there were security guards around and the only people allowed backstage were bands and crew, so I suppose he let himself get distracted.'

Caz rolled her eyes. 'Probably by a girl. He's easily distracted by pretty things.'

Nathan's phone rang once and then cut out mid-ring. He glanced at it. 'Matt,' he said to me. He turned back to Caz and Ian. 'Thanks again for your time. I'd better go and find a decent signal myself so I can return this call.'

We headed back up the hill, Nathan holding his phone out like a water diviner, although he was looking for 4G rather than an underground spring.

'What do you make of Ian's explanation?' I asked him, as soon as we were out of earshot. 'It might explain why Lee didn't have as much money as you'd expect, but it doesn't explain why he didn't have *any*.'

'No…' said Nathan, although he was more intent on

the signal. He stopped, satisfied, and hit redial. 'Matt, can you hear me okay?'

'Yes, Guv. Where are you? I thought you might be back at the food truck by now,' said Matt. I looked at my watch.

'Oh bugger.'

We rushed back to the truck, where Matt and PC Chrissie were waiting for us. No wonder Matt had told us not to hurry… They were both about to tuck into Soul Food Man's jerk chicken, and looked very cosy together.

'Have you had that before?' I asked Matt.

'No, but it smells amazing,' he said. Chrissie took a deep breath and smiled.

'It's just like my Nana Grace used to make,' she said. She took a huge bite and then nodded enthusiastically. 'Oh my God, *yes*, that hits the spot.'

Matt smiled at her and took a bite of his own. I counted in my head – *one, two, three* – and watched as his smile turned into a grimace.

'Hot?' I asked. He nodded.

'A bit,' he croaked. He swallowed and made a valiant attempt to speak, but no words came out. I patted him on the arm.

'I'll get you a glass of milk.'

'Water!'

'Milk's better, trust me.' I unlocked the food truck and turned the oven on to heat, then poured some milk into a mug and took it out to the others, where Matt was looking red in the face and Nathan was laughing at him. Chrissie smiled sympathetically.

'Sorry hun – I mean, DS – Matt, I should've warned you,' she said. Nathan and I diplomatically didn't mention her slip-up, because we were hardly in a position to comment about mixing personal and professional relationships.

Matt drank the milk and then eyed the rest of his chicken suspiciously. Nathan shook his head in amusement.

'Come on then, what have you got for us? Apart from indigestion,' he asked, herding his DS over to the food truck so that we could talk more privately (and so I could get some pies in the oven and eavesdrop at the same time). Matt forked some salad into his mouth, then set down his paper plate and reached for his notebook.

'Okay, so we got the preliminary stuff back on his finances, as you heard, but Sunil is trying to get hold of the victim's accountant to see if there's anything suspicious there,' he said. 'Obviously it's the weekend, and we've only got a work number at the moment, so we've left a message.'

'How did you find his accountant?' I asked.

'There were payments to him from Roskill's bank account. We got his bank details from Dougie McKay's assistant up in London, who works 24/7 by the sound of it. She also gave us his home address and mobile number, so we've put a warrant in for phone records.'

'Even if we don't have his phone, at least we can find out who he spoke to before his death,' said Nathan. 'And with his address we should finally be able to track down this Rebecca as well.'

'If they were living together,' I pointed out.

'Yep,' said Matt, 'that's what we thought. Only the address McKay had on file was his old one. He moved about two years ago and never passed on his new one. McKay's assistant said most of their contact over the last ten years has been via email, so it never came up that he'd moved. Sunil's looking into his emails and he's also put a trace on the phone, but obviously the signal is really bad down towards the beach and we're unlikely to get a ping, so unless someone stumbles across it, we're not going to find it.'

'It's in the sea,' said Chrissie, and we all nodded in agreement.

'The ME has had a chance to have a better look at the wound,' said Matt. 'Cause of death *was* the head wound, of course, but guess how it was caused?'

'By a rock,' said Nathan and I in unison.

'Well – yeah, obvs. But there are multiple contusions around the same area,' said Matt. 'Which means—'

'Which means his head came into contact with the rock more than once,' said Nathan. 'And if you fall over, you don't typically keep hitting your head over and over again, do you?'

'So it really was murder?' I said. Matt nodded.

'Looks like it. The ME reckoned he was on the ground, and someone knelt next to him and held his head—' Matt mimed the actions as he spoke '—and smashed it at least five times into the rocks.'

'So Lee's on the beach, arguing with someone,' I said, 'there's a scuffle and he's pushed over, or maybe he steps back and trips on a rock…'

'And then whoever he's arguing with doesn't let him get up again. Ever,' said Nathan grimly. 'This wasn't an accident. It wasn't even as if someone pushed him over and killed him unintentionally. They've made a point of finishing him off.'

'But who? And why?' I asked. Matt shrugged.

'Your guess is as good as mine at the moment. We're still checking alibis. I spoke to the drummer and the guitarist—'

'So did we,' said Nathan. 'The drummer, anyway. What do you reckon?'

'Their alibis check out. Danny, the guitarist, was live streaming during the murder window on some music social media site. Chrissie had a look at it and the times check out. He confirmed that Neil was there all night, and so were Caz and Ian until about half ten, quarter to eleven. We're trying to get a crew member or anyone else who was backstage to corroborate that as well, so we're not relying on them alibiing each other. I haven't spoken to Caz and Ian yet, have you?'

'We were just leaving them when you rang,' said Nathan, and he filled Matt in. He whistled.

'So Caz Harper had opportunity…'

'How'd you work that out?' I said.

'They're camping up by the yurts, you said?' Nathan nodded. Matt flipped his notebook to a page where he'd drawn a rough sketch of the campsite and showed it to us. 'They would've been at their tent around here?' He pointed at a biro-drawn forest of what looked like teepees.

'They've got a yurt at the edge of the site, just there,' said Nathan.

'Paul Dyer's tent, with the distinctive hoodie hanging outside, is here.' Matt pointed at his drawing again, where a small rectangle sat in the middle of the camping area with the letters 'PD' on them. 'Where do you reckon you bumped into the person in the hoodie?'

'Debbie's tent is down towards the beach,' I mused, looking at the sketch. 'Around there, maybe? And we came from the food truck over here, so we went around the bottom of the yurts and into the ordinary camping area just there, and headed downwards…'

'There,' said Nathan, reaching over and stabbing the paper with a finger. 'I reckon they collided with us there. They were heading back up the hill.'

'And what time was it?'

'I didn't really look at the time. Just gone midnight? Maybe a bit later,' I said. 'I know we left the food truck at eleven fifty, and what with the dog and it being dark and that, it took us a good twenty minutes to walk Debbie to her tent.'

'And what time did Caz say she got back to *her* tent?'

'She was a bit vague,' said Nathan, 'but around midnight…'

'Right,' said Matt. 'But from what you told me, Ian was half asleep and wouldn't necessarily have known what time it was when she left or when she came back, so he would probably just go along with whatever time she said it was.'

'Maybe,' I said.

'Probably,' said Nathan. Matt traced a route down the paper with his finger.

'It's practically a straight line down from their yurt to

the section of beach where Lee Roskill was murdered. It wouldn't have taken Harper more than fifteen minutes to get down there, probably less. She would've passed Dyer's tent, where she could've picked up the hoodie, and then down to the beach, to where she'd lured Lee.'

'How would she lure him?' I asked. I couldn't believe that she would murder him. Could I? I'd had a few suspicions about their relationship, but I'd talked myself out of them.

'They were old friends,' said Nathan. 'More than that, old lovers. She could've asked if they could meet up to talk about the court order.'

'She pushes him over, hits his head against the rocks a few times—'

'She wouldn't be strong enough, surely?' said PC Chrissie. 'It takes a lot of strength to beat someone to death.'

'Not if they're already on the ground,' Matt disagreed. 'She was above him, she could put all her weight behind it.'

'I suppose so…'

'She finishes him off, then she races up the hill to drop off the hoodie – which is a good disguise, by the way, because it's big enough to cover her up and disguise her shape, and anyone who sees it will do exactly what we did: assume it's the drug dealer.'

'She knew it belonged to the dealer, as well,' said Nathan. 'If you were looking to frame someone, he makes the perfect murder suspect.'

Matt nodded. 'On her way back to return the hoodie, she bumps into you there. But you carry on down the hill and she carries on up it, puts the hoodie back and then goes back to her yurt.'

Matt finished, looking very pleased with himself.

'Well, I'm exhausted just listening to that,' I said. 'One thing, though: that's a pretty fast and furious timeline.'

'She could probably have been gone up to an hour without Ian realising she'd got her timings wrong when she spoke to us,' said Nathan.

'Or Ian might know and be covering for her,' said Chrissie. And they were right, but I didn't want them to be.

'Okay, but even so: she's in her fifties, which hardly makes her old, but that's a pretty strenuous murder you've set out, *and* coming back it's all uphill. Could she really have done it?' I shook my head. 'I'm a bit younger and probably a bit fitter, and I don't think I could've done that, not in an hour. And not while I was high as a kite, either.'

'Maybe she wasn't as out of it as she claims she was,' said Matt.

'True, but…' I wasn't convinced. 'Anyway, even if she

had opportunity – which I still think is a stretch – why would she kill him?'

'We're back to who had motive, aren't we?' said Nathan. 'I don't suppose Sunil managed to track down what would happen to the song rights when Lee died, did he?'

'Still working on it, Guv,' said Matt. 'It's Saturday, none of these lawyers or accountants or whoever work at the weekend.'

'No. Which might also mean we don't get hold of his email and phone records until next week, either.' Nathan gave a groan of frustration. 'I know it can't be helped, but it would be so much easier if we could see who he last spoke to, or track down Rebecca, while all the others are still here.'

'You think it was someone in the band, then?' I asked.

'I don't know. They were all pissed off at him pulling the plug on their big reunion gig, weren't they? Neil reckons he's all right for money, but the royalties must start to run dry at some point, unless they start touring again or release a few new songs. And although Caz and Ian appear to be sorted financially pretty much for life, both Neil and Ian said she missed touring.'

'That's if the motive *was* financial, and not something else,' I said.

'Surely with Lee Roskill dead, that would make a tour

even less likely?' said Chrissie, and I got the feeling she didn't want Caz to be guilty either. She was younger than me, so probably hadn't been around when The Burners had been at the peak of their fame, but Caz had been a feminist, girl power icon for at least two generations of teenagers.

'No, because depending on the terms of Lee's musical estate, there's nothing to stop them using the name now, or playing their old songs,' said Nathan. 'There's plenty of old 80s and 90s bands out there, doing nostalgia tours with half the original line-up missing.'

'Yeah…' I said. 'Although everything will have to go through probate first, which could take months, or even years if anyone contests it.'

We decided that, other than getting Uniform to continue their canvas of festivalgoers to see if anyone had noticed anything untoward happening, there was nothing more to be done until Sunil received Lee's phone and email records. This would probably, frustratingly, take a few more days. Although Nathan could now ask for these urgently, as the medical examiner had pretty much confirmed it was murder, it wouldn't necessarily make the phone company move any quicker, especially over a weekend. Pro tip: if you're going to murder someone, do it over a weekend or bank holiday, or Christmas for preference, because it makes tracking down potentially incriminating evidence take that much longer; long enough for you to get on a plane to Brazil and disappear.

Matt and Chrissie left us to get back to our pies. I was beginning to think that if I never ever saw another pie again until the day I died, it would still be too soon.

I put a tray of Bruce Willises in the oven and then stood in the doorway of the truck, gazing across the festival site. Looking across to the stage and then to the yurts, I could see why Caz had become a bit disoriented, but the stage wasn't that far away; surely she'd have found it?

'It was dark and she was apparently off her trolley,' said Nathan, looking at me with a smile on his face.

'What?' I said, cursing the fact that he always seemed to know what I was thinking.

'You're measuring the distance from the yurts to backstage, and wondering how on earth Caz got lost on her way there,' he said. I reminded myself never to play poker with this man, unless it was strip poker, in which case I didn't mind losing. 'But now imagine it's dark, and you've taken something you shouldn't have, and the world is on a wonk…'

'Yeah,' I said. If anything, the stage being so brightly lit in the distance and the camp site being so dark around you would make it even more disorienting, or 'on a wonk', than if it had all been dark and just lit by the moon reflecting off the sea. 'Hang on, I thought just now you were convinced it was her?'

'I'm not convinced about anything just yet,' admitted Nathan. 'I don't *want* it to be her, but I'm preparing myself for the fact that it *might* be.' He pulled me into a gentle hug. 'I suggest you do the same.'

# Chapter Ten

Daisy turned up about half an hour later, Germaine snapping at her heels. She plonked herself down on one of the folding chairs out the back of the truck with a deep sigh. Nathan and I exchanged looks – *uh oh* – before I headed out to see what was up.

'Blimey, it's hot in there,' I said, sitting next to her and fanning myself. 'You on your own?'

'Just me and the dog,' she said.

'Right. No Jade? Or Ellie?'

'No.'

'Right… Everything okay?'

'Yeah,' she said. *Could've fooled me,* I thought, but I didn't say anything. I knew she'd tell me if I just waited. And sure enough… 'After all that stuff with Paul, Ellie only wanted to go and get some more pills!'

'What happened to the last lot? Did you take them?' I held my hands up. 'No, don't tell me, it doesn't matter. But you didn't want any more?'

'I didn't take any of the first lot,' she said, rolling her eyes. 'I'm not daft. This whole site is crawling with friends of yours and Nathan's, it's not exactly a place where I can let my hair down, is it?'

'Did you argue?'

'Yes. Me and Ellie, not me and Jade. Jade didn't say anything, she just sat there. I know she agreed with me but she didn't say a word.' Daisy looked annoyed, and a little bit upset. I leant over and grabbed her hand, giving it a squeeze.

'Don't take it personally,' I said. 'Ellie's her cousin, isn't she? She's family. It's difficult to argue with family, even when you know they're wrong. Especially when they're older and they're the only reason you were allowed to come here.'

'Yeah, I suppose so…'

'You wait,' I told her. 'Jade and you will make it up as soon as the festival's over, if not before. I bet she's sitting in the tent feeling rubbish.'

'They went to see the band,' said Daisy.

'Oh… well, she'll be dancing and that, but she won't enjoy it as much as she would've done if you were with them,' I said loyally.

'Good.'

I got up and gave her a hug. 'You're welcome to sleep here tonight, if you want to. You and me can sleep inside and Nathan can put the awning up and sleep out here.'

'You don't mind?' She suddenly sounded very young – fifteen going on sixteen, rather than fifteen going on thirty-five like she normally did.

'Of course not. You're still my baby. You'll still be my baby when you're forty years old and I'm an old lady.'

'Thanks, Mum,' she said, snuggling into me. I hate my daughter being upset, but if it means I get a cuddle I'll take it.

But I had to get back to work. I gave her a kiss and told her to just sit and chillax (she cringed at the embarrassing word, which I'd used on purpose to make her laugh), while I got on with a batch of Hans Gruber pies, which had proved inexplicably popular at lunchtime.

The evening dinner rush passed by uneventfully, other than a slight altercation with some kids who kept kicking a football at the truck – one of them booting it hard enough against the back window of the truck to make the whole thing shake and me and Nathan jump out of our skins. I ran outside to have a go at them, but Daisy was already standing there, telling them to stop being dicks and threatening to set the dog on them.

Germaine looked rather alarmed at this, but luckily the kids just laughed and ran off before she was forced to do anything more than bark.

By seven o'clock we were pretty much pied out, so we shut up shop and joined Daisy and Germaine. The burger van was still open – indeed it seemed to have been open 24/7 since we'd been there – so we bought burgers, Germaine got a sausage, and we all sat down to eat.

As we ate, Nathan and I discussed the case, going over what we'd already learnt, which didn't feel like much. Lee Roskill had annoyed his bandmates by pulling out of the gig, and then *really* annoyed them by getting the court injunction, but was any of that motive enough for murder? Or could it have been Caz, jealous perhaps of Lee's new relationship? Could it have been another band member, holding a grudge about something Lee had done in the past that they hadn't had a chance to retaliate for until now? Neil must've been hurt when the front man had 'stolen' his girlfriend. But that had been over fifteen years ago, and it wasn't like Lee had ended his marriage or anything; it hadn't been a serious relationship, although of course Neil might have seen it differently at the time. Until we had more background information on the victim it was going to be hard to work out who might have wanted him dead. Daisy listened, breaking bits off her burger bun and feeding them to Germaine.

'First his girlfriend dies in tragic circumstances, and then he does,' said Daisy, cramming the last bit of burger into her mouth. 'No wonder this new girlfriend of his doesn't want to be found, she's probably hoping she won't be next.'

'Hmm…' I said thoughtfully, because as usual my clever daughter had picked up on something that had been lurking at the back of my own mind. Nathan looked up.

'What does that "hmm" mean?' he asked. 'I recognise that "hmm", and it's never good.'

'No,' I said, 'it doesn't mean anything. It's just…'

'Here we go. I've been waiting for a bonkers theory from you.'

I elbowed him (not hard). 'Oi you, my bonkers theories have helped you out plenty of times in the past!'

'I'm not denying it,' he said, exaggeratedly rubbing his thigh, which was where my unaimed elbow had nudged him. 'I wouldn't dare.'

'I did think earlier, before we got caught up in who had opportunity and that: first his girlfriend dies, and then him. What are the chances of that happening? Really?'

Nathan stared at me keenly. 'You think there was

more to Emily's death in New York than everyone said? And that it's connected? But how?'

'I don't know,' I admitted. 'I mean, I'm sure the NYPD investigated it, but how thoroughly? I can just see McKay wanting to play it down, particularly if drugs were involved, and it wouldn't look good for the hotel either. And by all accounts she *was* a drug addict. How seriously would they have taken it?'

'Maybe not seriously enough. But like you said, she was an addict. It's not beyond the realms of possibility that it really was an accident.'

'Yeah…' I shook my head. 'I was thinking about that, too. Our window rattled a bit when those kids kicked their football against it, but it didn't break because it's made of toughened glass. Well, that's what coffee tables are made of, too. They're made to be strong enough to withstand a bit of weight on them, aren't they? They don't go around breaking the minute someone leans on them too heavily. And if someone tripped and fell onto it, the weight would be evenly distributed across the table top. It might tip over, but it wouldn't necessarily smash.'

'No, I suppose it wouldn't…' Nathan looked thoughtful.

'Years ago, when I was in Uniform, I got called to this domestic. The husband was going mental, smashing stuff up, throwing things at his wife. We found him in the dining room systematically smashing up this whole set of crockery.' I could see it clearly in my head as I remembered the call. 'Really, it was hideous stuff, he was doing his poor wife a favour. But of course we told him to stop, which made him more angry, because it was "his effing plates" and he could do what he wanted with them. And then he started on their big glass dining table, only he had real trouble smashing that up. He just about got it to crack, and that was only by repeatedly hitting it in the same place with a brass candlestick. By which time another patrol car had arrived and we got him on the floor before it completely shattered.'

'So you think there's no way the coffee table would have smashed when Emily fell onto it?'

'Not unless she fell on it from the roof,' said Daisy sardonically.

'It seems to me that both our victims could have been killed in the same way,' I said. 'Knocked over – in Lee's case onto the rocks, in Emily's onto the table – then their heads repeatedly bashed against the same spot. In Emily's case, with great force, causing the table to shatter and cut her, leaving her to bleed out. The murderer might not even have intended that to happen.'

Nathan looked at me seriously. 'Okay, but this was fifteen years ago. They might not have had the same safety standards back then.'

I shrugged. 'Maybe not. But I was a young PC at the time, so that domestic must have been at least fifteen years ago, probably even longer. And I'm guessing a fancy-schmancy hotel in NYC would have a bigger furnishing budget than the inhabitants of a council flat in Streatham Hill.' I sighed. 'But how can we check any of this? Not only was Emily's death a long time ago, it was on another flipping continent. We can't just ring up the NYPD and ask to have a look at the case files.'

'We could if we had a friend who worked there,' said Nathan, grinning.

'What? You've got a friend in the NYPD?' I asked in astonishment.

'You know I have.'

'Do I?'

'Well you should do, because I've told you about him. Craig? The DI I worked with in Liverpool? Who was my best mate from police college? The one I was talking about being my best man?'

'*Craig* Craig? The one you FaceTimed and you introduced me to? The one who…' I facepalmed. 'The one who lives in New York?'

'Yes.' Nathan shook his head, lips pursed. 'Honestly, woman, you never listen… He went over there about four years ago on some cultural exchange programme, so he could learn about different policing methods and that and then bring it back to Liverpool. Only he fell in love with a native New Yorker and decided to stay there.'

'Oh my God, I can't believe I forgot him,' I said. 'Although in my defence, you never said he was still a copper.'

'Yes I did…'

'Do you think he could get a look at the case file on Emily?'

'I don't know. I don't know what precinct would've investigated it, and of course it was a long time before he got there. And if it's closed, he'll need an excuse to get access to it.'

'I dunno, you got me all excited there and now it sounds like he won't be able to help us after all,' I muttered. Nathan laughed.

'Yeah, sorry. But I know Craig, and if anyone can get a look at that file, he can.' He looked at his watch. 'I don't know why I'm bothering to look at the time, because I have absolutely no idea what the time difference is between Cornwall and New York.'

'About forty years,' said Daisy. 'We only just got Wi-Fi.'

'I'll email him and ask if he can help,' said Nathan. 'I'll probably have to put an official request in, but you never know.' He held up his phone and squinted at the bars. 'Talking of the internet…I don't think I'm going to get enough of a signal here to get online,' he said. 'Fancy a walk?'

At that word, of course, Germaine pricked up her ears, so we *had* to go for a walk. I suggested we head down towards the stage – keeping at the back of the crowd, of course, otherwise one of us would have to carry the dog, which rather ruined the point of a walk for her – and swing by the backstage area, where I'd been able to get on to Google earlier when we'd spoken to Neil. They must have a mobile antenna or Wi-Fi or something set up for the 'very important' people. We might not be performers or VIPs, but Nathan was The Law, and that had to have some perks. Plus I needed the toilet and they were much nicer back there.

We made our way down the hill, listening to the performer currently onstage, a young white guy rapping, who, when you managed to make out his lyrics despite the machine-gun-fast delivery, was surprisingly erudite and funny. The crowd were lapping it up; a large swath of them even knew the words, although they weren't managing to keep up with him very well.

'I wonder if he talks that fast all the time?' asked Daisy. I laughed.

'He's probably lost his voice by the time he gets offstage,' I said.

We reached the gate to the backstage area. A huge,

slightly aggressive-looking security guard stood at the gate, arms crossed, barring our way. Nathan reached for his warrant card, but I patted him on the arm. 'I've got this,' I said.

I approached the security guard, who peered at me over the top of his black sunglasses, which seemed to be de rigueur for every bouncer and door person in the world. Then he smiled and whipped his shades off.

'All right, Jodie? Ain't seen you in ages. How's your mum?'

'Hiya, Mickey. Yeah, she's good. She's here, somewhere.'

The security guard chuckled. 'Why don't that surprise me?'

'How's your nan? She got an appointment for her knee replacement yet?' I could see Nathan and Daisy – and Germaine – watching the exchange with bemused expressions. Neither of them had quite got used to the fact that in a small town like Penstowan, everyone knew everyone else, or had been to school with their brother, or (in this case) done the catering for their nan's eightieth birthday party.

'Nah, I reckon they don't wanna do it, not at her age.' Mickey looked at my companions. 'Business, is it? Or something else?'

'Mostly business, but I also need to, um, "use the facilities",' I said, and he laughed.

'Oh God, yeah, the bogs up the hill are well rank. Come on through.' He waggled a meaty finger at Germaine. 'No causing trouble though, do you hear me?'

I laughed and clapped him on a massive bicep. 'We'll behave, I promise. Cheers, Mickey.' I led the others through the gate and turned to see them still watching me. 'What?'

Daisy did a big mock shudder. 'You were just like Nana then,' she said. She turned to Nathan. 'You know what you're marrying into, yeah?'

'Yeah, about that…' he said, and laughed at my outraged expression. He pulled me over and gave me a quick kiss. 'I'm very happy with what I'm marrying into. Now let's go and do what we came here for.'

So they waited until I'd used the toilet (which was definitely what I'd gone there for), and then we headed towards the backstage area, where the Wi-Fi suddenly kicked in. Nathan typed up his email to Craig in NYC, while Daisy and I watched the comings and goings of the stage crew. Germaine amused herself by sniffing around the various guitar cases and amps that were awaiting use. I thanked God she wasn't a drug sniffer dog, otherwise Nathan would probably have found himself very busy.

'All done,' said Nathan, hitting send. He grinned at Daisy. 'Want to go into the proper VIP bit? See if we can snaffle a few freebies?'

'Really? Could we?' Daisy looked at me for confirmation. I nodded. 'That would be so cool. It would almost make up for the fact that I'm here with my mum…'

I picked Germaine up and we headed into the VIP area. The first thing we saw was Neil, almost exactly as we'd left him, lounging in a bean bag drinking a bottle of beer. He saw us and raised it to us in a toast.

'I would get up,' he said, 'but I don't think I can.'

'Don't mind us,' I said. 'Pretend we're not here.'

'You're undercover, are you? The dog's a nice detail.' He gave a discreet burp. 'If you're looking for the others, they're round here somewhere.'

'Cheers,' said Nathan, and Neil used it as an excuse to raise his bottle to toast us again.

'Did Matt manage to corroborate McKay's alibi?' I asked, as we wandered away.

'Yeah,' said Nathan. 'Why?'

'I was just thinking about last night. The band all stayed here drinking after their set, but he left. He said he didn't really hang out with them these days, so he went back to his holiday cottage. But his car's stuck in the car park, isn't it? I wondered how he got back there. Did he walk?'

'No,' said Nathan. 'Matt checked with the owners of the holiday cottage, who live in the house next door. They share a driveway. They said they heard a car dropping someone off between eight-thirty and nine o'clock. They heard voices. He must've got a cab.'

'Hmm… He was lucky, then, because there aren't many taxis round here.'

'Maybe we should ask him,' said Nathan, nodding across the clearing to where the band manager was standing by himself, watching Caz and Ian as they talked to a couple of other performers. McKay looked up as if he'd felt us watching him. I turned to Daisy.

'You'd better make yourself scarce,' I said. 'It's enough of a push for me to be here, I don't think Nathan's boss would be as accepting of him having his stepdaughter with him too.'

'All right,' said Daisy, taking Germaine from me. 'I'll just be over there…' I followed her gaze, to where the rapper had just come off stage. He looked much younger in real life, as it were; not much older than Daisy. I grinned.

'Go and fan girl, but don't make a nuisance of yourself,' I said. And then added as an afterthought, as she walked away, 'And don't accept any free alcohol!'

'DCI Withers,' said McKay, as we joined him. 'I didn't expect to see you here.'

'We're just soaking up the atmosphere,' said Nathan.

'And using your loos,' I added. McKay grinned.

'Ah, yes, the soft toilet roll is a big draw, I hear.'

'While we've got you, could we just ask you a couple more questions?' asked Nathan, politely. 'Just concerning your whereabouts last night.'

'I told your DS, I was at my holiday cottage,' said McKay. 'Castaway Cottage, just up there.' He pointed vaguely in the direction of the hillside above the festival site.

'How did you get back there last night?' I asked. 'Did you get a taxi?'

'No, I didn't. I got a lift with a...' He paused. 'With a friend.'

'What friend was that?' asked Nathan, reaching for his notebook and then realising he didn't have it, because he was supposedly on holiday.

McKay looked awkward. 'I didn't get her name. I'd only just met her.'

'But she still gave you a lift?' Nathan looked unconvinced, but the other thing about living somewhere like Penstowan is that people do tend to give out lifts more easily, or even pick up hitchhikers, because everyone knows that public transport is few and far between.

'Believe me, DCI Withers, I wish I had got her name, because she's my alibi as well as my lift.' He gave us a rueful grin. I remembered what Caz had said about him earlier: *easily distracted by pretty things.*

'Where did you meet her?' I asked. 'Back here? Who was she, a wannabe singer, looking for a way into the business?'

He sniffed in mock outrage. 'Officer, if you're suggesting that I used my position in the music industry to lure her back to my cottage for a night of no-strings passion, then…' He laughed softly. 'Sorry. I know how it sounds. I'm only messing about because I'm a bit embarrassed about the whole thing. I'm far too old and boring to go hooking up with groupies, but…' He ran his fingers through his hair and looked around to make sure no one was nearby. 'Let me level with you. I told you before, I always wanted to be a rock star, yes? One of the things they always say about being famous is that it's great for picking up women. Well, being the manager is pretty good in that respect too, because I'm kind of famous by association. Only in the past I've never really gone in for that sort of thing.' He grinned. 'Don't get me wrong, I've always enjoyed a good flirt, but I never really went further than that.' He paused to reflect for a moment. 'Well, not very often.'

'But you did last night,' I said. He nodded.

'Yeah… In my defence, I'd just seen my wife – my ex-wife – on social media, celebrating marrying her third husband. You always hear about men dumping their wives for someone younger and prettier when they get successful, don't you? It was the other way around for me. She was a wannabe supermodel when we met. She wanted to hangout with Kate and Naomi, but she was never really in the same league as them. She thought when we got married that I could help with that, that her being friends with the band would make her cooler.' He grimaced. 'She soon realised that wasn't the case.'

'And last night…?' prompted Nathan.

'Last night I was feeling pretty sore about her marrying someone twenty years younger and several million pounds richer than me,' said McKay with a sigh. 'What an idiot.'

'You or him?' I asked, and he chuckled.

'Both. So when this young lady came over and started flirting with me, I was flattered. And I thought, why not? So I took her back to my place. Only now of course it feels wrong that I was having a good time while poor Lee was dying out on the rocks.'

'So she was with you all night, was she?' asked

Nathan. 'Only the neighbours seem to think the car dropped you off and then left straightaway.'

'It did,' said McKay. 'Oh, I see the confusion – she wasn't the one driving, it was a friend of hers. They'd arranged to drive home together, and the friend was a little bit put out when she said she wanted to be dropped off with me.'

'So, what time did she leave the cottage? Was she there all night?' asked Nathan. McKay nodded.

'Yes. She left about six-thirty this morning, because she said she had to go to work and needed to nip home first. I offered to call her a taxi, which she thought was hilarious for some reason—'

'You'll never get a cab round here at that time of day, not without booking it a week in advance,' I said.

'Is that right? She said that too. I thought she was just regretting sleeping with me and was keen to get away.' McKay gave a self-deprecating smile. 'Anyway, she said she was going to walk, so I assume she can't live very far away.'

'And that whole night, she never mentioned her name, gave you her number, nothing like that?' asked Nathan.

'I did ask her name, of course I did, I'm not a monster... Milly? Tilly? Something ending in "ly", anyway. We were both pretty drunk. And no, I didn't get her number. It was a one-night stand, DCI Withers. Neither of us was looking for love, we had a nice, consensual time and that was it.'

'Is there nothing else you can tell us about her? Hair colour? Piercings? Anything?' I asked.

'What about the friend, and her car? What make and model was it?' asked Nathan. McKay pursed his lips, musing, and then shook his head regretfully.

'What can I say? I wasn't paying that much attention. The friend… Nope, can't really tell you anything about her, other than it *was* a her. Oh, and she was wearing glasses. The car was a dark-coloured hatchback, quite old – a Nissan Micra? Something like that. Or a Peugeot of some sort.'

'And Milly or Tilly? What did she look like?' Nathan persisted. 'It would be to your benefit if we could track her down to corroborate your story.'

'I know, and I really wish I could tell you more. She had long blonde hair, in plaits—'

'Plaits? How old was she, twelve?' I asked.

'Of course not. Mid-twenties? Far too young for me. I couldn't believe my luck, to be honest. She was your typical twenty-first-century hippy festivalgoer. Cut-off jeans and a tight vest top thing. Big boots.'

'Tattoos? Piercings?'

'If she did, I never found them.'

'What do you think?' I asked Nathan, as we walked away.

'One: Dougie McKay really needs to get over his ex-wife,' he said.

'And two?'

'If you ever decide to get a tattoo, please get it somewhere I'll have to search intimately for it…'

## Chapter Eleven

We couldn't rub shoulders with the stars all night, however, so we headed back out to the crowd, Daisy reluctantly; she'd been chatting away with the young rapper, who turned out to be called Joe and was only seventeen. This had been his first big festival gig, and it was safe to say he'd aced it. I felt bad tearing her away from him – he seemed nice enough – but I didn't feel like backstage at a rock concert, surrounded by free booze and God knew what else, was a good place for me to leave her.

The headline act was about to start, a rock band that I'd heard *of* but never actually heard.

'Who's this lot?' asked Nathan, peering over people's heads to get a look at the four-piece who had just arrived onstage.

'Antwackie,' said Daisy enthusiastically. 'They're brilliant!'

'Better than Joe?' I teased. She smiled ruefully.

'He was really good, wasn't he? But this is more my sort of music…' She looked around at the crowd, and I guessed what she was thinking. Where was Jade? They'd probably planned to watch the band together.

'I'm sorry, sweetheart, but I do need to get the dog out of here,' I said gently, picking up my whimpering Pomeranian. 'It's too noisy for her. Maybe I could get Nana to look after her.'

'Daisy?' We all turned round to see Joe the rapper standing behind us, a little out of breath. Maybe he'd still not recovered from his set. Or maybe he'd run after us… He blushed as Nathan and I looked at him. 'Hi, sorry, I wondered if Daisy would like to watch the band with me?' he asked. 'From out here, I mean. It's a bit much, back there…' He nodded towards the back of the stage.

'I'd love to!' said Daisy, looking at me with a silent plea in her eyes. Nathan and I exchanged glances.

'Are you all camping together?' asked Joe, looking at me and Nathan. 'I promise I'll get her back to your tent safely afterwards.'

I half expected Nathan to get his warrant card out and show Joe just how much trouble he'd be in if he didn't get Daisy back to us in one piece, but he just raised his eyebrows. I nodded.

'That's fine. Just remember that she is still only fifteen.'

'Mum!' growled Daisy, and I knew she'd make me pay later for embarrassing her. 'I'm sixteen in two months.'

'I'm just saying, don't come back steaming drunk or anything, because if you end up with a massive hangover you'll get no sympathy from either of us.' I grinned. 'Have a good time and,' I bent closer to her, 'make sure Jade and Ellie see who you're with.'

She grinned. The two of them headed into the crowd and I turned to Nathan with a big smile on my face.

'What are you looking so pleased about?' he asked.

'My little girl's growing up,' I said. 'Look at her. She's so clever and funny and beautiful, isn't she? She deserves to enjoy herself. And I'll only worry about her a little bit, because she's sensible, too.'

'You were worried that she'd taken some of Dyer's pills last night,' he pointed out.

'Yeah, but she didn't. And they took them to be tested first.' I sighed. 'Part of being a parent is learning to let go, isn't it? Learning to trust your kids. I think I did a bloody good job with Daisy, even if I say so myself, and I trust her not to do anything daft.' I thought for a moment. 'Well, daft maybe, but not dangerous.'

'Yeah, you did a good job.' He leant forward and kissed me on the forehead – anything more passionate would've been tricky, with Germaine wriggling in my arms. 'But I think we should get our other baby out of here.'

We headed up the hill, but rather than go back to the truck we found a spot on the hillside where we could look down at the stage. It was a lot less noisy up there, so Germaine was happy, but it was still loud enough to hear the music properly. My phone vibrated in my pocket, and I checked it quickly in case it was Daisy, but of course it wasn't; it was Mum, asking where we were, because Tony and Carmen and Debbie – the whole gang, in fact – had been trying to find us. Before long we were all sitting on a blanket thoughtfully provided by Jocasta, who had also joined us, enjoying the music and eating a picnic pulled together by the others. Because food always seemed to find its way in to our gatherings.

'So what's been happening with this murder, then?' asked Mum. Tony laughed.

'I'm glad you asked that, Shirley, cos I reckon all of us have been sitting here trying to find a casual way of bringing it up.'

'You do know that none of you are actually police

officers?' I said. 'And that as such we're not supposed to share information with you?'

Debbie snorted. 'I don't know if you remember this or not, but you're not police either. You quit the force.'

'Yeah, but—'

'Twice.'

Nathan shook his head. 'I wish some of my actual detectives showed as much interest in their work as you do,' he said. 'All right, I realised a long time ago that it was impossible to keep anything from you lot. But we don't know much anyway. What do you want to know?'

'Was it definitely murder?' asked Tony.

'Yep. Next question.'

'Was it one of the band?' asked Carmen. I rolled my eyes.

'Carmen, I'm shocked. I thought you were above this sort of thing.'

'Me? Dear Lord, no. I don't know what gave you that impression. Was it the dog collar?'

'We don't know,' said Nathan. 'The band have all given us alibis.'

'But do they all check out?' asked Mum. This was what I got for letting her watch true crime documentaries on Netflix.

'Most of them,' said Nathan, carefully. Because we

couldn't really say for certain that any of them did, apart from Danny's, who'd been visibly online at the time.

'Oooh…' said Mum. 'Whose doesn't? Is it their manager? Is he one of those Svengali types? Like Colonel Sanders?'

'No he's not a Sven—' I started, then my brain caught up with my ears. 'Wait, what are you talking about? What's Colonel Sanders got to do with anything?'

'You know, Elvis's manager.' Mum helped herself – aptly enough – to a piece of chicken.

'I think you're thinking of Colonel Tom Parker, Shirley,' said Nathan, with extreme patience. 'Both he and the founder of KFC have alibis for the time of death.'

I laughed. 'Probably because they both died years ago. What are you like, Mother? Anyway, no, it wasn't their manager, because he was "entertaining a young lady" at his holiday cottage at the time.'

Debbie snorted. '"Entertaining"? Yeah, I bet he was…'

'Good-looking, is he?' asked Jocasta. Debbie mused for a second.

'Yeah, about an eight, I reckon…?' She looked at me for confirmation.

'I couldn't possibly comment,' I said, and Nathan laughed.

'Ooh, he's got a holiday cottage, has he?' said Mum. 'Nice. Whereabouts?'

'Up there,' I said, gesturing vaguely. 'He's rented Castaway Cottage for the weekend.'

'Castaway Cottage? Oh yeah, I know where you mean. They renamed it that to appeal to the tourists, but when I knew it, it was just number 54 Coast Road.' She sighed dreamily. 'Home to my very first love.'

'The Polish cabbage picker you told me about?' I asked.

'Who? No, not him. Or your father. No, it was Tom Wannacott.' She sighed again. 'He was a right looker. Wealthy an' all. His parents didn't approve of me, which just made him all the more keen. We used to sneak out at night and meet each other.'

'What happened?' asked Debbie, fascinated in spite of herself.

'He went off to university – he was clever an' all, see. Asked me to wait for him. I did try, but…' She suddenly cackled. 'Well, I've never been very good at resisting temptation.'

'Shirley Parker, you're a scarlet woman!' cried Jocasta. 'I knew there was a reason why I liked you.' We all laughed, and I started to think that maybe Jocasta was just the right sort of friend for my mum after all.

Down below us, the band were playing up a storm. They were a surprisingly old-fashioned sort of rock band, and Mum said they reminded her of the Rolling Stones, who she'd always preferred to the Beatles as they were a bit too goody-goody for her. The crowd were leaping around in a frenzy, and I thought with a pang about my little girl being down there among it. But she wasn't a little girl anymore, and at least I was nearby, in case she needed me.

'I bet Daisy's having a good time,' said Debbie, as if she was reading my thoughts.

'Yeah, I hope so. Joe seems nice,' I said. I really wasn't going to worry about my daughter, experiencing her first festival in the company of a boy, or rather young man, that she'd just met… Was I insane, letting her go off with him? Tony reached over to hand me a bottle of beer and smiled at me.

'Don't worry about her,' he said softly. 'She's sensible, and if she's got half your survival instincts she'll be just fine.'

'Survival instincts?' asked Nathan, pricking up his ears.

'Oh yeah, the stuff this one used to get up to…' said Tony, grinning. I wasn't sure if I preferred it when he and Nathan were all chummy and ganging up on me, or when Nathan was trying to arrest him for murder, which was how we'd met in the first place. 'Not sure if I should tell you about it though, what with you being Old Bill. And with Shirley here, too.'

'I don't care what she got up to,' said Mum. 'I always used to say, if no one's bleeding and you don't need bail money, then I don't need to know about it.'

I almost choked on my beer. 'What? You *never* said that, you always wanted chapter and verse on where I was going, who I was going to be with—'

'Never blooming told me, though, did you?' Mum sat back and stared up at the stars, which were just starting to come out above us. 'You came through the teenage years with no criminal record, no piercings and no tattoos, so I reckon I didn't do a bad job.'

The band finished their set, so we packed up our rubbish and the blanket and said our goodnights. Mum and Jocasta headed off to their yurt, both of them weaving slightly. Maybe I should have been more concerned about them than I had been about my teenage daughter. Nathan offered to see them back safely, but they both waved a contemptuous hand at him and Jocasta said it would be a sad day when they had to rely on a man to get them home. I rather thought my mum found it sadder to *not* have a man escorting her, but hey ho. Debbie, Tony and Carmen went their way, down the hill, and we went ours, up it, Germaine running ahead of us, barking happily.

We'd just sat down in the camping chairs outside the truck with a cup of tea when Daisy and Joe appeared, hand in hand. Daisy looked mortified that we were still up, but we were hardly going to go to bed until we knew she was back safe. Germaine wouldn't have let us, anyway.

'Hello,' I said. 'Did you have a good time?'

'Yes,' said Daisy. She turned to Joe, who was dividing his gaze between me, Nathan and his shoes. 'Thank you for walking me back.'

Joe looked up at her. 'Of course, I'm not gonna let you walk back on your own in the dark, there could be all sorts going on.' Nathan shot me an approving glance and I nodded. Joe had passed his first potential son-in-law test, although maybe it was a tad early to be thinking in those terms. 'So, you want to meet up and watch the surfing tomorrow?'

'Yes, definitely.' I could tell that she was trying very hard to play it cool, but was almost bouncing up and down on her toes. 'Meet you by the peace tent at ten?'

'It's a date,' said Joe, then he looked shocked. 'Er, I mean – you know.'

'Yeah, yeah,' she said. Then they both stood there, awkwardly. And we sat where we were, also awkwardly. *Oh, they want to kiss goodnight!* I thought. I nudged Nathan with my foot and inclined my head towards the truck.

'We'd better go inside and set up the sleeping

quarters,' I said. Nathan frowned at me, and then his face cleared as he understood.

'Oh yes, of course.' We both stood up. 'Night, Joe. See you again.' That earnt Nathan a glare from Daisy, because it made it sound like they were courting or something equally old-fashioned and lame.

I giggled and dragged him inside the truck, where the two of us immediately stood by the window and peered through the narrow aluminium slats of the blind, watching the young lovers. Joe moved in for the kiss, but then Daisy looked straight at us. We both jumped back guiltily.

However, it obviously didn't deter the course of true love, because it was a good ten minutes before Daisy opened the door of the truck; long enough, in fact, for Nathan to start getting a bit shifty, wondering about exactly how far things were going out there.

We decided that we'd put the awning up outside and Nathan would sleep on the spare airbed we'd brought with us, while Daisy and I (and Germaine) shared the double bed inside. But before we even started, there was a knock on the door of the truck.

'He's keen,' said Nathan, assuming as we all did that it was Joe coming back. But it wasn't. A repentant-looking Jade and Ellie stood at the door.

'I'm so sorry, Daisy,' said Jade, and she burst into

tears. And then Ellie did too. Daisy looked a bit startled, because while these two had been feeling guilty she'd been having the best night of her life, but then she burst into tears too. They all had a hug and after an intense but heartfelt chat, Daisy went back to the tent with her friends.

'All's well that ends well,' said Nathan, hugging me as we watched the little gang troop off back down the hill, arm in arm.

'The night isn't over yet,' I said to him, giving him what I hoped was a seductive look but which might have looked more like a facial tic. It didn't matter because it worked, anyway. Much to Germaine's disgust.

The next day we woke up at eight, which was a proper lie-in for us. Even Germaine was still snoozing, although she leapt off the bed and scratched at the door to be let out as soon as she felt me stirring. I threw on some clothes and took her for a walk to relieve herself; poor thing must've had her paws crossed for some time, going by the amount of time I had to stand, eyes averted, as she did her business. But it did mean that Nathan had time to heat up some water for washing in; there were only two portable shower blocks to cope with the whole festival site, and even though most people didn't bother there were still always queues to use them, and the hot water always ran out, so we'd taken to washing in a bucket. I was very much looking forward to washing my hair when we got home.

After a quick wash and a hearty spray of deodorant, we sat down with tea, yoghurt and fruit. Nathan checked his emails, wandering down to the stage area to use their Wi-Fi, but there'd been no reply from Craig in NYC. It was probably a bit too soon, even if he could get access to the file. Nathan wandered back, looking disappointed.

Nathan also checked in with Matt, but he was only just waking up himself and had nothing to report. Crime shows on the telly always have the police working diligently all night to clear up the case and find the bad guy, but in real life there comes a point where, having made the most of those first golden twenty-four hours after the murder to find leads and secure evidence, all you can do is wait; wait for phone records, wait for CCTV footage, wait for DNA and other medical or forensic tests to come back, wait for financial stuff, wait, wait, wait…

We cooked a couple of batches of pies, admittedly with rather less enthusiasm than when we'd baked the first lot on Friday, and plastered on cheerful smiles for our morning customers. The breakfast rush started closer to lunchtime than it had the day before, and our customers were starting to look worse for wear, battling with the late nights, lack of sleep, and an excess of alcohol. Except the younger ones, who all looked bright-eyed and bushy-tailed. 'Probably on drugs,' I said to Nathan, and he laughed.

Caz and Ian swung by for a breakfast pie. They both looked exhausted, particularly Caz, who was pale and had dark circles under her eyes.

'Morning,' I said, and she smiled wanly.

'Is it? I feel like I'm losing track of time here,' she said. 'It doesn't feel like real life.'

'It's not, it's a festival,' I said. 'Have you thought any more about trying to go home early? The police don't need you here, and you're only up the road if they need to speak to you again. You look like you could do with sleeping in your own bed again.'

'That's what I said,' said Ian, but she shook her head.

'I'm fine, I told you.'

'Did you find your phone?' asked Nathan, handing another customer a pie.

'No,' said Caz. 'Ian did Find Your Phone but nothing came up.'

'There are a lot of spots round here where the mobile signal drops out,' said Nathan. 'Or whoever's nicked it has taken the SIM out.'

'Have you tried the security tent?' I said. 'Someone might've handed it in.'

'Yeah, we already asked there.' Caz shrugged. 'It

doesn't matter. I can get a new one, it's just a pain transferring all my numbers and everything over.'

I became aware of a persistently cheerful tune playing from inside the truck.

'Talking of phones,' I said to Nathan, 'is that yours ringing?'

It was. 'Craig's FaceTiming me,' he said. We excused ourselves and left Caz and Ian to eat their pies, and went out the back of the food truck, where the mobile signal seemed to be slightly stronger.

'All right, you crazy kids?' Craig's cheeky grin and broad Scouse accent leapt out at us from the screen of Nathan's phone. 'Youse still at that festival?'

'Yeah, you all right, mate?' said Nathan, wiping his free hand on his apron. Craig squinted, peering closer.

'What *are* you wearing? Is that a pinny?' He shook his head. 'She's got you well domesticated.'

'She' popped her head into shot so he saw her. 'Hiya, Craig,' I said.

'Oops! There she is!' Craig laughed. 'Nah, only joking, Jodie. How are you?'

'Good, yeah, we're all good,' said Nathan, impatiently. 'You manage to get any info for us?'

'Always straight to the point,' said Craig, winking at me. 'I hope he's not like that in bed.'

'He might've been for you, but he's not for me,' I said, and he roared with laughter.

'Touché.'

'I'm more worried about our dodgy phone signal cutting out before you get to the good bit,' said Nathan.

'I can't talk for long anyway,' said Craig. 'I'm due at work in an hour. I had a look into the Emily Logan case, and I discovered that the NYPD don't like foreigners who weren't even in the country at the time going through their closed case files.'

'Ah, right,' said Nathan. 'Bugger.'

'But was I dismayed? Was I put off? Was I 'eck.' Craig looked smug. 'Guess who just happened to know the detective who was in charge of the case?'

'You do?'

'No. Ha! Not me, but my partner used to be at the same precinct. He was a good cop.'

'*Was* a good cop?'

'Yeah. Oh, he ain't dead, he's retired. And one thing retired cops love to do is talk about their old cases…'

I sat down on a camping chair, and Nathan followed suit, drawing his next to mine so we could both see the phone.

'I went round to see him last night after work,' said Craig. 'He remembered the case straightaway. Turns out he wasn't very happy with it.'

'No?' Nathan and I exchanged looks. 'What was he unhappy about?'

'Couple of things. For starters, he said he was never completely convinced about the table.'

I looked at Nathan. 'I told you!'

'He said it was a big, posh hotel, with expensive furniture. This coffee table was built to last, it wasn't some cheap crap from Home Depot. And Emily Logan was a skinny little thing. So why did the table break?'

'What did he think? That someone bashed something against it – probably her – until it smashed?' asked Nathan.

Craig shrugged. 'That or there was a fault in the glass. Which apparently is possible. And that's what went on the report.'

'What about forensics?' I said. 'Surely if someone had bashed her head on the table, it would've shown up in the post mortem?'

'Do you know what date this happened?' asked Craig. 'Thirty-first of October. Halloween.' We both groaned, because even in the UK, where Halloween is nowhere near as big an event as it is in the States, it's still one of the busiest nights of the year for the police, certainly in the cities. 'All the crazies crawl out of the woodwork at Halloween over here,' said Craig. 'It fell on a Saturday that year too, so double crazy. I get the impression that they were so overstretched that they took her death almost at face value. The tox screen showed she had a large amount of Class As in her system. There was no sign of forced entry into her hotel room, no sign anyone else had been there at the time. Everyone connected to her, all the band members, the roadies, everyone, they were all accounted for, all alibied. Much easier to put it down to her being a junkie, and then get on with the next stiff.'

'It does happen,' admitted Nathan. 'But your detective still wasn't happy about it.'

'No, he wasn't. And not just about the table. There was no CCTV from the hotel.'

'None at all? Surely there would be cameras in the lifts, maybe in the corridors…?'

'There were cameras in the lobby and the lifts. Not in the corridors, because the hotel prides itself on being "discreet" – half their clientele is probably there with people they shouldn't be. But, surprise surprise, there was no CCTV footage at all of that night.'

'Was it wiped?' I asked.

'He didn't know. He asked the security guard who was on duty that night, and he said he'd been watching the monitors all night, saw people going in and out but didn't spot anyone or anything suspicious, and he'd assumed that it was recording like it always did. But he realised after the police were called that it wasn't.'

'Did he know why that might've happened?'

'Nah. Said it must've been a Halloween prank or something. Or the ghost.'

I rolled my eyes. 'Of course there would be a ghost.'

Craig laughed. 'Yeah, that's what I thought. But the hotel's been there for about two hundred years, there's gotta be a ghost or two, ain't there?'

'What did your detective think?' asked Nathan.

'He certainly didn't think it was a ghost pissing about with the security cameras,' said Craig dryly. 'But there was no reason to think the security guard – or anyone else who had access to the system, which was quite a few members of staff by the looks of it – had anything to do with it. Why would they tamper with it?'

'So it got left off the file?'

'No, but it wasn't given the importance he thought it should have had. You know what it's like. Cases aren't always cut and dried, are they? You have to go on the balance of probability, and his boss thought the balance of probability showed that a junkie had got off her face and had an accident.'

'Right,' said Nathan. 'I can see why they might have thought that, I suppose. But your detective – he's still not convinced, is he?'

'No, and I'll tell you why not. He decided to check with the security guard a few weeks later, to see if they'd found out why the cameras hadn't been recording, but the guard had quit two weeks after the death.'

'Is it me,' I asked, 'or is that a bit sus?'

'It does sound suspicious,' said Craig. 'But apparently the guard had been working his way through college, and he'd decided to quit and concentrate on his studies.'

'Which is feasible,' pointed out Nathan.

'Yeah. Only he also moved house and didn't give a forwarding address.' Craig smiled thinly. 'Which is still feasible.'

'It wouldn't be enough to keep the case open,' said Nathan, 'but I wouldn't like that, either.'

'No. And the other reason my detective friend still isn't convinced it was an accident is that I'm the second person to ask him about it in the last week.'

## Chapter Twelve

'So someone else was interested in Emily's death,' said Nathan. I nodded.

'Another Brit as well, according to Craig's retired detective.' We'd closed the truck – we were pretty much out of pies by now, with about two batches left that we planned to cook for the dinner period later on – and were sitting out the back. I pulled the crust off a leftover Nakatomi Plaza chicken pie and tossed it to Germaine. I'd have to put the entire family on a healthy eating plan when we got home, after the number of pies we'd consumed. 'I wonder who that could've been?' But my question was rhetorical, because there was surely only person who cared about Emily Logan's death. Or rather, there *had* been.

'Lee Roskill hired a private detective to look into it,'

said Nathan. 'But why? Why now and not fifteen years ago?'

'That must be what was behind him pulling out of the gig,' I mused, picking out a piece of chicken and eating it, much to Germaine's disgust as, not happy with just a bit of crust, she'd been eyeing it up for herself. I relented and gave her some. 'He had suspicions about – something.'

'So he hired someone to go to the States and dig up the dirt,' said Nathan. 'They found something that confirmed his suspicions enough for him to apply for a court injunction to stop them playing. And then what?'

'The PI found even more and passed it on, and that was enough to make Lee come here and confront the band,' I said. 'And, unwittingly, his killer.'

'Well, if we ever manage to get hold of this private detective, hopefully he'll be able to tell us all about it,' said Nathan. 'Thank God Craig got the guy's name and phone number.'

'Shame it goes straight to voicemail,' I said. Nathan shrugged.

'He could be travelling, or his phone could be out of juice.'

'Or he could be dead, too.'

'God, let's hope not or we'll never find out what's going on.'

'Hello? Shop!' Matt's voice came from around the front of the truck.

'Round the back,' called Nathan. Matt came round and stood in front of him.

'Got something for you, Guv,' he said, holding out a plastic evidence bag. 'I'm on my way back to the station, thought I'd pop over and show you first.'

'What's that?' I asked, shading my eyes against the sun, which was sparkling off the object in the bag.

'Mobile phone,' said Matt.

'Lee Roskill's?' Nathan sat forward and held out his hand to take the phone. He turned it over and studied it, the light glinting again off the screen.

'We don't know yet. But one of the plod found it near the crime scene, down on the beach.'

I grinned. 'I hope you don't call them "plod" in front of your girlfriend.'

Matt laughed. 'God, no. I don't have a death wish.'

'It was by the crime scene, but they've only just found it?' Nathan looked up at his DS, and I could tell that he wasn't impressed. 'How did they miss this? I thought they'd searched the area.'

'They did, thoroughly. I dunno, maybe it was under a rock or something and the tide dislodged it as it came in and went out again.'

'Or maybe they didn't look hard enough,' said

Nathan. Matt looked like he was going to defend Chrissie and the other uniformed PCs, but wisely thought the better of it. Nathan sighed. 'Never mind, we've got it now. Before you take it back to town, see if one of the other band members can identify it as his. They might not be able to, but it's worth a shot. Otherwise it might just belong to another festivalgoer. See if anyone's reported one like this missing at the security tent.'

'Will do.' Matt bustled away.

'Don't be too hard on Uniform,' I said. 'Especially the new ones, like Brett. They're not used to dealing with stuff like this, not down here.'

'That's not really an excuse, is it? If that really is Roskill's phone, that's potentially an important piece of evidence, and they missed it.' He looked at me and chuckled. 'All right, I won't go banging any heads together. I'll just treat it as one of those, what did they call it on that management course…'

'A teachable moment,' I said. He laughed.

'Yes! I'll teach them they need to make sure they've searched the area thoroughly, otherwise they might get a senior officer's boot up their backside.'

'Which is always a valuable learning experience.' I leant in to kiss him, and he pulled me close. 'You know what, you are so sexy when you're being all tough and in charge…'

'Ahem…' We both turned to see PC Chrissie standing behind us. I hoped she hadn't heard Nathan's comments about Uniform's search skills. 'Sorry to interrupt, Guv…'

'No, it's all right, go on,' said Nathan, hastily rearranging himself into a more professional pose.

'I just found something.' She held up her own phone. 'I was watching Danny Harris's live stream, the one he did during the time of the murder?' We nodded. 'Well, the timing checks out fine, but there's something in the background you might want to take a look at.' She tapped the phone screen and held it out for us to see. 'Or rather, someone…'

Neil was in his usual spot, flopped on the bean bag drinking beer. I'd wondered earlier if he ever actually moved from it, other than when the band had been onstage, but we knew now that he had.

'Back so soon?' he asked.

'Couldn't stay away,' I said.

'No,' said Nathan, 'not when we saw this.' He passed his phone over to the drummer. On the screen, Danny was talking to a musician from another band while someone else recorded it. Neil watched for a moment, looking confused.

'Oh yeah, young Daniel loves his social media stuff,' he said. 'I can't get the hang of it meself.'

'Yeah, he's a natural,' said Nathan. 'Very interesting. Not as interesting as what's going on in the background, though.' He paused the video. 'That's you, isn't it? Outside the VIP area, heading away from backstage, where you told us you'd spent the entire night. See the time stamp on the video? Right around the time of Lee Roskill's death.'

'Ah, yeah…' said Neil. He sat up straight, or as straight as was possible on a bean bag. 'I know they always say this in the movies, but I can explain.'

'Go on, then.' Nathan put his phone away and folded his arms, waiting. 'Where were you between eleven forty-five and twelve forty-five? Because you weren't in the VIP area, as you claimed.'

'I went back to the camper van,' he said. Nathan shook his head.

'No you didn't. Because the camper van is in the opposite direction to the one you were walking in, and there's no sign of you walking back in the video.'

'I got lost.'

'Really? You and your bandmates all seem to have a terrible sense of direction,' I said.

'I was quite drunk at that point,' protested Neil, with a grin. Nathan raised an eyebrow but didn't speak. Neil looked at both of us, then suddenly laughed. 'Oh all right. I wasn't lost, I was on a mission.'

'Oh God, not *another* booty call,' I groaned. He looked surprised.

'What, me? The missus would kill me.' His face froze. 'Sorry, poor choice of words… No, it wasn't a woman. I was out for revenge.'

'Revenge?'

'Yeah. Me and the drummer from Bladestar – they played after us – we had what you might call an altercation. So I decided to go and pee on the door handle of his trailer.'

'Eww!' I said, and Nathan wrinkled his nose in disgust. Neil had the decency to look slightly ashamed.

'Yeah, I know… I didn't do it in the end.'

'Thought better of it?'

'Nah, couldn't work out which trailer was his.' He sighed and flopped back in his seat. 'I'll be honest with you, all that business with Lee, even before he died, really got to me. Got me on a bit of a short fuse.'

'Because seeing Lee reminded you of Emily?' asked Nathan.

'What? No.'

'It must've really hurt when your best mate stole your girlfriend,' I said. Neil shook his head.

'He didn't "steal" her, how the hell do you steal a person?' He sighed again. 'I *was* a bit put out when he brought her on tour with us, but after a while I realised I'd dodged a bullet.'

'What do you mean?'

'I was pretty serious about Emily, but we weren't together that long. Lee came and told me after we'd split up that he liked her and was going to ask her out, if I didn't mind. I *did* bloody mind, but I wasn't going to let them know that, so I said it was fine. By the time we were on tour I didn't really care until I saw the two of them together. That…that hurt. But after a couple of weeks I realised just how manipulative she could be. Don't get me wrong, I think she loved Lee, but… I didn't like the way she went on with people.'

'Like who?

'She was weird with Caz. Like she wasn't sure if she hated her for being with Lee first, or if she liked her and wanted to hang out with her. She was thick as thieves with Dougie's ex, and *that* woman was a nasty piece of work, I can tell you. Absolute gold-digger.'

'Okay…' said Nathan. 'But you were still upset enough about the past to disappear for the best part of an hour?'

'I told you, I was drunk and looking for trouble. And then I got a text from my wife, saying she was about to go to bed and wishing me good night, and I had an overwhelming urge to ring her up and talk to her about it all.'

'And did you?'

'Yeah. I walked round the back of all the trailers and somehow found the camper van, then rang up my lovely lady wife and talked to her for at least half an hour. Check my phone records, you'll see it.'

Nathan sighed and shook his head. 'Why didn't you tell us this when we asked for your alibi?'

'I don't think you fully appreciate just how drunk I've been since about nine-thirty on Friday night, Chief Inspector,' said Neil, and there wasn't much we could say to that.

We left him to get even drunker.

'So, what do you think of that?' I asked, but Nathan didn't get a chance to answer as my own phone rang.

'Jodie, you two need to come down to the drugs tent right now,' said Debbie on the other end. 'There's someone here Nathan needs to talk to…'

The young woman sitting with a friend on the other side of the tent was in her mid to late twenties, with long blonde hair tied back in a ponytail, held by a tie-dyed scrunchie. There were thick pink streaks in her hair, and she wore a loose flannel shirt, unbuttoned, over a tight-fitting vest top and cut-off denim shorts. Debbie nodded towards her and then spoke in a low voice.

'Lucy came in here about half an hour ago,' she said. 'She didn't have any drugs to test, but she wanted to know about the effects of Rohypnol.'

'Roofies?' Nathan looked shocked. 'Does she think someone spiked her?'

Debbie nodded. 'Yeah, but she's not sure. She wasn't going to report it, but she told her friend, who persuaded her to at least come and talk to us.'

Debbie led us over to Lucy. She wasn't visibly distressed, but she did seem uneasy. As we approached, her friend threw a protective arm around her shoulders and glared at us. Germaine, who we'd been forced to bring with us, trotted over to Lucy and put her front paws on her knees, gazing up at her sympathetically. The young woman relaxed a bit, reaching down to pat her.

'Lucy, love, this is Nathan, and this is Jodie. I told you about them. They're with the police. Well, Nathan is – Jodie's sort of—' Debbie floundered a bit. I couldn't blame her.

'I'm kind of a liaison person,' I said. 'And I own the emotional support fluff ball.' I gestured to Germaine, and

I swear that dog would've done a little bow if she could, because she definitely understood that I was talking about her.

'Can you tell us what you told Debbie?' asked Nathan, gently. Lucy looked doubtful.

'There's not really much to tell,' she said. 'And he didn't do anything, so I don't want to get him into trouble if I'm wrong.'

'Let us be the judge of whether he should get into trouble or not,' said Nathan. Lucy looked at her friend, who nodded.

'All right, well, I met this bloke and we spent the night together,' she said.

'When was this?'

'Friday night,' said Lucy. 'I s'pose it's my own fault, I didn't know him—'

'No!' said Debbie and I together, vehemently.

'It might have been a bit unwise,' I said, 'but that doesn't mean you deserved to be drugged and then…' I let the sentence trail off. Lucy looked surprised.

'Oh, I wasn't assaulted or anything like that,' she said. 'At least I don't think I was.' She frowned. 'I don't *feel* like I was.'

'Go on,' said Nathan.

'We went back to his place, and we were messing about on the sofa and – you know – and then I just felt really funny, like I was awake but I couldn't move or anything. I tried to get up but my legs wouldn't work. I remember he carried me over to the bed, and then I passed out.'

'Had you taken anything earlier in the evening, before you went back to his house?' asked Nathan. She shook her head.

'No. I did have a bit to drink, but I wasn't drunk, not even close.'

'And what about when you got back to his house?' I asked.

'We had some wine. It was this posh sparkling stuff. He had some too. But only one glass.'

'Do you know how long you were asleep?'

'I slept all the way through until six o'clock. I still had all my underwear on—'

'Just your underwear?' I asked.

'Yeah. Before I passed out, we were snogging on the sofa and we'd started taking our clothes off.' She frowned again. 'That's why I'm freaked out. I don't know why he would spike my drink, because it was pretty obvious he was going to get lucky. He didn't need to drug me.'

'Okay,' said Nathan. 'When you woke up, was he there? Did he say anything?'

'Yeah, he said, like, "Thank God you're awake, I was worried."'

'He was worried?'

'Yeah, he said I'd passed out and he didn't know what to do. He said he'd nearly called an ambulance, but he didn't want me to get into trouble if I'd taken something dodgy at the festival. But I hadn't.' She stared at Nathan, wide-eyed. 'I honestly hadn't taken anything.'

Nathan looked at Debbie and nodded discreetly to the other side of the tent, then turned to Lucy. 'Let me just have a word with Debbie, Lucy, and we'll be back in a minute.'

We left the two girls fussing over the dog and muttering about how useless the police were. (Probably. Not for the first time, I wished Germaine could eavesdrop and then pass back to us what people were saying.)

'What do you think, Debs?' asked Nathan. 'Are we looking at Rohypnol or something less suspicious?'

'We've taken her blood pressure and given her a quick examination,' said Debbie, 'and although of course there's only so much we can tell from that, she seems as fit as a flea. She says she did vomit when she woke up, which could mean food poisoning, but it would have to be a pretty bad case to cause her to pass out, and if that was it

I'd have expected a lot of chundering, probably for several hours after ingestion. And with the floppiness of the limbs, it sounds more like a muscle relaxant of some sort to me.'

'Just like Rohypnol, in fact. Can you test for it? Would there be any left in her system now?' asked Nathan. Debbie shook her head.

'We'd normally do a urine test, but if it happened on Friday night that's at least thirty-six hours ago now, so most of it will have gone. We can do a hair test, that can work up to two weeks after, but only if it was a high dosage, and I'd say we're probably not looking at *that* high.' She frowned. 'I don't understand why anyone would spike her drink, if it was obvious she was going to have sex with them.'

'Because it's not about sex for some men, is it?' said Nathan. 'It's about control.'

Debbie shuddered. 'That's horrible.' She turned to look across the tent at Lucy. 'But she's adamant he didn't assault her.'

'If she's been home and had a shower since then, there won't be any evidence left anyway,' said Nathan. 'Let's just get the bloke's details and pull him in for a friendly chat.'

'You have got to be kidding me.'

We were standing outside the drug-testing tent, having got some more details from Lucy.

'Do you think he was being deliberately vague when he described her?' I asked. Nathan shrugged.

'Maybe. Lily is pretty close to Lucy, so it could've been an honest mistake. And he did say she looked like a typical twenty-first-century hippie festivalgoer. He wasn't wrong.'

'But he forgot to mention that she was unconscious for most of their "night of passion",' I said. 'Why would he do that? Come on, we need to go and talk to Dougie McKay.' But Nathan put out a hand to stop me.

'No. Sorry, babe, but this is a serious allegation and I can't have you there.'

'But—' I protested, but I knew he was right.

'I can't. When we spoke to him before, Matt had already taken a statement and we were just having an "unofficial" chat, weren't we? But this is different. Matt and I will talk to him.' He grinned. 'I'll give you a full rundown afterwards, don't worry.'

'Okay…' I said. 'You're right.'

'Blimey, can you say that again so I can record it?' He held his phone out and I swatted it away.

'Cheeky bugger. I'm not *that* bad.'

'No? I mean, no, of course you're not…'

'I still don't get why he'd roofie her. He was on a

promise, wasn't he? He'd already got her back to his place.'

'Yeah. And she's still absolutely adamant that she wasn't assaulted. She's got no unexplained bruises, no soreness down below, nothing to suggest that anything was done to her while she was out of it.' Nathan shook his head. 'I know you can never tell, but Dougie McKay doesn't strike me as someone who would drug a woman.' We turned back to look at the tent. 'I don't doubt that *something* happened to Lucy, I'm just not sure what.'

So Nathan called Matt, and they went off to interview Dougie McKay and left me stewing (or, more accurately, baking more flipping pies. This was definitely the last lot I was doing, I decided). I was itching to know what was going on, and I didn't even have anyone to talk about it with, as Tony and Carmen were dealing with burnt-out festivalgoers in the peace tent, Daisy was making the most of her time with Joe and her friends, and Mum was having a gong bath with Jocasta. I did tell her I didn't think it involved an actual bath, with water, and it was unlikely that she would need to take her clothes off for it, but she wouldn't listen. I hoped PC Chrissie wouldn't be arresting her for indecent exposure. Germaine listened to me banging stuff around in the truck in a huff for a while, and then wisely decided to sit outside in the sun and look cute for passersby.

After what felt like an eternity but in reality was about an hour and a half, Nathan and Matt joined me at the truck. As Matt tucked into a Bruce Willis – I noticed that Nathan was giving the pies a wide berth and I knew he'd reached his limit, just like I had – Nathan filled me in on what I'd missed. Having conducted interviews myself in the past, and having sat in with Nathan several times, I could see it all in my head.

Dougie McKay had tried to hide his alarm when Nathan had told him that they'd tracked down his alibi for Friday night, Lucy. His eyes had widened, but he'd quickly wiped the shock off his face and given them a rueful smile.

'Lucy! Of course, yes. I was close though, wasn't I? How is she?' The nervousness that accompanied that last line gave him away.

'She's fully recovered from her "illness",' Nathan had said. McKay had relaxed, but only slightly.

'Oh, good. Yes, she wasn't very well at one point…'

'She seems to have been a bit more than "not very well",' said Matt. 'Try "unconscious" for several hours.'

'Ah. Yes. Although I wouldn't necessarily say "several" hours…'

'Can you tell us, Mr McKay, why you didn't mention

this when we interviewed you earlier?' Nathan had been polite but firm. I could almost hear his tone of voice now.

'I can't wait to hear this,' I said. Matt grinned through a mouthful of meat and pastry.

'You owe me a tenner,' he said to Nathan.

'What?'

'I bet him a tenner you wouldn't get through the whole thing without interrupting,' he said. I rolled my eyes.

'How come your DS knows me better than you do?' I said. 'Anyway, carry on.'

McKay had kept quiet out of respect for the lady, he said. He'd been concerned that she'd taken something she shouldn't have, and that if he'd mentioned it she could have ended up in trouble with the law. Drugs charges or something. Further questioning revealed that he was also covering his own arse, because he realised he probably should've called an ambulance but hadn't. The relief on his face that Lucy had described when she'd woken up was genuine; she'd been out of it long enough that he'd started to worry about her not waking up ever again, and he really hadn't wanted *that* landing on his doorstep. All he'd wanted was a night of consensual adult fun. He hadn't laid a finger on her – well, not after she'd passed out – because he much preferred his sexual partners being able to move about and, you know, join in.

'Did you believe him?' I asked. Nathan and Matt exchanged glances.

'I don't know,' admitted Nathan.

'I think he genuinely thought she might die of an overdose, and that he'd be held responsible because he hadn't called an ambulance,' said Matt. 'He'd had a bit to drink himself and wasn't thinking that clearly, and when she passed out he just assumed that she'd throw up and get it out of her system, or sleep it off and be all right in the morning. But as the night went on he started to worry that he should've got help.'

'Right. But do you think he drugged her?' I asked.

'We don't really have any evidence either way,' said Nathan. 'But I'm inclined to believe that Lucy didn't knowingly take any drugs. She told Debbie she hadn't taken anything, and there was absolutely no reason for her to lie to her, even if she thought she should lie to us. And if you *had* taken something, wouldn't you automatically assume that's what you were reacting to? You wouldn't think someone had slipped you something, you'd think you'd taken a bad pill or that it was a lot stronger than you were used to.'

'True,' mused Matt. 'So does that mean we think he *did* drug her?'

Nathan sighed. 'Not necessarily. What would be the point? I don't think he's lying about not touching her. She seems certain he didn't. Maybe someone else slipped something into her drink before they left the festival, planning to go off with her themselves, but then of course she left with McKay and it only kicked in when they got back to the cottage. That's quite possible.'

'Did you ask McKay if he had access to Rohypnol?' I asked. Nathan nodded.

'Yes. He said no, of course, but he said he'd heard of it and that if she suspected he'd spiked her drink then it's no wonder she was so keen to get away from him next day. And he was so freaked out by the whole thing that he wasn't exactly in the mood anymore.' He grinned. 'I reckon he'll be thinking twice about casual hook-ups for a while, at least.'

'And of course he's washed up the wine glasses and the bottle for recycling, so we won't find anything there,' added Matt.

'So what do we do now?' I asked.

'What *can* we do?' said Nathan. 'Not a lot. We don't even have proof other than Lucy's testimony that anything happened, let alone proof of who did it. Even Lucy isn't sure what happened.' He shook his head. 'I don't like letting it go any more than you do, but we've hit a brick wall. If anything else comes up then we'll pursue it, of course, but for now we need to concentrate on who killed Lee Roskill.'

'Talking of which,' said Matt, 'I still need to get someone to identify the phone we found as our victim's. I didn't ask McKay, I didn't want to muddy the waters by bringing up that case while we were questioning him about a separate incident.'

'Caz might be the best person to ask, anyway,' I said. 'She seems to have been the closest to him.' A thought occurred to me. 'You must have Lee's number?' Matt nodded. 'Well, why don't you just try ringing it, then? Does it still have some juice in it?'

Matt took the phone, still in its plastic evidence bag, from his pocket and shook it. The screen lit up. 'Yes. Why didn't I think of that?' He handed Nathan the phone and took out his own, then dialled a number written in his notebook. We all stared expectantly at the phone…which stayed resolutely silent.

'So it's not his,' I said.

'Nope,' said Nathan. 'But going by where it was found, it could belong to whoever was on the beach with him.'

'Whoever bashed his head against the rocks…' I started in surprise as Nathan moved his hand and the screen lit up again, giving me a closer look at it. The phone's owner had set a photograph as the lock screen image, a photograph taken from the top of a hill, by the looks of it; of the sea glittering in the sunlight, and in the foreground the rooftops of a Cornish town. To one side of the frame the spire of St Botolph's church rose from the hillside and looked down upon the town. It was Penstowan.

'I know that view,' I said. 'And I think I know whose phone this is...'

## Chapter Thirteen

Caz and Ian were outside their yurt. A large rucksack and a holdall, overflowing with clothes, were on the ground next to them as they zipped up the canvas flap.

'Heading home?' asked Nathan. They both jumped and looked round at us. Nathan, Matt and I had decided to pay them a visit, and it looked like we'd timed it just right.

'Oh, yes,' said Caz. 'Ian managed to find someone to pick us up. Neil's staying for now and taking the gear back with him.'

'We can't do anything here,' said Ian, 'so we might as well be at home. Caz might actually get some sleep back in her own bed.' She smiled at him, but the smile was interrupted by a huge yawn. She rested her head on his shoulder and he put an arm round her. 'Ollie, our son, has been calling me every five minutes to make sure we're okay. He's on his way down from London to see us.'

'You just want to have your loved ones close when something like this happens, don't you?' said Caz. I nodded.

'Yes, you do…' We needed to mention the phone, but I didn't want to be the one to do it. Because I didn't want to believe what it could mean.

'I'm glad we caught you, then,' said Nathan. 'I wanted to show you something before you leave.' He took the phone out of his pocket. 'Do you recognise this?'

Caz looked surprised. 'Yes, that looks like my phone!' She reached out to take it, and Nathan handed it to her in the plastic envelope. She turned it over in her hand, and the screen came to life. 'Yep, that's my phone. That's a picture I took of the view from our garden. Where was it? I looked everywhere.'

'Down on the beach,' said Matt. And now she looked confused. It looked genuine to me.

'On the beach? How did it get down there? I haven't been anywhere near it. We didn't have time on Friday, and then after Lee…well, it's not somewhere I really wanted to be after that.' She looked at Ian, and then at me. 'How did it get on the beach?' She went to take it out of the plastic bag, but Nathan stopped her.

'Where did you last see it?'

'I told you, I left it backstage with all the others, but when I went back to get it the next day it was gone.'

'Just yours?' I asked. 'Ian's was there?'

'I picked mine up on Friday night before we came back here,' said Ian. 'We were buzzing when we came offstage, so I didn't think about it until later. When I went and got it I didn't see Caz's there, so I assumed she'd already picked it up. I was a bit miffed, to be honest, that she hadn't got mine while she was at it, but I didn't say anything because we were celebrating, not arguing.'

'And I completely forgot about mine until we got back here, and then of course I tried to go back to get it but we all know how *that* turned out.' Caz smiled sheepishly. 'I am *never* doing drugs again.'

'Until next time,' said Ian. Then he quickly turned to Nathan and Matt. 'Only joking, officers. There won't be a next time.'

Nathan cracked a thin smile. 'Did you hear from Lee Roskill after the argument that afternoon? Before you went onstage, maybe?'

'No, nothing.' Caz shook her head. 'I was going to call him, but Ian stopped me.' Nathan looked at him, eyebrows raised.

'I didn't want her ringing him up and having a go at him,' he said. 'She was angry and I didn't want her doing something she might regret.'

'Like what?'

'Oh great,' said Caz. 'Thanks love, you've made it sound like I wanted to kill him. I was just going to shout at him for a bit, nothing more.'

'Can I get you to unlock your phone, please, Mrs Holt?' said Matt.

Caz and Ian exchanged worried glances. '"Mrs Holt"?' said Caz. 'This is all getting very formal.'

'And then we'd like to check your messages and emails, if you give us permission? We can get a warrant if you don't.' Nathan took the bag from her, opened it and offered her the phone. Matt had already checked it for fingerprints – he had a portable kit in his car, as working in rural and often quite remote areas can mean the nearest forensics team is a few hours away, and sometimes every second counts. However, it had been exposed to sun, sand and sea water, and it had proved impossible to find anything.

'Of course you don't need a warrant,' said Caz, sounding bewildered. She entered the passcode, which Matt made a note of, and handed the phone back. She went to sit down but Nathan stopped her.

'If you'd like to stay there, please, Mrs Holt, so you can see what we're doing.'

Caz looked at me, and I took her arm.

'Caz, it'll be fine. This is just eliminating you from the enquiry, that's all,' I said. 'Your alibi was a bit hard to corroborate, wasn't it? With any luck there'll be something on here to prove it.' Although what that might be, I couldn't say. It seemed unlikely.

Nathan tapped the text message icon, and drew in a sharp breath.

'What is it?' Caz and I both said at the same time. Nathan didn't answer immediately, but showed the phone to Matt, who nodded and stepped forward.

'Carol Holt, I'm arresting you on suspicion of the murder of Lee Roskill. You do not have to say anything, but anything you do say will be taken down—'

'What the hell?' Ian looked furious. 'Get your hands off my wife!' This to Matt, who had taken his handcuffs out and was about to clap them around Caz's wrists. I looked at Nathan.

'Come on, Nath, she ain't going to run away, is she? How far's she going to get without a car?'

Nathan hesitated for a moment, and then gestured for Matt to remove the cuffs. Then he gently moved me out of the way and took Caz's arm, and marched her away to a waiting police car.

• • •

'What in the name of the sweet baby Je–ustin Bieber is going on?' asked a shocked Debbie. I think she'd been about to say 'Jesus', but Carmen was with us and in deference to her position with the church we tried (mostly unsuccessfully) to avoid blaspheming in front of her. Not that we needed to bother, really; she knew we were all heathens. Good-natured, but heathens.

I'd headed over to Mum's yurt – Nathan and I had dropped off Germaine there on our way to talk to Caz – after trying to comfort Ian. I hadn't known what to say to him, because what *do* you say in that situation? "Sorry, your wife might've murdered one of your friends"? Because the evidence didn't look great. Mum had listened to my shocked "They've arrested Caz", and then immediately rallied the gang around, because she could see I was upset.

And I *was* upset, not just because Caz had been my teenage idol, but because I liked her now, as a person. She'd been funny and kind when I'd done her dinner party, never talking down to me like I was the hired help (even though I was), which couldn't be said of some of the people I'd worked for. The fact that I hadn't even realised who she was, even though I was easily the right age group to have seen her at her prime, just pointed to how down to earth and modest she was. And yes, I was aware that it was starting to sound like I had a girl crush on her, because at age seventeen I had had one.

We sat on cushions outside the yurt while Jocasta brewed up some 'special tea' (you could hear the quotation marks around it as she offered to make some. I didn't want to think too much about what might be in it). Tony shuffled over and put his arm around me.

'You all right?' he asked.

'Yeah. I just don't want it to be true,' I said.

'So what exactly did the text message say?' asked Carmen, moving closer. They all leant towards me, all the better to hear the tea being spilled (not literally – by the smell of it, if Jocasta spilt any of *her* tea it would set fire to the grass). I rolled my eyes.

'It didn't take long for you to be assimilated into the group, did it, Vicar?'

She laughed. 'I'm trying to show my parishioners that beneath this dog collar I too am just a woman of flesh and blood.'

'I can vouch for that,' grinned Tony, and then he grimaced slightly as she elbowed him. Jocasta handed me a small enamel mug of something that was definitely hot but I wasn't convinced was tea, then held up the pot.

'Anyone else?'

Everyone else looked at me, obviously not willing to

accept a drink until the lab rat here had tried. I took a tentative sip and braced myself. And…it was delicious.

'That is *lush,*' I said enthusiastically.

'It's masala chai,' she said. 'I learnt the recipe when I was in an ashram in Pondicherry.'

'Really?' I asked, and then she gave a sudden cackle.

'No, not really. I had a fling with one of the waiters at this Indian restaurant I used to go to in Muswell Hill.'

There was a pause before we all roared with laughter. I smiled gratefully at her; I'd needed that, after the day I was having. I could definitely see why my mum had taken to her. Underneath the tie dye and scarves and New Age nonsense, she was funny and intelligent.

Jocasta finished handing round cups of tea and sat down with her own. 'So come on, then. Shirley tells me you love a good gossip—' she gave Mum a bit of side eye '—can't think where you get *that* from… But so far you've been disappointingly discreet.'

Everyone laughed again – the cheek! Although they had a point.

'All right,' I said, 'but it goes without saying that what is spoken about in the yurt stays in the yurt, okay?'

'Okay,' they all said, nodding dutifully. Honestly, they'd have agreed to anything for a bit of gossip. And *I* was the one with the nickname Nosey Parker!

'Lee Roskill texted Caz and asked to meet her,' I said.

'He said he had something he needed to talk to her about, and that she shouldn't tell anyone about it until she'd spoken to him.'

'Oooooh!' said Mum. 'Did he say what he wanted fo talk about?'

'No.'

'But she went to meet him?' asked Tony. I nodded.

'Looks like it. She texted him back and said to meet on the beach at midnight. She said it was the only way she'd manage to get away on her own without anyone noticing.' I sighed. 'She told us she was completely out of it and needed to go for a walk at about eleven-thirty, but she must've been putting it on so Ian wouldn't wonder why she wanted to go off on her own for a bit.'

'Wow…' said Debbie, and the others nodded. 'I wouldn't have imagined that she could be so scheming. She seemed so nice! But then she's used to performing, I suppose.'

'That's what Nathan said,' I said.

'How come none of the others saw the text?' asked Carmen. 'If they were all together, surely she would've looked a bit shocked or surprised and one of the others would've noticed?'

'Not necessarily,' I said, 'and anyway, she received the text at seven-twenty, when they were onstage. She'd left the phone backstage. She claims to have lost it, but she must've picked it up and seen the text, because she replied three hours later.'

'But no one saw her reply?' persisted Carmen. 'They didn't see her on her phone?'

'She could've been in the loo when she did it,' said Debbie.

'Yeah, that's what I thought,' I said. 'Plus there was a lot of drink and drugs circulating backstage, which doesn't make for very observant bystanders.'

'No, I suppose not.' Carmen frowned, and Tony put his arm around her.

'I love how you always look for the best in people,' he said, 'trying to make allowances for them and that, but sometimes people just do horrible things.'

'I know,' said Carmen. 'But she seemed so upset when she was in the peace tent with her husband, upset and completely bewildered. I didn't really talk to her, but she seemed to be genuinely grieving.'

'Or suffering from a guilty conscience,' said Tony. I rolled my eyes.

'Let's not convict the poor woman just yet,' I said. 'Do you actually *want* it to be her?'

'No, of course not,' said Tony. 'No more than you do. But you know better than any of us that in the right circumstances – or maybe that should be the wrong circumstances – most people are capable of murder.'

'Yeah,' I said. 'So what were the circumstances? If she *did* meet him, and she *did* murder him, why? Maybe she thought they could overturn the court injunction against the band with him out of the way.'

'More likely that it would be far more complicated with him dead,' said Jocasta. 'Not my area of expertise, but I expect they would need to appoint an executor or someone to manage his musical estate and represent his interests, or rather the interests of his beneficiaries. The best way to get a court injunction overturned is to appeal to the person who brought it in the first place. Hard to do when they're dead.'

'Although maybe she didn't realise that,' I said. 'But then of course, there's the murder of his ex-girlfriend in New York all those years ago. She was killed in pretty much the same way.'

'On a beach? In New York?' asked Mum.

'What? No, of course not,' I said, rolling my eyes. 'Does New York even have a beach?'

'Coney Island,' said Jocasta.

'Oh yes, of course. Anyway—'

'Hallett's Cove,' added Jocasta. 'South Beach, Brighton.'

'What? Really?' I was surprised. 'How do you know all this?'

'I worked for a law firm in Manhattan for a couple of

years,' she said. 'Fantastic place. I had an apartment in Greenwich Village, right above one of the biggest gay nightclubs in the city. I used to let the drag acts come up and use my bathroom as the one in the club was disgusting.' We all stared at her, incredulous.

'How on earth did you end up in Penstowan?' asked Debbie.

She shrugged. 'Americans have never got the hang of pasties.'

'Anyway…' I said, getting the discussion back on track. 'Lee's ex-girlfriend died after someone bashed her head repeatedly against a glass table. At least,' I admitted, 'we think they did. Same MO, could point to the same killer. But why would Caz kill her?'

'Backtrack a minute,' said Tony. 'If she texted him at, what, ten-thirty? and they arranged to meet at midnight… Lee must've been staying nearby. Near enough to get back at short notice.'

'Yeah, you're right…' I said thoughtfully. 'I don't know if Matt was able to track where he went after the argument, but he can't have gone far. If he was staying in town, or in Bude, even, unless he had a car he would've found it difficult to get back here by midnight.'

'Maybe he was staying at the festival?' suggested Debbie. 'Maybe he's got a tent somewhere on site.'

'Yeah… I wonder how we could find that out?' I said. Mum laughed.

'Oh *yes*! At last. If you want us to do a sweep of the camp and then secure the perimeter, count me in.'

'"Secure the perimeter"? We're in Cornwall, not 'Nam,' I said, but at the same time I was thinking, *Could we do that…?* Maybe somewhere there was a tent with all of Lee's stuff in it. And maybe amongst all that stuff would be a clue, something to tell us just what he'd wanted to talk to Caz about that had to be kept secret from the rest of the band…

'Morwenna might know,' said Debbie. 'Callum's sister works for the festival organisers, I think she was doing ticketing or something. I don't know if she'll still be here, but she was definitely here Friday and Saturday because we asked her to babysit so Callum could come with me, and she said she couldn't cos she was going to be here too.'

'Worth a try,' said Mum.

'Okay, but Lee did pull out of the festival,' I pointed out. 'Would he still have paid for a camping spot? Or been given one by the organisers?'

'The tickets sold out ages ago,' said Tony. 'They must've already allocated him a camping spot before he pulled out, and there might not have been time for them to resell it.'

'Maybe they allocated him a yurt, like Caz and Ian,' said Carmen.

'Maybe, *if* he'd been planning on staying here,' I said. 'He might have preferred to stay in a holiday cottage, like Dougie McKay.'

Debbie rang her sister-in-law, who as it turned out had gone home but was due back tomorrow to help clear up, which she really wasn't looking forward to.

'We could do with some volunteers,' said Morwenna, hinting. Debbie had put her on loudspeaker so we could all hear. 'You know, I probably shouldn't really be helping anyone but the police…'

'Jodie's practically the police,' said Debbie.

'And we'll all stick around in the morning and help you clear up,' I added. An audible groan went up amongst the others, but I waved them down and mouthed 'Shh!' at them.

'All right, I'll see what I can find. I'll call you back.' Morwenna rang off, leaving us staring at each other and wondering what to do next.

'What do we do next?' asked Carmen. Germaine, who up until this point had been a very good girl, leapt up; she'd obviously had an idea. I laughed.

'I think Germaine wants to do a sweep of the camp, like Mum said,' I said. 'She needs a walk.' I looked around. 'I wish I could let her off the lead and let her have a run around, but I can't do that here.'

'You could take her out onto the coastal path,' said Mum.

'We'd have to walk all the way to the main gate to get out onto that though, wouldn't we?' I said.

'No you wouldn't,' said Jocasta, pointing up the hill. I hadn't noticed when we'd descended upon Caz and Ian earlier – I'd had other things on my mind – but behind their yurt, which was right on the furthest edge of the glamping area, there was a small gate in the temporary fence that enclosed the festival site. A solitary and bored-looking security guard sat next to it, reading a book.

'Anyone else fancy stretching their legs?' I asked, standing and gathering up Germaine's lead. Mum decided to come, but the others were too settled on the floor cushions to move. 'Lazy,' I said.

Mum, Germaine and I headed up the hill to the gate. The security guard looked up from his well-thumbed Terry Pratchett novel, surprised. I couldn't blame him – Mum did give off an air of Nanny Ogg, although I wasn't sure if that made me Granny Weatherwax or Magrat.

'Hello,' I said. 'If we go out, can we get back in again?'

'You got your wristbands on?' he asked. Mum and I

both held ours out. 'Yeah, that's fine. I'm just here to stop anyone coming in without a ticket.'

'Have many people have tried?' I asked. He shook his head.

'Nah, not really. We had a big group on Friday afternoon try to sneak in, but other than that the only people I've seen have been a couple of walkers trying to cut through to the other side of the coastal path.' He grimaced slightly. 'Didn't go down too well with 'em when I told them they had to go the long way around.'

'Well, they did want a walk,' I said, and he laughed.

'Yeah, maybe I should point that out if anyone else asks,' he said.

'Why have a gate here at all, though?' asked Mum. 'You could just have a big fence, with barbed wire.'

'And dogs patrolling.' I laughed. Germaine barked. I don't think she liked the idea of being a watchdog.

'Well, I ain't told you this,' said the security guard, 'but I think the organisers are on dodgy ground here.' Mum and I both looked down at our feet before we could stop ourselves. 'No, I mean, it's a public footpath so they're not really supposed to block it off. Legally, like. But then it's only one weekend, and everyone round here knows about the festival, so most people are avoiding it anyway. But if anyone complained and the council came out to have a look, we could point to the gate and tell them people still have access.' He winked at me. 'Even though I'm not meant to let them through it.'

We left him to get back to the Discworld and walked out onto the hillside. I stopped to get my bearings while Germaine relieved herself by a gorse bush.

'Okay,' I said, facing towards the sea, 'so Bude and Penstowan are…that way.' I pointed to my right. 'Which means Boscastle's that way,' I pointed to my left, 'and the road is behind us.'

'And Ireland's over there,' said Mum, pointing forwards. I laughed.

'Yeah, I don't think we'll go that way,' I said. 'Bit too far, and I don't fancy a swim. Unless you brought your broomstick,' I added, thinking of the security guard's book.

'Eh?'

'Never mind, Nanny.'

We headed up the path which would, eventually, take us home to Penstowan. Nathan and I had done this walk in the opposite direction a few times in the past with the dog, but most of the time we didn't get this far. We always seemed to get waylaid by the café at the end of Bude canal, and by the time we'd scoffed a cream tea we were ready to turn round and go back again. The sun was out – we'd been lucky this weekend with the weather – and away from the cluster of tents and the noise (and smell) of the festivalgoers, it felt fresher up here, with a cool breeze that carried the tang of the ocean on it. I realised that I'd felt slightly greasy all weekend, what with spending so much time surrounded by bloody pies, and it was nice to be away from it all, albeit only for a little while, and not even that far; we could still faintly hear the music.

Mum stopped and sighed.

'Are you all right?' I asked, concerned. I sometimes forgot that she wasn't getting any younger, and she wasn't quite as fit as she had been.

'Oh, I'm fine,' she said. 'Just taking a trip down memory lane.' She smiled, gazing out to sea. 'I haven't been up here for ages, not without your dad.' I didn't say anything, just reached out and put an arm around her. 'I do miss him, you know.'

'I know. So do I.'

'Although to be fair, this wasn't really "our" place. We used to get as far as Widemouth Bay and then stop for a cuddle on the beach.' She grinned. 'That's where you were con—'

'Don't tell me!' I said, sticking my fingers in my ears, but I wasn't really that freaked out. No one likes to think of their parents, you know, doing *that*, but I quite liked the idea that I'd started life on a Cornish beach. Mum grinned wickedly.

'Of course, the beach down *there*,' she said, pointing, 'that was mine and Tom Wonnacott's special place.'

'Oh God no, don't ruin every beach in the area with tales of your sordid teenage shenanigans,' I said, and she laughed.

'"Sordid teenage shenanigans"? You were a saint when you were that age, of course…'

'I bloody well was compared to some of your stories,' I said.

'Nah, I was a good girl really. Your dad and I were married and well out of our teenage years by the time you came along. And Tom never got to – what do they call it these days? – second base.' She looked thoughtful. 'Is second base top or bottom? Or both, but under your knickers rather than over them?'

'Please, stop now.'

She laughed again. 'You're such a prude. I'm kidding anyway. All poor old Tom got was a snog on the rocks.'

'Down there?'

'Yes. Well, actually near where that poor man died. That's where the path goes.' She turned and pointed back towards the festival. 'It goes through the campsite, like that security guard said. And from there, of course, it branches down to the beach. But up there—' she turned and pointed behind us, up the hill '—up there it branches off and comes out on Coast Road. There used to be a car park up there, with a tearoom next to it. One of Tom's friends used to borrow his dad's Ford Cortina and drive me and Sheila Farrell up there, and Tom used to sneak out and meet us.' She grinned. 'And *that's* where Davey Trelawney was conceived.'

'Bloody hell, did nobody use a bed in the old days?' I asked. Davey Trelawney was one of my dad's old police recruits, one of the few just about young enough to still be serving. He had a Rock-like physique ('Rock' as in the wrestler turned actor, rather than a solid lump of granite, although he wasn't too dissimilar to that, either), with so many muscles that it looked like his biceps had their own biceps, but he was the calmest, sweetest-natured man in the country. Most of the time. 'I bet he couldn't fit in the back of a Ford Cortina now.'

'Nor could Sheila,' said Mum. 'Not without putting her new hip out.'

My phone beeped. Daisy was checking in with me. I felt a rush of pride; I didn't even have to ask her these days, she just knew that I'd be worried if I didn't hear from her all day, so she would send me a text every now and then to reassure me that she hadn't been abducted by aliens or fallen down a well or something.

'Daisy having a good time?' asked Mum. I nodded.

'Yeah, she's with that Joe, and Jade and Ellie. They've

been watching the surfing and now they're going to watch a band.'

'She's a good girl,' said Mum. 'You used to do the same with me, remember? You'd always give me a call from your friend's house, just to let me know you were going to the cinema or whatever.'

'Yes...' I said, suddenly going cold as I remembered what I'd *actually* been doing when I'd rung my mum. Safe to say I hadn't always been going to the pictures... But my Daisy wouldn't lie to me. Would she? I forced the thought from my mind – after all, even if she *was* up to no good, then she was only following in my footsteps, and I'd turned out all right. I called to Germaine, clipped her lead on, and we headed back to the festival.

## Chapter Fourteen

We arrived back at Mum's yurt to find Debbie on the phone, with everyone gathered around her.

'Oh, hang on,' said Debbie into the phone, 'she's just got back. Sticking you on speaker phone.' She turned to me and mouthed, 'Morwenna.'

'Well it just so happens that we have to keep a register of people staying, for health and safety reasons, in case we have to evacuate the site,' said Morwenna. 'Well, the name of whoever made the booking and how many people are in their group, anyway. Actually, Jodie, I'm surprised that fiancé of yours hasn't already asked for it.'

'So am I,' I said, 'but then he was meant to be on holiday, and he's been distracted by pies. Is Lee Roskill on the list?'

'Yeah, he must've checked in on Friday afternoon,

because his wristband was issued,' she said. 'When you got to the entrance gate you had to show your ticket and get a red wristband, yeah? That's a vendor's wristband, and because you needed a special site for your truck we allocated you one. The ordinary campers get a green wristband and a map of the site and are just told to camp wherever they can find a spot.'

'Oh, great…' We'd never find his tent, then.

'But anyone staying in a yurt gets a yellow wristband with the number of their yurt on it,' said Morwenna. 'And Lee Roskill got yellow number thirteen.'

'Unlucky for some,' muttered Tony.

'Unlucky for him, definitely,' I said. 'Morwenna, you're an absolute star.'

'You're welcome,' she said. 'Unfortunately I can't tell you the name of the person he was with.'

'Hang on, you mean he wasn't on his own?' I asked. It had never even occurred to us that Roskill could have had company, because no one had come forward to report him missing, even after his body had been discovered and news had spread around the site that someone had died. Now why would they do that…? 'You're sure he was with someone?'

'Well, I wasn't on the gate all day and I wasn't the one signing people in, but it's a two-person yurt and both wristbands were issued, so I'd say he must've been.'

'Do you know who was on the gate? Would they be able to identify who was with him?'

'I don't think so.' Morwenna sounded doubtful. 'I can see here who issued the wristbands, but in the two hours he was on the gate he gave out over a thousand of them, so the chances of him remembering are pretty low.'

'Right… Can you ask him anyway? Just on the off-chance?'

Morwenna promised to ask and hung up, after reminding us of our promise to stick around tomorrow and help her clear up. I thought back to the body on the beach; I didn't recall seeing a wristband, but maybe it had come off when the tide had come in. They were only paper, after all. I gave my own an experimental tug. Paper, yes, but surprisingly tough. And his hands, as far as I could remember, were above the tideline and had stayed dry. Maybe the killer had cut it off, and thrown it away with his wallet and phone to make identification harder? Or, more likely, Lee had taken it and just hadn't put it on. Maybe he hadn't intended to stay, but he'd had to show his ticket in order to get in and confront the band. He wouldn't have been on the list of performers anymore, having pulled out, so how else would he have gained entry to the festival site?

I was just about to speculate aloud as to where yurt number thirteen was when Mum held up her own wrist, pulled back the sleeve of her kaftan – which had been specially purchased for the festival – and revealed the number on her wristband.

'We're number eight,' she said. 'It must be just over there.' She leapt to her feet and everyone else followed suit, apart from Germaine, who looked up with a bewildered expression. She was probably thinking, *More exercise?! But I just got comfy!* I admired everyone's eagerness, but…

'Hold up!' I said, jumping up and getting in front of them. 'Where do you think you're going?'

Mum rolled her eyes. 'Er, duh,' she said. She'd obviously been listening to Daisy. 'Where do you think?'

'We can't go in there,' I said. Everyone else groaned. 'What? You didn't really think we could just storm into a murder victim's tent and help ourselves, did you?'

'What was the point of us finding it, then?' asked Debbie.

'So we can tell Nathan and get him down here,' I said, and everyone moaned again and told me I was boring. But Tony stood next to me, shaking his head at them.

'Nah, I reckon Jodie's right,' he said. 'There could be evidence in there, and if we go in unauthorised and trample all over it, any barrister worth their salt will see to it that it's classed as inadmissible.' He looked very pleased with himself.

'When did you study criminal law?' I asked him. He grinned.

'Ten years of watching *Law and Order* on the telly,' he said, and then followed it up with the epic 'DUN DUN!' sound from the theme tune. Jocasta laughed.

'I was in criminal law for twenty-five years,' she said. 'And I can confirm that Tony's right.'

'What *are* we allowed to do, then?' asked Mum.

'Well…' I really had to stop my own nosiness getting the better of me, but it was difficult when everyone else was just as bad. They all leant forward, sensing weakness, but I couldn't give way. 'No no, we *can't* go in, I told you that. But you heard Morwenna. There was someone else with him. Mum, Jocasta – have you seen anyone coming in or out of that yurt, at any time over the weekend?'

'No,' said Jocasta. 'But that doesn't mean anything. We haven't been here all the time, and to be honest, even if we were here and someone *had* come out, I don't think we'd have paid any attention. Why would we?'

'That's what I thought. They could have left already, but they *could* still be lurking in the tent, waiting for a moment to slip out unnoticed, so we don't want to risk any of us getting hurt or letting them escape.'

'You mean they could be the murderer?' cried

Carmen. I waved my hands at her in a 'calm down' gesture.

'Shh! Yes, they could be. Or,' I said, because something even less savoury had just occurred to me, 'or they could be another victim.'

As one, we all turned our heads to look at the yurt again.

'If they were murdered around the same time as Lee Roskill,' said Debbie, 'that's, what, almost forty hours ago? And it's been very hot.'

'So what?' asked Tony, and then his eyes widened as he clicked. 'Oh, right. It'll be starting to smell…' He winked at me. 'I watch *CSI*, too.'

'And there'll be flies,' said Debbie. 'Lots of flies, in this heat.'

Mum pulled a face. 'Maybe you should ring Nathan after all,' she said, which was exactly what I did. Except he was probably still questioning Caz, so I texted him with what we'd discovered.

He rang me back almost immediately. 'How did you find his tent so quickly?' he asked, before he'd even said hello. He sounded slightly exasperated. 'We put in a request for information with the promoters and they haven't got back to us yet.'

'The Penstowan grapevine,' I said, and he snorted.

'Penstowan mafia, more like,' he said. 'All right, whatever you do, don't let any of that lot go inside.'

'What lot?' I asked, trying to sound innocent, and he laughed.

'Yeah, right, they're all there with you, aren't they?' he said. Damn, he knew us so well. 'Roskill's tent is a yurt, so I take it you're all sitting outside your mum's, yeah? Just keep everyone together, and sit tight until I can get a Uniform there. I think Chrissie's still around. I can't imagine that anyone's holed up inside, but just watch and wait until she gets there. She can go in and have a poke about.'

'Okay,' I said. I looked around at the others, who I knew had all been eavesdropping but were suddenly very busy looking elsewhere. I wandered a little way away from them and asked in a low voice, 'How's it going with Caz?'

Nathan sighed. 'We're just taking a break. So far, it's not going well. She swears blind that the first she knew about any text messages to or from Lee was when I showed them to her. And she's sticking to her story about going for a walk and getting lost.'

'It might not be a story,' I said. 'It might be true.'

'Yeah, I know. But until we get financials and that back on Lee, what little evidence we've got points to her, and she *did* have opportunity. And possibly motive, even if it feels like a weak one. Everyone else connected to our victim has an alibi, apart from Ian. I'm not ruling him out, either.'

'And of course this mysterious person who was in the tent with Lee,' I said. 'Why didn't they report him missing? Why not come forward to the police?'

'Yes,' said Nathan. 'Someone else being there does throw a bit of a spanner in the works. But that's if there really was someone. The bloke on the gate might just have seen it was a two-person tent and handed over two wristbands, regardless of whether there was a second person.'

'Yeah, I suppose so,' I said, reluctantly, because I still didn't want it to be Caz. We ended the call after saying the usual soppy stuff to each other (I assumed Nathan was out of earshot of his colleagues), and I went back to the others. 'We're to wait,' I said, which was met with moans.

But we didn't have to wait for long, because soon PCs Chrissie and Brett whatever-his- name-was arrived. Brett nodded at me, while Chrissie took charge.

'All right, Jodie?' she said. 'Nathan's filled me in. Do you want to wait over here, or is that a stupid question?'

'It is a bit,' I said, and I followed her and Brett over to the yurt, stopping en route to tell the others (who were right behind me) to back off and give the Law room to breathe. Germaine took no notice and carried on trotting after me, stopping to sniff at the entrance to another yurt nearby, to growl at a large green weed that was looking at her funny, and to pee uncomfortably close to some fellow campers, until Tony jogged back and grabbed her collar.

I was relieved to find no swarms of flies wafting around the tent, no buzzing and none of the stink that would normally accompany a dead body that had lain undiscovered for a couple of days. Chrissie raised her hand to knock at the yurt, but of course it was made of canvas and there was nothing to bang her fist on. Instead, she looked at Brett, who nodded and headed around the back of the tent, although as far as I was aware there wasn't another way in or out. Then she called out.

'Hello, is anyone in there? This is the police, we'd like to have a word.' She paused. No answer, and no movement from inside the tent. She repeated herself, and then looked at me, and with a shrug reached out to unzip the tent. I stepped forward but she put a hand out to stop me. 'Nathan said you were allowed to come in and have a look, but I'm going in first just in case, okay?'

'Okay,' I said, feeling a bit daft. She was right; I kept forgetting I wasn't a copper anymore. She held back the tent flap and stepped inside, staying alert as she gazed around; but then she relaxed.

'It's all right,' she called back over her shoulder. 'It's clear.' Brett came round the front of the tent and we both went to step inside, getting in each other's way. We had a split-second stare-off to see who would go first, but Chrissie solved it by calling me in. 'Jodie, look at this.'

I smiled apologetically at Brett and went in. Inside, there was a big double bed – a proper one, not a camp bed or blow-up mattress, because this really was glamping. The sheets were pulled up but rumpled, like someone had been lying on it but had hurriedly attempted to make it. There were two empty beer cans on one side, but on the other was a bottle of water and an empty cardboard coffee cup. I bent down to get a look under the bed and sniffed; not coffee after all, something less pungent like tea, or even green tea. Under the bed was empty except for a thin strip of glossy paper. I recognised what it was by the brand name printed on it.

I straightened up and looked around. There was a sports bag on the floor on the other side of the tent, still full of something by the looks of it. Chrissie pulled on latex gloves and squatted down to open it. 'Clothes,' she said, 'men's.'

'Lee Roskill's,' I said, and she nodded.

'Presumably.'

I hooked a thumb at the bed. 'There's something

under there,' I said. 'Looks like the backing paper off a panty liner.'

'Hmm, or a sanitary towel,' said Chrissie. Brett looked embarrassed. I don't know why – if it wasn't for periods none of us would be here – but some men just seem to get a bit squeamish about it.

'Nah, that brand's for what they euphemistically call "light bladder leakage",' I said. 'Wait until you're pregnant, or you've had kids and you hit forty. You'll know all the brands, when you can't sneeze without a little bit of pee coming out.' Brett now looked so uncomfortable I thought he might pass out. He spoke quickly, probably to stop us talking about any other lady issues.

'So not just Lee Roskill, then,' he said. 'Whoever he was with has cleared out in a hurry and left his stuff here.'

'A mysterious female companion,' said Nathan, when I called him and reported back. 'What's the betting it was this girlfriend of his we still haven't been able to track down?'

'Rebecca? Yeah, that's what I wondered,' I said. 'Because wherever she is, she must've heard he's dead by now. It's been on the news and everything. You'd think she would've been straight on to the police to find out what happened or help with the investigation.'

'Unless she did it,' said Nathan, and I could've cheered. Maybe Caz really was as innocent as I wanted her to be. 'She could've been planning it for some time, which is why she's proving impossible to find now.'

'Yes!' I said. 'I mean, it's a gutsy move, but killing someone at a festival full of people drinking and misbehaving and making themselves look like potential suspects…'

'Even though we've pretty much ruled out a random killing or mugging gone wrong,' said Nathan.

'Yeah, but obviously she didn't know how clever the police round here are,' I said.

'And sexy.'

'And sexy, of course, goes without saying.' I said. 'I take it you're not in the office surrounded by people, then?'

'I'm actually on my way back to you,' he said. 'We're leaving Caz to stew for a bit and then Matt and Sunil are going to carry on questioning her. We've got enough to hold her until tomorrow, by which time we should have financials and phone records back, although I'm not sure they matter so much now we have Caz's phone. But they might help us finally track Rebecca down.'

I passed the phone over to Chrissie so he could give her instructions, then said goodbye and sat with the others, watching as the two uniformed officers sealed the tent back up and stuck a piece of sticky incident tape across the zip. Chrissie waved me over as they finished up.

'There doesn't appear to be anything in there of interest,' she said. 'We're taking Lee's bag back to the station, but it looks like it's just clothes. We've sealed it up to stop anyone having a nose about.'

'Not me, Officer,' I said, as sweetly and innocently as I could, and she laughed.

'The thought didn't even cross my mind,' she said. Yeah, right. 'I was thinking more about your posse over there.'

'I'll keep an eye on them,' I promised, and Brett muttered under his breath.

'That fills me with reassurance,' he said.

Dusk had started to fall. During the summer it didn't get *proper* dark that far west until much later in the evening, but the heat had started to go out of the sun and everyone's thoughts had turned to dinner. Well, mine had anyway, but they're never that far from food at any time. Pie Hard was officially shut; we'd pretty much sold all the ready-made pies, and I couldn't face making any more even though the fillings and the pastry were all in the freezer. My friend Sean had said that the frozen stuff was really for emergencies only, and that we should have enough ready-made to see us through, so despite me and Nathan abandoning the truck at every opportunity we must've sold almost as many as Sean normally did. Maybe he liked to duck out and have a bit of a dance? I was guessing he didn't tend to investigate as many murders as we did.

Daisy had sent me a text asking where I was – funny how she seemed to forget all about me until it was time to eat, or she'd run out of money or something – and now she, Joe, Jade and Ellie were sitting outside the yurt with us. Tony had suggested that after the excitement with Lee's yurt we should go and watch a band or something, but we'd all groaned and sunk lower into the floor cushions, even Germaine; we were all out of energy, and, watching my teenage daughter and her mates, I suspected they were too. Although in their case it was probably because they'd already spent most of the day watching the surfers and then leaping around in front of the stage to whoever was playing, and not because they were really too old for this camping malarkey. I was pleased to see that Daisy and Jade had forgotten their argument and were BFFs again, notwithstanding that Joe was occupying a lot of Daisy's attention as well. I wondered what would happen when the festival was over. Would he go home, or on tour? Where was home, anyway? He had a London accent, but then half of the population of Cornwall these days came from upcountry, so that didn't necessarily mean anything. And of course she wasn't even sixteen yet, so it would probably be one of those young love, holiday romance things, and she would more than likely end up with a broken heart. I knew it was inevitable that she wouldn't get through life without it happening at least once, but if we could just put it off for as long as possible that would do for me.

Tony and Joe did a run to the nearest food outlet – it was the closest Tony would ever get to being a hunter-gatherer, and Joe was obviously after brownie points – and brought back two bags of chicken, beef and veggie burgers, with lots and lots of chips. Debbie and Daisy took Germaine for a last (reluctant) walk, and picked up some cans of soft drink. Then we all sat and tucked in, occasionally still glancing over at the yurt that had almost been the final resting place of Lee Roskill.

Nathan still hadn't arrived, so I called him; Tony had brought him a burger, but if he wasn't there soon someone else would probably eat it.

'Sorry, babe,' he said. 'I just popped back to the house for a shower. I'm leaving right now, I'm in the car.'

'Noooo!' I cried, horrified. 'That means you'll be able to smell me when you get here. I haven't had a shower since Friday morning.'

He laughed. 'I had to, I've been working and I could see people keeping downwind of me. I don't care what you smell like.'

'Good.'

'Within reason.'

'Cheeky git.' I heard him start the car and the sound of the engine as he pulled away.

'So, have you managed to keep that lot out of the tent?' he asked.

'Yeah,' I said. 'They've all lost interest in it by now. Too busy eating burgers. Which reminds me, we got you one so you better—'

'Mum!' hissed Daisy, urgently. I looked at her, then followed the nod of her head towards Lee's yurt. A man stood in front of it, looking at the tape across the zip. Then he reached up and tore it off. The others had of course also heard Daisy's cry, and they looked up too, gasping as he ripped the sticky tape away and threw it on the floor. Or tried to, anyway; it was stuck to his hand.

'You still there?' asked Nathan.

'Yeah,' I said. 'Some bloke's just gone sniffing around the yurt…' I covered the phone and hissed at the others. 'Stop looking! Don't make it obvious we're watching him!' They all dragged their gazes away, but it was too late; he obviously felt someone watching him, because he looked straight over at us. I gave him a friendly smile, while gritting my teeth and muttering, 'Shit…'

Nathan groaned. 'Don't tell me, he's seen you watching him.'

'Yeah… Oh God, Mum's waving…'

Nathan sighed. 'Why does that not surprise me? What does he look like? What's he doing?'

The man looked quizzically at us, then turned away. He took out a phone and dialled a number.

'He's on the phone,' I said. 'IC1 male, mid-thirties, short dark hair, smart clothing – too smart for a festival, really. What do we do?'

'What do normal people do when a man they don't know is on the phone, minding his own business?' said Nathan. 'Pretend you're normal and ignore him. Hang on, someone else is trying to call me. I'll ring you back.' He disconnected the call and I floundered for a moment like an idiot, before sitting down next to Mum.

'What's he doing now?' asked Mum, whirling around to look at him. I shot out my arm to stop her.

'Will you behave, Mother!' I said. 'Stop looking at him and eat your chips.'

'He's still on the phone,' said Jocasta, risking a fleeting glance. 'He's – oh bugger.'

'What?' I looked up to see the man, still on his phone,

looking straight at us. As he spoke, he began to approach us.

'Should we run away?' asked Carmen. I looked at her and she shrugged, looking slightly embarrassed. 'Sorry, I don't know why I suggested that. I'm not used to this sort of thing. Tense, isn't it? The worst thing I've had to deal with recently was a large seagull flapping about in my vestry.'

'Ooh, Matron!' said Mum in her best Kenneth Williams *Carry On* voice, but I could tell her heart wasn't really in it, too intent was she on the man on his phone.

'Your family is *awesome,*' said Joe to Daisy, a chip paused halfway to the large but bemused grin on his face. 'Are they always like this?'

She rolled her eyes. 'Don't encourage them.'

The man stopped in front of me, still on his phone. He looked me up and down and spoke to the person on the other end of the phone. He had a Thames Estuary accent and up close I could just see the edge of a tattoo poking out from beneath his shirt collar. 'The one in the T-shirt with a biscuit on a computer screen on the front and the words "accept all cookies" on it?'

'It's a *cookie,* not a biscuit,' I said grumpily, self-consciously rearranging my T-shirt, 'otherwise the pun doesn't work.'

'Yeah,' said the man into the phone, grinning, 'she

just said that. Here.' He passed the phone to me and I took it, bewildered.

'Surprise,' said Nathan on the other end.

'What the – do you know this guy?' I asked. 'Is he another copper?'

'No,' said the man in front of me. 'I'm a private investigator and I just flew in from New York.'

'Ooh, get you,' said Mum. 'Fancy a chip?'

## Chapter Fifteen

'So were you looking for Rebecca?' I asked. We were sitting outside Lee's yurt on some folding chairs that had been inside, waiting for Nathan, who had texted me to say he was parking the car and would be with us shortly. The private investigator, whose name was Adam, had made himself quite at home, eating our chips and accepting a can of Coke. It sounded like he literally had just got off the plane from NYC and made his way straight to the festival. He looked knackered.

'Yeah,' he said. 'Do you know where she is?'

'We didn't even know where she *was*,' I said. 'We had no idea she was here. She definitely came with Lee?'

'Yes. They were supposed to wait for me to get here before they did anything, but…' He shrugged. 'Looks like they decided not to.'

'Did you know what Lee was planning to do?' I asked, although I probably shouldn't have, because Nathan would no doubt be asking exactly the same questions.

'He told me he was going to confront the band,' said Adam. 'He said he wanted to talk to Caz, but it was difficult getting her on her own.'

'Well, he definitely did confront them,' I said. 'I saw it with my own eyes. What were you investigating in New York?'

Adam hesitated. 'I'm not sure I should be telling you that,' he said. 'I think I should wait for your DCI to get here.'

'Yeah…' I decided not to mention that Nathan wasn't 'my' DCI, as such. Adam grinned suddenly.

'I knew it! You're not police, are you? You're ex-Job, like me. You can always tell. Where were you?'

'I was a sergeant in the Met, out of Stockwell. Twenty years, or near enough. You?'

'Brighton. Ten years, until I got kicked out for drug abuse.'

'Sorry,' I said, although it was hardly my fault.

'It was my own doing. Even when I got clean, I was too much of a risk. You can't have someone who could potentially be bought off by drugs or blackmailed or whatever dealing with criminals, can you? I didn't really give them much choice. And it did make me realise I had to get my shit together. I went into rehab and that's where I met Lee. He was a good bloke.'

'You stayed friends?'

'Yeah, sort of. We didn't see each other socially, but we kept in touch, made sure we were both staying clean, that sort of thing.' He looked at me. 'He *was* clean, before you ask.'

'So we've been told.' Nathan stood in front of us. 'Mr Burridge, I presume?' Adam jumped up and held out his hand to shake.

'DCI Withers? I got your message. Sorry I couldn't speak to you before, I was in the air when you phoned. You can call me Adam.'

'And you can call me DCI Withers,' said Nathan, shaking his hand. I hid my grin. If Adam was taken aback he didn't show it. Nathan sat down and gestured for him to follow suit.

'So, Adam, can you tell me exactly what you were doing in New York?' asked Nathan, although we already knew some of it from our own man in NYC, Craig.

'Of course. I was following up an inquiry on behalf of my client, Lee Roskill.'

'I thought he was your friend?'

'He was. Client *and* friend.' Adam casually reached for a chip. I watched, fascinated: Nathan held the upper hand here, the power dynamic in his favour, but Adam had information we wanted, information that he obviously thought was valuable, and he wasn't going to be intimidated by Nathan's rank.

'I believe you were looking into the murder of Emily Logan at the Madison Suites hotel fifteen years ago,' said Nathan, a statement rather than a question. Adam looked surprised, but then recovered quickly.

'I'm impressed, DCI Withers. Yes, I was. Lee didn't think the police had investigated it thoroughly enough at the time, and in light of other recent discoveries it seemed like he could be right.' Adam leant back, attempting nonchalance.

'The hotel's CCTV footage from that night had disappeared,' said Nathan. Again, there was a brief flash of surprise from Adam, but he didn't say anything. 'I'm assuming you found it? Or at least what happened to it?'

'I might have done.'

'But it didn't occur to you to present what you'd found to the NYPD so they could reopen the case?'

Adam hesitated for a moment, and then laughed.

'All right, mate, you win. I was trying to keep it close to my chest, because, to be honest, if Lee hadn't blundered in and got himself killed we probably would've used what I found to blackmail a certain person into doing the right thing, rather than us going down the legal route. But it don't matter now, does it?' He sat forward, alert. 'I may have taken a few…liberties, shall we call them, and not necessarily followed the strict letter of the law, but I did follow what you'd call the *spirit* of it.'

'You did stuff that ain't legal but it was to get at the bad guys,' I said, and he nodded.

'Yeah, you get me. Only I have to warn you, I'm not exactly sure which one of 'em *is* the bad guy.'

'Of course you're not,' said Nathan. 'It's never that simple, is it? Tell us what you know.'

'Okay, well, Lee thought there were discrepancies with the investigation into Emily's death. At first he put it down to junkie paranoia, but after he got clean he got a little bit obsessed with it. When he found out I used to be a cop, he started really bending my ear about it. I dismissed it at first, but after a while I did think it sounded like the NYPD had been slapdash about it.' He looked frankly at both of us. 'You know what it's like, though. From the police point of view. You know what happened, but there's not really enough evidence to prove it. Shit, there might even be stuff that goes against what you think you *know*, deep down, happened. So you don't lie, you don't falsify anything, but you – you know.'

'You fudge it,' said Nathan. Adam nodded.

'Yeah. What can I say? Stay in the job long enough and you'll probably do it yourself.'

'I nearly did,' said Nathan, looking at me, and I knew he was remembering the case that had brought us together, where he'd been absolutely convinced of Tony's guilt, but I'd known otherwise. And for a while neither of us had been able to prove which one was right.

'So you're NYPD, it's Halloween, when all the nut jobs come out and cause bloody chaos. It was bad enough in Brighton, and we don't even really do Halloween here, do we? But this is New York City. So everything's going bonkers, loads of weirdos about, crazy stuff happening, and in the middle of it some junkie bangs her head on a glass coffee table, smashes it and bleeds to death. Everyone connected to her has an alibi, she never left her hotel room so it can't even be some random homicidal maniac. Accident, right? Gotta be.'

'And no CCTV footage to prove otherwise,' said Nathan.

'Exactly. That's a bit weird, but it's Halloween, people playing stupid pranks, things going wrong, some old bollocks about the hotel ghost… What would you do?'

'Investigate it properly,' I said stubbornly, but Adam shook his head.

'But there's not many lines of inquiry, and they all

come up blank, and when you get down to the nitty gritty it's just one more dead junkie.' He spread his hands wide in a what-you-gonna-do-about-it gesture. 'Overworked coppers make mistakes or take things at face value. I'm certain that's all it was, rather than some big conspiracy on their part.'

'What about the missing footage?' I asked. 'Did you find it?'

'No,' said Adam. 'I tracked down the security guard who was working that night, and he told me a very interesting story.' He grinned. 'Actually, he told me two. The first one was about the hotel ghost, who had a habit of messing about with technology. Very entertaining. After he finished telling me about that, I asked him to cut the crap and tell me the truth, and eventually he did.' He gave Nathan a sideways glance. 'And that might be where I veered slightly from the prescribed police interview techniques.'

'You beat him up?' I asked. He looked shocked.

'What? No, of course not. He was bigger than me… No, Lee was foresighted enough to sign off on a very generous expenses allowance for me. I bribed the bloke. He told me that the night of the murder – because we're all agreed that Emily was murdered, yeah?' Nathan and I both nodded, although at this point we still didn't have anything that backed that up. 'That night, after the body was discovered and the police were on their way, an English bloke found him in the security office and offered him a huge amount of money in return for him losing the footage.'

'An English bloke? Did he get a name?'

'Someone's offering you ten thousand dollars to delete a bit of video, you're not going to ask questions, are you?' said Adam.

'Those are the *exact* circumstances where you should,' said Nathan. 'But in view of the fact you might not like the answers and you might end up losing the money, no, I'm guessing you wouldn't ask. But what about the money? If it was a bank transfer there'd be a trail, a name at least…'

'Cash,' said Adam. 'Which is suss in itself, innit? Who just happens to have ten grand in readies sitting in their wallet?'

'So all you got is that they were male, and English. No other description?'

'Nothing specific. White, possibly mid-thirties but our witness admits he's terrible with ages, so could be anything from twenty-five to forty-five. Which means now they could be forty, or they could be sixty, or anything in between. Medium height, medium build, brown hair.' The sort of description cops *love* (not), because it could apply to half the male population of the

UK. And it also applied to pretty much all the men connected with this case.

'And the footage is gone?' asked Nathan.

'He deleted it, just like he was asked to,' said Adam. 'But there is this…' He took out his phone. 'He took a couple of screenshots as "insurance". I sent them to Lee, just before he was killed.' He clicked on the photo app, and passed the phone over.

On the screen was a very grainy black and white still taken from the security camera that overlooked the hotel lift, down in the foyer. On it, a man in dark trousers or jeans – it was impossible to tell which – was about to get into the lift. He wore a dark baggy hoodie with the word 'CREW' emblazoned on the back. The hood was up, covering his hair, which might have looked suspicious but for the fact that it was October in New York and therefore probably quite cold outside.

'Swipe onto the next one,' said Adam, so we did. Here, the same man was getting out of the lift. The floor number above the door said twenty-five. 'That's him getting out on the floor the band's rooms were on.'

'Is that a crew sweatshirt from the tour?' I asked, and Adam nodded.

'Yeah, I checked. They all had them. It's hard to tell from the photo, but I went to the hotel and I reckon, using the lift doors as reference, he's not that tall. Five eight at the most.'

'The same height as the hooded man we saw the night of Lee's murder,' I said. 'Ian Holt's about five eight. Remember what Neil said, about him not getting on with Lee or with Emily, because they were persuading Caz to take drugs again?'

'Yeah…but he also said they'd got past it,' said Nathan. 'You know who else is that height? Dougie McKay, and Neil Hiller. And Caz, in her heels.'

'The person in that picture isn't wearing heels,' I said, although truth be told it was actually really difficult to say that for certain, with the angle of the camera shot. The other thing you couldn't see because of the angle (and the hoodie) was the person's face. But that would've been far too helpful.

'Does the security guard think the person in this photo is the same person who went to see him?' asked Nathan.

'I asked him that, but he said he didn't know. He said he couldn't really remember that night now, it was so long ago. Although it was surprising how much his memory improved when I gave him some money.'

'How much did you give him?' I asked. 'Just out of curiosity.'

'Not as much as he was given to lose the footage,'

said Adam, dryly. 'I don't blame him. The bloke told him the death was an accident, but it would be very embarrassing not just for the band but for the hotel and the security company as well if the police started looking into it. He said that the security team would be blamed for letting a drug dealer into the hotel.'

'That's who he said was in the footage?' I asked. 'A drug dealer?'

'Yeah,' said Adam. 'One providing a different sort of room service to the one the hotel offered. Our security guard didn't really care about that, of course, but he was working his way through college and he didn't have much money, so that ten grand would've really helped.'

'But he quit a few weeks later, didn't he?' said Nathan. 'So he obviously had some suspicions, and wanted to put a bit of distance between him and the hotel.'

'Not that it worked,' said Adam, looking smug. 'I tracked him down in Florida.'

'Okay,' I said, thinking over what we'd just been told. 'Back up a bit. What was it that made you take Lee seriously about this? You said "in light of recent discoveries". What discoveries?'

'I don't know the ins and outs of it,' said Adam. 'But Lee told me someone had swindled him out of some money.'

Nathan and I exchanged glances. Ian had admitted that he'd helped Lee with some investments after they started making big money, and that Lee had lost a lot of it. But he'd told us that he'd advised Lee against it. Maybe he hadn't? Maybe he'd found a way to get that money paid to his own account. Or maybe he'd just wanted to get back at Lee for putting Caz at risk of getting a drug habit.

'He said he'd only realised when he'd asked his lawyer and his accountant to get together and work out how much his estate was worth, and they raised questions about it,' said Adam. 'From what his accountant said, it had to be someone with an in-depth knowledge of both the music industry and financial planning and investments.'

'Ian Holt worked in the City before the band,' said Nathan, and I nodded, feeling sick. Because I didn't want him to be guilty any more than I wanted his wife to be. But it did all add up.

'And now you have his wife in custody,' said Adam.

'How did you know that?' asked Nathan.

'It's probably all over social media,' I said. 'She got escorted from the festival in a marked police car. Even though she wasn't in cuffs, it wouldn't take a genius to work out what was going on.' Ian had been desperate to follow and was apparently currently doing everything he could to get her home. Was that down to a guilty conscience? Or was it just because she was his wife, and he was just doing exactly what any other husband would do?

'What have you got on her?' asked Adam. Nathan snorted.

'You seem to be under the impression this is a partnership,' he said. 'You're a private investigator and I'm a copper. The information only flows one way, you know.'

'Fair enough.' Adam sniffed, like he wasn't that bothered. 'I reckon Lee arranged to meet Caz Harper down on the beach, but it was Ian who turned up instead, and then he killed him. Am I close?'

'Not even,' I said, but I felt cold, because I was starting to think the same thing. 'But how does any of that tie in with Emily's murder?'

'Because Emily was with Lee when the band had their most successful album and tour,' said Adam. 'She realised – or suspected – that he wasn't getting as much money as he should've done. Something like that, anyway. He said that she told him she thought someone was screwing him over, but he didn't believe her. She even said it in front of the rest of the band, and they all dismissed it. But it looks like she was right.'

'And whoever was doing it shut her up before she

could make the others believe her,' said Nathan. 'We must be talking about a lot of money, if it was worth killing two people over.'

I shook my head. 'It probably was a lot of money, but only the first murder would've been about that. If Lee realised that this person had killed Emily, that's what *his* murder would be about: not getting put away for Emily's death.' I turned to Adam. 'Because Emily's death was more important to him than the missing money, wasn't it?'

Adam nodded. 'Yeah. He said it was his fault she died, because he didn't take her allegations seriously. He did what everyone else did – underestimated her.' He yawned and gave a big stretch. 'Now, if you don't mind, I'm cream crackered and I need to get me head down.' He glanced towards Lee's yurt, and Nathan laughed.

'In there? Dream on, sunshine.'

In the end Nathan got PC Brett to give Adam a lift into Penstowan, where he would (hopefully) be able to find a bed for the night. I gave him Margaret Tiddy's number – she ran a B&B in town – and told him to mention my name, but if she was full, then she was full.

'Not my problem,' said Nathan. 'My problem is waiting for me back at the station.'

'What do we do now?' I asked. 'By "we" I mean "you" and then you tell me all about it.' He laughed.

'Yeah, I knew what you meant… As much as I hate to admit it, our new friend might have cracked it. These are the facts.' Nathan sat back and counted them on his fingers. 'Fact number one. Lee Roskill texted Carol Holt née Harper and asked to talk to her, and she texted back arranging to meet him on the beach at midnight. We have proof of that. Fact two. Everyone connected to Lee had an alibi at midnight, apart from Caz and Ian, who alibied each other. Up to a point. Their whole story is vague.'

'But is it deliberately vague, or is it true?' I asked. 'You know as well as I do that watertight alibis are the most suspicious, because most people can't remember what they had for breakfast yesterday, let alone what they were doing "on the night of"… They could be telling the truth.'

'They could, but Caz goes for a wander among the yurts and no one else sees her? How likely is that? I know it was dark and most people were probably either watching the band or drinking or whatever, but there must have been someone around. She's either trying to put herself as far away from the beach as she can without running into witnesses, or she's drawing attention to her own actions so we ignore Ian.'

'Who at this point is supposedly tucked up in their

tent, but is actually down at the beach in the festival drug dealer's hoodie, bashing Lee's head in…' I sighed. 'I don't like either of those options. And it doesn't explain how Ian killed Emily, either, if we're going with just one murderer. Because they all had alibis for that night, too.'

'Yeah, which we could do with getting our hands on,' said Nathan. 'I'll talk to Craig again, and put in an official request for the file. But fact number three: same MO for both murders, even down to disguising themselves in a hoodie.'

'Yeah…'

'Our next move is re-interviewing both of them, seeing if we can get one of them to crack.'

'What, and dob the other in?' I shook my head. 'Unlikely. I don't know if they're murderers or not, but they're loyal. They won't turn on each other.'

'I know, but all we need is for one of them to get a detail wrong in their story, just enough for us to pull it apart. And of course let's not forget that we still need to track down Rebecca, because her doing a runner and not making herself known to us is definitely not what I'd expect a grieving partner to do.' Nathan yawned. 'But that can wait until tomorrow. Shall we go to bed?'

'Are you staying?' I asked, surprised. He nodded.

'Of course. I thought I'd drive the truck home in the

morning. I came back specially because I know you don't like driving it.'

'Aww, babe…' I leant over and kissed him. 'Let me round up Daisy and the dog and make sure they're okay, and then I will let you seduce me in our pie-scented love truck one last time…'

# Chapter Sixteen

Nathan left early the next morning after having a word with the festival organisers, who cleared a path for the truck and let him exit via the emergency vehicle access. Anyone who needed an emergency pie was in luck.

I hadn't forgotten my promise to Debbie's sister-in-law Morwenna, however, so Germaine and I waved him, Pie Hard and a few crumbly remnants of Bruce Willis and Hans Gruber off with a sigh of relief (no more pies! Hurray!) and made our way over to Mum's yurt, stopping en route a few times to sniff at some interesting piles of rubbish left behind by departing campers. The dog sniffed at a few, too…

I hadn't really expected any of the others to stay behind and help clear up, apart from Debbie, of course, but when I got to the yurt Tony was already there, helping Mum and Jocasta pack their clothes, get rid of their rubbish and strip the linen from their beds. Although the last thing wasn't strictly necessary, Mum *always* stripped the beds whenever we stayed anywhere, even in posh hotels, and I'd picked up the habit. Daisy had asked me once why we did it, because obviously the housekeepers would be in to clear up after we'd checked out, and I told her what my mum had told me: regardless of how expensive the hotel was, you could bet your life the housekeepers would all be women working for the minimum wage. And a lot of them would be mums, who no doubt would finish clearing up after guests and then go home and have to pick up their kids' rubbish too, only they wouldn't get paid for that. If someone's doing a hard job – whether that's physically, mentally or emotionally hard – then we should all do what we can to not make it even harder for them, especially when they're not earning much from it.

Except in this case it was *Tony* doing what he could to not make it harder for them, despite the fact he'd been staying in his own tent using a blow-up mattress and a sleeping bag, which he'd already packed up. He looked slightly bewildered.

'She's roped you in to help, has she?' I grinned at him. He nodded.

'Yup. I should've expected it from your mum,' he said. 'I'm meant to be helping Carmen. I left her and the other volunteers taking down the peace tent.'

'Oh dear,' I said. 'I think as a vicar, though, she's legally obliged to understand and not have a go at you.'

He laughed. 'Oh, if only that were true… Nah, it's all good. I pointed out that helping Shirley would be the Christian thing to do, so she didn't have a leg to stand on.'

'You not finished that yet?' said Mum, coming over. 'We haven't got time to stand around chatting.' Behind her, Jocasta mimed a whiplash and Tony and I laughed. Mum whirled round in time to see her friend assume an innocent expression. 'What?'

'Nothing, Shirl,' said Jocasta. 'I was just admiring your managerial skills.'

Daisy arrived on her own. I pulled her in for a hug to say good morning and she even let me give her a peck on the cheek. It's amazing how demonstrative I'm allowed to be when none of her friends are around to see it. I suspect she even still enjoys it.

'Home time soon,' I said. 'Where are the others?'

'Jade and Ellie are sticking everything in the car,' she said. 'I think it'll take a couple of hours before they can move it, though. I got up early to say goodbye to Joe.'

'Right,' I said, thinking, *Is this it? My daughter's first holiday romance and subsequent broken heart?* But I needn't have worried because—

'Is it all right if he comes round next Saturday?'

I looked at her in surprise. 'Who, Joe? Yes, of course. Where does he live? In London? Because that's a long old drive, as you know.'

She laughed. 'What? No, he lives in Exeter. His family moved down from London about eight years ago.'

'Ah, okay. I thought he had an accent.'

'Yeah, he's not from our neck of the woods, though.' She pulled a face. 'North of the river.'

'Oh *no*. Never mind, we'll try not to hold it against him.' And that was it. Heartbreak averted, for now at least. Phew.

Debbie arrived with Morwenna, who was wearing a T-shirt emblazoned with the festival logo on the front and 'volunteer' on the back, and carrying a walkie-talkie. She looked like she meant business. It was weird; physically, she really resembled her brother (and Debbie's husband, and the boy in my old high school that all the girls and probably a few of the boys had had a crush on) Callum, with dark, curly hair and beautiful eyes. But Callum was a complete softy, very gentle and laidback, whereas Morwenna… Well, she was nice, and of course she had been very helpful with finding Lee's yurt, but she prided herself on being super-organised and a real go-getter and I, for one, would not have liked to get in her way.

She was just explaining what jobs needed doing, and how she'd organised (or more likely press-ganged) all the volunteers into groups, when I spotted Adam Burridge, our friendly neighbourhood private detective, sauntering over to Lee's yurt. I watched as he unzipped the tent and stepped inside.

'Back in a minute,' I whispered to Daisy, who seemed surprised to have been dragged into volunteering but was now too firmly caught in Morwenna's net to escape. I slipped away and followed Adam into the tent.

'What you doing?' I said loudly, and he jumped. He turned around with a hastily assembled smile on his face.

'Oh, you know, looking for clues, that kind of thing,' he said, obviously hoping that I'd be satisfied with a vague explanation. But then, obviously, he didn't know me.

'Yeah, you see that police tape over the zip? The stuff you had to tear off in order to get in here? I think that's meant to stop anyone coming in.'

'I'm not "anyone", though, am I?' he said, with what he probably thought was a charming smile, but I lived with Nathan and I knew what a charming smile really looked like. I looked at him with my eyebrows raised but didn't speak. He groaned. 'Bloody hell, it's really difficult dealing with other ex-cops, innit?' he said. 'I don't suppose you'll just bugger off and pretend you ain't seen me?'

'Not a chance,' I said. 'Not unless you tell me what's going on. You know more about this than you're letting on, don't you? Where's Rebecca? Why has she done a runner?'

He hesitated for a moment, and then plopped himself down on the bed. 'What do you know about her?' he asked.

'Absolutely nothing,' I said, 'or near as dammit. According to the rest of the band, Lee was madly in love with her, but she seems to barely appear in his life. We've got his address, but there doesn't appear to be anyone else living there, no bills in joint names, nothing.'

'No,' said Adam. 'He was being cautious. He didn't want what happened to Emily to happen to her. Especially not now.'

'"Not now"? What does that mean?'

'You'll see for yourself when you meet her.' He looked around. 'She said Lee had left a bag here.'

'You've spoken to her?'

'She texted me last night. I've been trying to get hold of her since I heard about Lee.' He got up and started looking around the tent again, but it wasn't that big and it must've been obvious fairly quickly that the bag wasn't there.

'The police have taken it,' I said. 'What did she say? Did she tell you why she left?'

'Yeah, she said when she realised Lee had been killed she was terrified. She said Lee had told her that if anything happened to him she should lie low, so she grabbed her stuff and legged it.'

'Why? If she was worried for her own safety she should've come to us. I mean the police,' I corrected myself. I gave Adam a tight grin. 'Force of habit. You know how it is.'

'Yeah.'

'Running away just makes her look suspicious, like she's hiding something. I mean, it could even make it look like she did it.' Adam laughed, irritatingly. 'What's so funny?'

'Like I said, you'll see when you meet her.'

'Okay. Nathan's *very* keen to meet her, or even just talk to her for starters. Did you give him her phone number?'

Adam shifted his feet. 'No. I forgot, okay? I meant to. There was just a lot going on last night when I got here. And jet lag—'

'Balls. Why are you keeping stuff from the police? Or even from me? I'm unofficial, just like you.'

'Because he wants to help his friend, and he's not convinced the police will do it properly,' said Tony, from the doorway of the tent. Adam rolled his eyes.

'Now who's this?' he said, exasperated.

'I'm someone who would probably be in prison now if Jodie hadn't got involved, because the police had got it wrong,' said Tony, and I thought, *I'm not sure that's helping…* 'She gets it, all right? She gets that you want to get justice for Lee and help his girlfriend, and you can trust her. You can even—' he swallowed hard '—you can even trust DCI Withers. Even if he is police, and a bit flash now and again.'

'Oi!' I said.

'Well, he is, ain't he? Not all the time, just when he's in police mode. It's all "you're nicked, sunshine" and that,' said Tony, and I had to stifle a giggle because Nathan *did* do that, only I liked it. 'But he's good as gold. A nice bloke and a good copper.'

Adam looked at the two of us for a moment, and then shook his head and sat down again. 'I give in. I'll tell you what I know, which ain't that much, to be honest. But I don't want you passing any of this on unless I say so, all right?'

'All right,' said Tony, going to sit down. 'But—'

'Tony, love, where are you?' called Mum. I looked at him and he sighed.

'On my way, Shirley,' he said, resigned, and headed back to the tent flap. But he stopped and turned to me first, and said in a low voice, 'You all right on your own here? Or shall I get Nathan?'

'Nah, it's all right, *sunshine*,' I said. I squeezed his arm to show him that I really did appreciate him looking out for me, and he left. I turned to Adam. 'Right, talk to me.'

'Okay,' he said. He took out his phone. 'I called Lee from Florida and told him that I'd tracked down the security guard and got his story. I told him I was emailing him the screenshots, but that he should wait until I got back and we could meet up at his house next week to discuss where we go from here.' He smiled thinly at me. 'I said to your DCI before that we'd decided to keep everything close to our chest, so that we could blackmail the guilty party into doing the right thing, the right thing being to pay back the money they'd embezzled. But I realised that Lee was more bothered about getting justice for Emily, and that would mean getting the police involved sooner or later. I told Lee I didn't know who was in the pictures, but if he did recognise them we should focus our investigation on getting a confession out of them or something, because, to be honest, proof is going to be almost impossible to come by, this long after Emily's death. And if we couldn't get anything tangible enough for the police, maybe we could still stick to the blackmail plan.'

'Okay. What did he say?'

'He agreed in the phone call to wait until I came home. He never replied to the email, so I assumed he couldn't identify who was in the photos either.'

'But it looks like he did,' I said. Adam nodded.

'Yeah, that's what I think. I think he confronted them, told them he knew what they'd done.'

'And they killed him.'

'Yes,' said Adam. He looked suddenly very sad, and very guilty. 'I can't help thinking I should've just kept the pictures to myself until I got back,' he said. 'I should've known how Lee would react. If someone killed one of your loved ones, how could you stop yourself confronting them?'

'It's not your fault,' I said. 'Most of us would *want* to confront them and say, "I know what you did," but most of us wouldn't actually do it. Most people would go to the police if they had proof. You can't blame yourself for Lee's reaction.'

'Up here—' Adam tapped his head '—I know you're right, but in here…' He placed his hand on his heart. 'I told DCI Withers that he was a client and a friend. Well, he was, but he was a friend first and foremost. We were accountability buddies. We checked in on each other to make sure we were both staying clean. I had a few wobbles when I came out of rehab, but Lee kept me on the straight and narrow. If it wasn't for him, I'd be back in rehab. Or worse.' He nodded towards the tent flap. 'I can understand why your friend out there came running in to your rescue. You saved him.'

'No I didn't,' I said, waving it away and trying not to feel uncomfortable.

'Yes you did,' insisted Adam. 'His life would've been completely ruined.'

'Anyway…' I tried to get the conversation back on track. 'What time was this phone call? What time did you last speak to him?'

Adam held out his phone to show me. 'I called him around lunchtime in Florida, so that would've been five o'clockish here. We only spoke for a couple of minutes, because I was sending him the photos and all the information again in the email. Which I sent…' He clicked on the mail icon on his phone and scrolled through. 'About an hour later.'

'Why the delay?'

'I was on my way to the airport. I hadn't expected to go to Florida, so I'd booked a return trip from London to New York. I had to get from Tampa to JFK to catch the flight back to London and I didn't have a lot of time. I waited until I was airside and I had twenty minutes before I had to board. It was a real rush.'

'Okay. And then you didn't hear from Lee again?'

'No, I didn't *talk* to him again. Later on he sent me a brief text asking me to come straight here rather than going home.'

'Did he say why he'd changed his mind?'

'No, but I assumed that he wanted the chance to talk it through with me while everyone was still here. Everyone connected with the band, I mean. Maybe he'd decided to do a big Hercule Poirot reveal in front of everyone, I dunno. I didn't see the text until later, though.

'I got back to New York,' he continued. 'I had some loose ends there to tie up before I got on my flight home. I wanted to see if I could get my hands on the original NYPD case file for Emily, but of course they wouldn't let me have a look and I didn't have enough time to argue about it. I wanted to go through the band's alibis, see if there were any that were less than watertight.'

'Yeah, that's Nathan's next move,' I said.

'I hope he has better luck than me.'

'Did Lee think it was someone in the band, then? It seems the most likely explanation,' I said. 'The person in those screenshots *could* be Ian Holt. He's about the same size and he used to work in investment banking, so he'd probably have the skills needed to embezzle money from Lee.'

'Yeah,' said Adam. 'I haven't met any of them, so physically I couldn't say who that looks like, but going by the background I have on them Ian is right up there on the list of suspects.'

'Did Lee think it could be him?'

'I don't know.' Adam frowned. 'I think he might have done, but at the same time he thought they were friends, so I don't think he wanted it to be him. I think they'd had a falling out in the past, but Lee thought that was all sorted.'

I knew what that falling out had been about – Lee, and later Emily, persuading Caz to take drugs. Maybe that was why Ian hadn't been as keen as Caz to resurrect the band and start touring again. 'Okay, so what happened next?'

'I got off the plane at Heathrow and there was a voicemail from Rebecca, telling me Lee had been killed and she didn't know what to do, and another one from Penstowan CID.' He looked at me grimly. 'And of course that text from Lee, telling me to come here. So I did. I kept trying to call Rebecca back, but there was no answer.'

'Why didn't you call CID until you got here?'

'Because I wanted to find out what the bloody hell

was going on first. I don't like being at a disadvantage.' He smiled. 'You strike me as the sort of person who likes to be kept in the loop, too.'

'Yeah. Living with the local DCI does have its advantages,' I said. 'But anyway, Rebecca: she texted you back last night? What exactly did she say?'

Adam found the message on his phone and held it out to me.

*Hi, sorry I didn't return your calls, been lying low with friends. So scared after what happened to Lee. Can you do me a favour? I was in a hurry to get away and I left Lee's bag at the yurt (#13), can you get it for me and text when you have it? And then we can meet?*

'Rebecca's got friends here, has she?' I asked. I didn't know Rebecca, but something about the text didn't ring true. Why was she so bothered about his bag? Nathan had checked and it was literally just three pairs of clean underpants and some T-shirts.

'She must have,' said Adam. 'Maybe she made friends with people staying nearby. She's from California, so I doubt she's got relatives or anything here.'

'She's American?' I asked. 'Has she lived over here a long time?'

'Not long. She was over here travelling when she met

Lee, and she just didn't go home again. About a year, I think. Why?'

I pointed to the text message. 'She's written "favour" with a "u" in it.' Adam looked blank. 'That's the British spelling. The American one would end in "or".'

'She might've got into the habit of spelling it our way,' said Adam, but he didn't look convinced. It would surely take more than a year for someone to integrate so completely into the British way of doing things that they spelt words differently.

'Maybe…' I swiped back to the message screen on Adam's phone and was about to hand it to him when I spotted something and did a double take. 'Is this the last text you got from Lee?' I said, selecting it.

'Yeah. Why?'

'He sent it at two in the morning,' I said. 'When he was already dead.'

## Chapter Seventeen

'Overlooking the fact that he should've come straight to me after Rebecca texted him,' said Nathan, his disapproval evident down the phone, 'this is very helpful. I'll be back as fast as I can.'

We were sitting in the security tent, which was still serving as an unofficial outpost of Penstowan Police. I'd rung Nathan, who had told me not to let Adam out of my sight under any circumstances until he got there. Lee Roskill's phone and financial records had finally come in (seriously, don't get yourself murdered over a weekend, because it really can hold things up; the legal departments of most phone companies and banks only work Monday to Friday, and we can't get a look at your records until they say so), and DC Sunil was already poring over them. Nathan had left Matt to have another chat with Caz, and then they would decide whether they had enough to charge her. The evidence against her said yes – just about – but I got the feeling that Nathan's gut said no. Mine said the same, but it could've been wishful thinking. Not that my gut could think – it didn't have a brain – although it did occasionally seem to have a mind of its own—

'Earth to Jodie,' said Adam, waving a hand in front of my face. 'What are you thinking?'

'I'm wondering who knew the password to get into Lee's phone,' I said. 'Even allowing for the fact that we can't pin down the exact time of death, Lee Roskill was definitely dead when that text message was sent to you. The killer must have sent it.'

'Yeah, I was thinking about that,' said Adam. 'If the killer told me to come here, then they want something from me, don't they?'

'Have you got a USB stick drive or something with the screenshots saved on it, and the security guard's statement?' I asked. 'Maybe they want that.'

'Of course I haven't. Who uses those nowadays? I saved everything on my phone, which also automatically saves it to the cloud, and I emailed it to myself as well, just to make sure. Belt and braces.' He looked serious.

'The best they could do to get rid of the evidence is to get rid of me and destroy my phone. It would still be in the cloud, of course, but they wouldn't necessarily know that.'

'If you were killed in suspicious circumstances, coming so soon after the death of your client, then we – I mean the police – would be sure to dig into your digital records anyway,' I pointed out. 'Even if they had your phone and deleted everything off it, there'd still be a trace of it left and Tech would be able to recover it eventually. If they knew what they were looking for, of course.'

'So our murderer might know all about swindling money out of people, but they don't know anything about modern policing,' said Adam. 'It's crazy how many people don't realise you can never really get rid of anything digital. It's all there on your hard drive, even after you delete it.'

We both looked up as Nathan came into the tent. He sat down next to me and slapped a file on the table in front of Adam. Adam raised an eyebrow.

'Is this the case file? I thought information only flowed one way,' he said. *Cheeky*, I thought. Nathan gave him a level stare.

'I haven't decided if I'm going to share it with you

yet,' he said. 'So I was wondering, if someone sent you a text message pretending to be Lee—'

'How would they get into his phone?' I interrupted. 'I know, we were just talking about that. They'd need his passcode.'

'They couldn't just use his fingerprint to open it?' asked Adam. Nathan shook his head.

'No, doesn't work on dead tissue,' he said. He turned to me with a smile on his face. 'Do you remember that time I pretended I'd cut off the victim's thumb and brought it back to the station with me so we could look at his phone…' Adam looked horrified. 'It was in the early days of our relationship,' Nathan explained quickly, 'and she wouldn't butt out of my investigation.'

'You surprise me,' said Adam, dryly.

'But anyway…who would know his passcode? I know yours,' I said to Nathan. 'What? Don't look so worried, I know you're not hiding anything from me. Believe me, I've checked… And you know mine, anyway. You know what it's like. One of you's driving and your phone goes off, so you get the other one to unlock your phone and read out the text message, that sort of thing.'

'Yes, that's what I'm thinking,' said Nathan. 'So for Lee, who could that be? Rebecca, probably.'

'Rebecca hasn't killed anyone, least of all Lee,' said Adam firmly.

'You know this how?'

'You'll understand when you meet her.' The private detective was adamant.

'If she's still around for us to meet,' I said. 'Show Nathan that text you had from her.'

'The little information we've finally found on her says Rebecca Greene is American,' said Nathan, reading it. 'But that's the British spelling.'

'Exactly!' I cried triumphantly, and then reined it in a bit, because if the text *wasn't* from Rebecca but from someone pretending to be her, then that could be very bad news indeed. 'So not only could the last text from Lee actually be from the murderer, then that one could be, too.'

'Shit,' said Adam. 'If anything's happened to her and the—'

'And the what?' asked Nathan, but it suddenly clicked why Adam was so convinced she hadn't murdered Lee. It also explained why Lee had suddenly started looking into his financial wellbeing.

'And the baby,' I said. 'She's pregnant, isn't she?'

Adam looked at us both for a second, and then nodded. 'Yeah, she is. Six months gone. So I know she wasn't out there on the rocks bashing the father-to-be's head in.' He sighed. 'Lee was so excited when he found he was going to be a dad. He hadn't told the band, because at that point he hadn't spoken to them for a while, but when it looked like he was going to play at the festival with them he decided he was going to introduce her and the bump to them.'

'Poor Rebecca,' I said. 'I can't imagine losing your partner anyway, but to be heavily pregnant at the time as well…'

'Is that why Lee started looking into his finances?' asked Nathan. 'You said he'd got his lawyer and his accountant to work out what his estate was worth.'

'Yeah, he wanted to make sure that the baby would be taken care of after his death,' said Lee. 'Not that he was expecting that to happen so soon. He told me he was going to leave his musical estate to his kid.'

'And that's how he realised that there was money missing?' I asked. Adam nodded.

'Yeah, I assume so. I don't really know anything about that side of it, other than it looked like what Emily had told him all those years ago was true. Someone was taking money that should've been going to him.'

'Okay, so let's take Rebecca off our list of suspects,' said Nathan. He didn't add 'for now' but I knew it was there anyway. 'Who else could get into his phone, and presumably hers as well, if we're following this theory?'

'Hold up,' I said. 'Along the same lines… What if Caz

is telling the truth and she really didn't get her phone back after the gig?'

'What?' Adam looked confused. 'What's *Caz's* phone got to do with anything?'

I hesitated and looked at Nathan, but he nodded. 'Go on.'

'Lee texted Caz on Friday night, asking to talk to her. This was while they were onstage, so she didn't see it straightaway. It would also have been after you sent him the email with the screenshots on it,' I said. 'Caz says she left her phone backstage, just as she always does during a gig, and when she came off stage she forgot all about it. When she went back the next morning to get it, it was gone.'

'But there's a text from her phone, replying to Lee and arranging to meet him on the beach at midnight,' said Nathan.

'Where he was then killed,' said Adam. I nodded. 'Shit. And that's why you've arrested Caz?'

'Yes. That, and her alibi is pretty vague. Her phone was found on the beach, that's how we saw the text messages between her and Lee,' I said. 'But that bothers me, as well. Uniform searched round the rocks before, and they didn't find it. A member of the public spotted it and told us. Chrissie – that's one of our PCs,' I told

Adam, 'Chrissie swears blind that they were really thorough. I know it's possible to miss things, but what if they didn't? What if the killer stole Caz's phone, replied to Lee's text message and lured him down to the rocks, and then planted the phone later on, so we'd find it?'

'But why not plant it when they killed him?' asked Nathan.

'I dunno. Maybe they were hoping we – I mean, you – would think it was an accident. They wouldn't want to leave anything that would make the police poke around. Without it, there was a chance that the police would just think Lee had got high and then fallen over on the rocks.'

'Just like they did with Emily in New York,' said Adam.

'Yes…' said Nathan, thoughtfully. 'And when it became obvious that we were treating it as murder, they planted Caz's phone to make her look like the murderer. That could be true. But that would mean the killer would have to have had access to Caz's phone after she left it backstage. They'd have to know her passcode, and Lee's, and possibly Rebecca's, too.'

'*Possibly* Rebecca's?' I asked.

'Because we shouldn't assume that she's dead,' said Adam. Nathan nodded.

'No, we shouldn't. She could be being held against

her will, or even be staying with the killer voluntarily, unaware of who they are. But that's if we really think that message wasn't from her, and we haven't got much to go on there.'

'That British spelling is doing a lot of heavy lifting,' I admitted. 'She might just spell it that way. And Caz might've dropped her phone while she was murdering Lee, and Uniform didn't find it.'

'But you don't think so,' said Nathan.

'No, I don't.' I sighed. 'But I don't know how far we can follow this line of reasoning at the moment. I think we should concentrate on finding Rebecca.'

'Me too,' said Adam.

'Me three,' said Nathan, 'which is why I have this.' He opened the folder in front of him. 'Lee's phone records.' He turned a piece of paper around so Adam and I could both read it. 'This is Rebecca's number, isn't it? Luckily she and Lee have the same phone provider, so while they were feeling cooperative we were able to go back and get her records, too.' He turned over another sheet of paper. 'My DC, Sunil, is worryingly good at sweet-talking organisations into giving us more information than we actually asked them for.'

'You wouldn't think it to look at him,' I said, 'but he is a total *master* at it.'

'We haven't had a chance to look at it properly yet,' said Nathan, 'but I see that Rebecca rang you, Adam, on Saturday morning at five past eleven. That's not long after word started getting out that a body had been found on the beach. That call lasted just under thirty seconds, long enough to leave you a voicemail.' Adam nodded. Nathan tapped at the paper. 'Twenty minutes later she rang someone else, and spoke to them for almost five minutes. Do you recognise that number? We will find it, of course, but I think we need to move as quickly as possible on this, just in case Rebecca is being held somewhere.'

'Let me have a look,' said Adam, taking out his phone. 'Lee gave me the band's contact details…' He looked up, surprised. 'That's Dougie McKay's number.'

'Did she know him?' I asked. Adam shook his head.

'No. Like I said, Lee hadn't spoken to any of them that much until just recently, while they were organising the festival gig, and he hadn't seen any of them in person for ages. I can't see how she would've met Dougie, or even spoken to him on the phone.'

'When we spoke to Mr McKay on Saturday he said he didn't know her,' said Nathan. 'And that would've been after she called him.'

'Hmm…' Adam thought for a moment. 'I don't know how much Lee told her about what was going on,' he said. 'I know he had this thing about protecting her from anything bad while she was pregnant, in case it stressed her and the baby out. But say he tells her he's going to meet Caz. When he doesn't come back, she assumes that Caz, and maybe Ian, have done him in, and she's scared.'

'You think he gave her Dougie's number and told her to call him if something bad happened?' I asked. Adam shrugged.

'I don't know. Maybe. Maybe he had the number written down somewhere and she found it.'

'So she rang McKay and told him what had happened, and he promised to hide her until it was safe for her to come forward,' mused Nathan. 'But if that's the case, why not come clean when we spoke to him?'

'Not everyone trusts the police,' said Adam. 'But that is still a bit weird.'

'Not if she thinks the killer is still on the loose,' I said. 'You've arrested Caz, but what if she thinks it was someone else? They're still free while you're concentrating your investigation on the wrong person. So she's not safe, is she?'

'But who else…?' asked Adam. 'I thought everyone else had an alibi?'

'Neil was supposedly on the phone to his missus—' I started. Nathan stopped me.

'He *was* on the phone to her. We checked.'

'Okay, but that doesn't mean he was where he says he was. He could have been down on the beach while he was talking to her.'

'Having a chat while he murdered someone?' said Nathan. He wasn't convinced, but at the same time I could see there was a spark of doubt in his eyes.

'Of course, there is one other theory,' I said, hesitating. Adam looked at me, curiously. 'Although it's not going to be a popular one. Maybe Rebecca *did* have something to do with Lee's murder, and she's convinced Dougie she's next or something so that he hides her until she can get away.'

'You're right,' said Adam, glaring at me. 'That's not a popular theory.'

'I'm just thinking aloud,' I protested. 'I'm not saying she was down there on the rocks herself, but she could've known about it or even organised it. We can't rule anything out.'

'And that's why not everyone trusts the police.' Adam stood up abruptly, and I realised I'd royally pissed him off. 'This isn't getting us anywhere. We need to find her. Where's Dougie staying? That's if he's not already left.'

'Up on the hill—' I started, stopping as I saw Nathan's tiny shake of the head. We didn't want Adam blundering in there. But we needn't have worried, because at that moment the private detective's phone beeped. We all looked at each other, stupidly, until I said, 'You should probably answer that.'

'It's Rebecca,' said Adam. 'Another text message. She wants to know if I've got Lee's bag yet.'

'Why is she so keen to get this bag?' I asked. 'I thought it just had his clothes in it.'

'Maybe she – or the killer,' said Nathan, looking at Adam apologetically, 'thinks there might be something in there that could incriminate them.'

'Is there?' asked Adam. Nathan shook his head. 'Would you tell me if there was?' Nathan shook his head again.

'No, probably not. But in this case there's nothing to tell. It really is just his clothes.' He held his hand out for Adam's phone, and after a slight hesitation Adam gave it to him. 'She wants to meet you on the cliff path,' said Nathan, reading the text. 'That's a nice, isolated spot.'

'Now *that's* not at all suspicious, is it?' I said. 'Particularly as we think the killer wants to get rid of Adam, as well. You do know what this means though, Nath? It means it's not Caz, because she's still in custody. And she was in custody when the first text from "Rebecca" came through.'

'I know,' said Nathan. 'Ian isn't, though. They could be in it together.'

'Or they could not be in it at all,' I said. 'So what do we do now?'

'We meet Rebecca, or whoever sent that text, on the cliff path,' said Nathan. He turned to Adam. 'How do you feel about being bait?'

## Chapter Eighteen

Contrary to what you might read in murder mysteries, or see in crime movies, the police really do not like using people as bait. You've only got to look at what normally happens in those stories to understand why. Normally it'll be the heroine offering herself up to draw out the killer. It always works; the killer is always daft enough to turn up, and it usually turns out all right in the end, but there's normally a moment when the heroine is left dangling by her (carefully manicured) fingertips over a pool of crocodiles or, literally in this case, off the edge of a cliff.

The Health and Safety Executive would have an absolute *meltdown* if the police actually did such a thing. So although Adam was going to agree to meet her, the might of the Penstowan police force (okay, I know that doesn't sound terribly threatening) would be lying in wait to jump Rebecca or Ian or whoever bloody turned up well before they got near enough to the private detective to lay a finger on him. Let alone push him off the edge of the cliff.

I found Daisy, Mum and the others, who were quite rightly a bit miffed that I'd volunteered everyone to help Morwenna clear up and then buggered off. Germaine was pleased to see me, but that was because she'd really enjoyed barking at piles of rubbish and then running into them, scattering them around so that they had to be swept up again. I was willing to bet Morwenna would not be offering to help me or the police again any time soon.

Everyone of course wanted to know what was going on, but there was no way I was going to tell them anything; they'd all be up on the clifftop themselves if I did, wanting to get a piece of the action as it happened. I made sure everyone could get home, Daisy with her friends as originally planned (the car park had thinned out now, and they could actually move Ellie's ancient Ford Fiesta), while Mum and Jocasta hitched a lift with Debbie. Tony and Carmen had arrived on a minibus with the other peace tent volunteers, and would be going home the same way.

Germaine, however, was going to stay with me, as she

had an important role to play. I was going to take her for a walk along Coast Road posing as 'innocuous dog walker #1', and see if I could spot any movement at Castaway Cottage. Matt had checked with the owners of the holiday cottage and discovered that Dougie had booked it until the following day, so as far as we knew he was still there. But was Rebecca with him? Had she holed up there to evade the police, or avoid becoming the next victim?

I'd overheard Nathan discussing the missing pregnant woman with Matt, along with the possibility that she could have been involved (somehow) with the murder, and that was why she was lying low.

'Being pregnant don't mean she couldn't have bashed his head in,' said Matt. 'My mum was still getting up and bringing the herd in for milking when she was in labour with my sister. She only started pushing once the last one was in the shed.' Matt had grown up at a dairy farm a few miles outside Penstowan, and it had come as a complete shock to his family that he'd joined the police rather than devote his life to cows. Having met his mother on a few occasions, it didn't surprise me in the least that she hadn't let a little thing like (literally) having a baby stop her from getting up at dawn and doing her farm chores. She was tough and determined, and she scared the hell out of me.

'Yes,' said Nathan diplomatically, 'but I think we're looking at Rebecca Greene being a co-conspirator, at most. There doesn't seem to be any obvious motive for her to want him dead, but the way she's disappeared is worrying. It *could* be seen as suspicious, but I think, to be honest, she's more likely to be in danger.'

I left the two men to organise the rest of the crew and headed across the site with Germaine. Sunil and Davey Trelawney would be in an unmarked Rover, parked in the car park of a café on Coast Road that had closed down the previous winter. PCs Brett and Chrissie would be on foot, posing as birdwatchers further down the path. I assumed 'posing as birdwatchers' simply meant they'd be in their civvies and carrying binoculars, which would come in very handy. Adam would be waiting somewhere near the cliff edge, where he could be seen by whoever had arranged to meet him (but not *too* near the edge), while Nathan and Matt lurked close at hand ready to leap out and shout, 'Gotcha!'

I reached the edge of the festival grounds, where the Terry Pratchett-reading security guard was still sitting. He looked more cheerful today though, the end of what must've been a very boring weekend finally in sight, and smiled as he spotted us approaching.

'All right?' he said.

'Yeah, all right?' I replied. This, for anyone not from

the UK, is the standard greeting when you meet someone, being neither aggressively unfriendly nor too sincere and emotional. It's an all-purpose acknowledgement that can be used on anyone from total strangers to your oldest and dearest friend. 'Almost time to go home?'

'Yeah, thank God. Not the most exciting job, but I got a lot of reading done.' He held up his book.

'Great book,' I said.

'Yeah. Love his work.'

'Yeah,' I said. He opened the gate in the security fence and let us through, Germaine giving him a friendly bark as she passed. 'I hope they paid you properly. Did you have to sit here all night as well, or did someone else take over?'

He laughed. 'Nah. Pay's all right but not enough to keep me sitting here in the dark, and no one else volunteered. But if anyone was brave enough to come along that cliff path in the pitch black just to get in here for nothing, well, let 'em in, I reckon.'

'Yeah, I reckon you're right,' I said, and we walked on. I stopped as Germaine sniffed at a bush and looked around. Up the hill, the path would eventually lead to that car park where Sunil and Davey were waiting. Down the hill, the path got closer to the cliff edge and then veered away towards Penstowan.

We walked on, Germaine enjoying the freedom after being kept on the lead so much over the last couple of days.

That car park up on Coast Road, I mused absentmindedly, must be the one Mum had told me about. I wondered if Davey knew that was where the twinkle in his father's eye had become too much for his mum to resist, and that he'd been conceived there. Weird. We turned up the path. In the distance, to my left, Castaway Cottage lay still and quiet. It really *was* quiet after the noise of the festival, although the faint sounds of people leaving, the stage being dismantled and roadies and bands packing up their equipment still reached my ears. But over that, the cries of the seagulls, waves breaking on the rocks below, and the hum of insects were a welcome respite from the *thud thud thud* of music that had been the main soundtrack to the weekend.

I couldn't risk getting too close to Castaway Cottage, not from here, where the gorse bushes had been cut back recently to keep the path clear, and weren't high enough to hide me. I headed up the path towards the road, keeping a discreet eye on the cottage, but there was nothing.

Until there was. Germaine, who had been running ahead of me and nosing in the bushes, had tried to pick something up in her mouth, but instead it had stuck to her muzzle. I watched as she comically tried to lick it off, her tongue not quite long enough to get to it. I laughed, and then stopped as I realised what it was. A festival wristband. Yellow, with a number 13 on it. Lee's or Rebecca's? It was a tough walk for a pregnant woman, especially in the heat of a summer's day, and we'd all kind of assumed that if Rebecca *was* with McKay then she'd got a lift there. Damn. I should've asked the security guard if he'd seen her. But I couldn't imagine walking up here when I was six months pregnant (to be fair, I had been *huge* with Daisy). If it was Lee's…well, he hadn't been wearing it when he was found, and we'd speculated that maybe the murderer had taken it, along with his wallet and anything else that might identify him easily. If so, had they dropped it as they made their escape?

And then I spotted the trail – not a true path that would be marked on the map we'd looked at earlier, when we'd been working out everyone's positions, but one that generations of feet had picked out and flattened, leading from the cottage onto the stony path that I now stood on. The one that led up to the road, or down to the festival. Where someone could easily climb over the gate in the dark, with no security guard to stop them, and follow the path that wound its way through the campsite, past the drug dealer's tent with the handy hoodie draped over a guy rope, there as an advertisement for Mr Dyer's pharmaceutical services but just ripe for using as an impromptu disguise. Because this murderer had done it before, hadn't they? They'd worn a 'Crew' hoodie in that New York hotel, one that every crew (and band) member had, that would have rendered them almost invisible amongst the other genuine crew members.

I stopped and took out a doggy poo bag, then hunkered down next to Germaine. She gave me a pathetic look.

'I know, sweetheart,' I said, 'Mummy's going to help you.' Using the poop bag as a glove, I pulled the wristband off her snout and wrapped it in the plastic bag; ideally, I'd have left it in situ, but not when the situ was a dog's nose. I took my phone out and dialled Nathan's number. As soon as he answered, I said, 'I've just worked out why you'd take someone home and spike their drink with no intention of assaulting them. And how you could unlock someone's phone without knowing their passcode…'

So the plan hadn't changed, but at least now we had an idea of who we were waiting for. And sure enough, at the time arranged, Dougie McKay opened the door of

Castaway Cottage and headed down the path. Chrissie, who like me had eyes on the cottage, radioed everyone, so Adam was ready. He headed up the path to meet McKay half way. McKay glanced down to the holdall in Adam's hand.

'You meeting Rebecca?' he asked. Adam's own well-hidden Airwave radio was on, so we could hear the exchange.

'Yeah. Who are you?' said Adam, tightening his grip on the sports bag, which was actually Matt's and held nothing more than his sweaty gym kit.

'I'm a friend of hers. She asked me to come along and make sure everything was okay.' He nodded back down the path. 'She's waiting for you down there.' He sounded charmingly convincing.

'Is she? I didn't see her,' said Adam.

'No? She'll be there in a minute,' said McKay. It was clear that he really wanted Adam to move; so they could talk somewhere more private, or so the cliff edge would be close enough for it to just take a quick shove and all his problems would be over? Probably both. 'She went for a walk earlier to get some fresh air. She said she'd meet us both there.'

'I'm in a hurry,' said Adam. 'The police have been trying to get hold of me. Just take the bag and I'll be off.' He held out the bag. McKay didn't reach for it, and from what I could see of his body language, from my position crouched behind a gorse bush further up the path, it looked to me like he didn't quite know what to do. This wasn't going how he'd expected it to.

McKay sighed and shook his head. 'This is awkward,' he said, in a reasonable tone of voice. 'Look, I know Lee hired you to look into a few things—'

'The death of Emily Logan? Yeah.' Adam dropped the bag on the ground in front of him. 'Don't you want to open it? See if there's a hoodie in there you can disguise yourself in?' McKay looked at him, hesitating. 'Yeah, that footage you wanted destroyed? It wasn't. Not completely. But you knew that, didn't you? Lee told you, when you met him on the beach.'

'Bloody Emily!' burst McKay. 'She was a manipulative, conniving cow. Pretending to be friends with my ex-wife, Natasha, who was too bloody stupid and self-obsessed to know what she was doing – digging for dirt on me, which she was only too happy to give her. And all the time, dripping poison into her ears, telling her she was better off without me. Emily Logan was just a pathetic bloody junkie, and then suddenly she's going on like she's some hotshot accountant, accusing me of stealing money from Lee—'

'Which you were,' said Adam, calmly. I wondered when Nathan and Matt would step in, but as McKay was doing a sterling job of confessing so far, I guessed they would wait. It was all being recorded on Adam's Airwave, so the more he talked, the better.

'Nothing I did was ever good enough for her!' snarled McKay. 'Natasha was constantly moaning that I didn't know the right people, I didn't take her to the right parties or drive the right car—'

'So you stole money from the band to fund the sort of lifestyle she wanted,' said Adam.

'None of them have ever had any idea how much I do for them!' spat McKay. 'Neil would be a washed-up alcoholic if it wasn't for me. Caz and Ian, swanning around like love's young dream and leaving me to pick up the pieces with Lee all the time – he was their bloody friend, not mine!'

'Pick up the pieces?' said Adam, incredulously. 'You never let him get clean. He told me, you made sure there were always drugs floating about. You knew the dealers in every single city the band played in, and you made sure they always got backstage or into the hotel. It suited you to keep Lee off his tits so you could manipulate him. Because you knew he was at the heart of the band. If he agreed to do something, the others would eventually follow, because he was their leader.

'On the night of Emily's death you made sure you were wearing a crew hoodie during the gig, so that you'd blend in. You told the NYPD that you were backstage at the time of Emily's death, and the crew went along with it because they couldn't say for certain that you weren't. But you slipped out and went back to the hotel, which was right next door, and went up to her room. Maybe you didn't mean to kill her, maybe you just meant to talk to her, but it all went wrong. Afterwards you realised you'd been picked up on the security cameras, so you did what you always did – you went and "picked up the pieces", found the security guard and bribed him with the money that you always had on hand to pay drug dealers. You thought you'd got away with it, because the others in the band didn't like her and were too self-absorbed to really care, and the NYPD had enough on their plate without worrying about another dead junkie.'

Adam took a step forward, until his nose was almost touching McKay's. 'But you reckoned without Lee. You wrote *him* off as a stupid junkie too. But he knew it wasn't right, and he found you out. *I* found you out.'

McKay stepped back, and I thought for a moment he would turn and walk back to the cottage. But then he drew something out of his pocket: a carving knife, probably taken from the kitchen of the holiday cottage. Its long blade glinted in the sunlight.

'Knife!' I shouted, leaping up. Germaine started to bark her furry little head off, and suddenly, where there had apparently just been gorse bushes, there now stood almost the entire Penstowan police force. McKay looked bewildered and dropped the knife, as Chrissie and Brett tackled him to the ground and Nathan looked down at him in satisfaction.

'You're nicked,' said Adam, just as Nathan opened his mouth to say it himself. Nathan looked at him and grinned.

'All right, sunshine, I'll let you have that one,' he said.

'Rebecca!' said Adam, yanking hard on McKay's arm. 'Where is she?'

'I never hurt her,' said McKay. 'She's at the cottage.'

Nathan felt in the now subdued man's pocket and drew out a door key. I grabbed it and raced up the path towards Castaway Cottage, Germaine following hard on my heels. I could hear Chrissie following behind me, but I had a head start and got there first.

I burst in through the front door. 'Rebecca?' I cried. 'Where are you? It's the—' I hesitated, but then for the sake of expediency finished 'the police!'

Germaine yapped and rushed up the stairs. I looked at Chrissie, who was in the doorway behind me. She shrugged, and both of us followed the dog, who was by now flinging herself at a closed door. It was locked. Chrissie gently moved me out of the way and shoulder-barged it, forcing it open, and I ran in as she recovered.

A heavily pregnant woman in her thirties was propped up awkwardly in a chair, hands and legs tied together and a strip of fabric forming a gag in her mouth. I pulled it away and held her as she took some deep breaths, brushing straggly strands of her long, sweat-soaked dark hair away from her face.

'Are you okay?' I asked, although it was a bit of a daft question. Chrissie tugged at the rope around her hands and legs, freeing them. 'Did he give you anything?'

'No,' she said. 'He threatened to drug me if I didn't do what he wanted. He said it would hurt the baby, so I did it. I unlocked my phone so he could send Adam a text. Is Adam okay?'

'Yes,' I said.

'Lee…' she began, and then dissolved into tears.

'Come on,' I said, 'let's get you to the hospital and get you checked out.'

# Chapter Nineteen

So *of course* I wanted to be in on the police interview back at the station, but *of course* I wasn't allowed to because I was a caterer, not a police officer anymore. But as I'd said to Adam before, being engaged to the local DCI did have its perks (other than him being a complete hunk of sexiness).

We'd eaten dinner and washed up by the time Nathan got back from the station, and I was having my usual end-of-the-day cup of tea, sitting on the stone wall that separated our back garden from the sheep field behind our house. Mum's granny annex was finished by now, and out the back of it was a lovely little patio garden which she'd filled with pots of flowers; the only ones I could name were the geraniums, which had been my grandmother's favourite, but there were many others, all bright, colourful and fragrant. It had been a complete surprise to see her tend these pots so carefully, because I couldn't recall her ever showing any real interest in gardening before. We all change, I suppose. But one thing that didn't change was that I would always end up on that wall, usually facing the other way, looking above the heads of our sheep neighbours and over the field to the sea that lay beyond.

Nathan had his own mug of tea in hand as he settled on the wall next to me.

'So that's that,' he said, and then – infuriatingly – shut up. He sipped his tea and waited for me to say something. I struggled not to, but you know what I'm like.

'Oh come on! You can't leave it like that! Was I right?'

Nathan laughed. 'Yes, your theory was pretty much correct from what Dougie McKay coughed up, although we are still waiting for forensics on Dyer's hoodie and that to back it up in case he suddenly decides to plead not guilty. And we're tracking down his ex-wife, because apparently she knew what he'd done with the money and had let it slip to Emily.'

'He did Lee out of a lot of royalties, then?'

'Yeah. I don't really get it, but there's a team of

forensic accountants going over his accounts as we speak.' He frowned and looked at his watch. 'Well, they will do, in the morning. It sounds like he stitched the whole band up when they signed the deal for their third album, right around the time his marriage was getting into difficulties. They got paid a massive amount upfront for the recording studio and all that, but he managed to channel a lot of it his way. Not into his bank account, of course, but various shell company accounts and the like. You know he said he was friends with the band, and that's how he became their manager? Well, that wasn't strictly true. He worked with Ian, and he used that to worm his way into a few gigs for free. He did help make them a success, but he certainly paid himself well for it.'

'All that time we suspected Ian could've been defrauding Lee…,' I said. 'If only we'd known Dougie had exactly the same financial skills.'

'If not better,' said Nathan, 'because he was higher up in the company than Ian was.'

'He told us that he mothered the band and did everything for them when they were on tour,' I said. 'Is that how he knew Caz and Lee's phone passcodes?'

'Yep. He knows Ian and Neil's, too. To be fair, they might've just used their birthdays, like everyone else does,' he said, looking at me meaningfully. Because yes, I was guilty of using things that were easy for me to remember, and potentially easy for other people to guess. 'He tried to get into Lee's emails, but Lee had changed his password, probably because he suspected McKay knew it.'

'So Lee got the email from Adam, with the screenshots attached,' I said. 'Lee recognised Dougie, and texted Caz that he needed to talk to her about something on her own. McKay can't have known what that was, but he must have suspected.'

'Guilty conscience,' said Nathan, nodding. 'Maybe Lee said something during the argument earlier on that made him realise that he knew about the fraud, even if he didn't know about Emily.'

'McKay saw the text come through, saw it was from Lee and decided to read it, in case it incriminated him,' I said. 'When he saw it, he knew he had to stop Lee telling anyone else what he suspected, so he stole the phone and waited until he was back at the cottage, when he texted Lee back pretending to be Caz.'

'Yep. He waited until he was back at the cottage, because he wanted to make sure he had an alibi.'

'That girl, what's her name—'

'Lucy. Yeah. He picked her because, in his words, she looked like a "typical tattooed junkie festivalgoer".'

'Nice.'

'I get the impression she reminded him of Emily, which made it easier for him to drug her. He really hated Emily, because he blamed her for his marriage failing. He already had Rohypnol with him because he sometimes has trouble sleeping. He gave Lucy enough to knock her out, thinking that she'd probably taken stuff at the festival, and, if she couldn't remember what happened that night, she'd put it down to whatever drugs she'd voluntarily taken. So he could use her as an alibi and she'd confirm it.'

I snorted. 'But he picked the wrong "junkie", because she hadn't even had that much alcohol, let alone taken anything stronger. And then he threatened Rebecca with it too, so he could use her fingerprint to open her phone without her permission.'

'Yes, but he didn't, thank God, because that could've hurt the baby. I think he'd planned to, but when he saw her baby bump he locked her in the bedroom and told her she'd go the same way as Lee if she didn't unlock her phone for him.'

'He was hardly going to let her go though, was he, even if she cooperated. He must've been planning to kill her too.'

'Yeah, he won't admit to it but he couldn't let her live.

I think a part of him is relieved he got caught and didn't have to kill her. Like us, he hadn't even known she was at the festival until she called him. Apparently Lee had given Rebecca the band's numbers, in case anything happened to him, so she had someone she could call if she needed help. He told her he was meeting Caz, so when he didn't come back she jumped to the same conclusion that we did – that Caz or Ian or both of them had done him in. So she called McKay, who arranged to meet her and take her back to the cottage. Do you remember, when we spoke to him on Saturday morning he was on the phone? Well, you won't believe it, but he was organising a lift to take him and Rebecca back to the cottage.'

'Bloody hell,' I said. 'It was happening in front of our noses.'

'Yeah.' Nathan grinned. 'You must be losing your touch, Nosey Parker.'

'Cheeky!' I said. 'So why was he so obsessed with getting Lee's bag?'

'Oh, he wasn't. It was just an excuse to get Adam onto the clifftop. He needed to make sure he had all the evidence Adam had collected, and then he was going to get rid of it.'

'And Adam.'

'Yeah, he hasn't admitted to that last bit being part of

the plan, but going by the fact he pulled a knife on him in front of all of us, he can't exactly deny it.'

'So the night Lee died – he got a lift back to the cottage with Lucy and her friend, made a point of making a lot of noise so the owners in the cottage next door would hear them, and then drugged her,' I said. Nathan nodded. 'And once she was safely asleep—'

'Unconscious.'

'That's what I meant – he texted Lee. Then he walked down the path and through the side entrance of the festival. How did he even know about the path? It's not very well signposted. I didn't even know it went up near the cottages.'

'The owners told him about it,' said Nathan. 'They thought he might want to go birdwatching or something.'

'I'd file him in the "or something" category,' I said. 'Did he know the side entrance would be unguarded?'

'No, he didn't even realise there was a gate. He was expecting to climb over the fence,' said Nathan. 'But he had worked out the route down to the beach. He'd been to Caz's yurt earlier and saw the path through the campsite.'

'Where he found Paul Dyer's hoodie,' I said.

'Yes,' said Nathan. 'We'll check for his DNA on it, and Lee's, but he's already admitted to borrowing it.'

'What about Adam? How is he, after having a knife pulled on him?'

'Oh, don't worry about him, he'll be dining out on this case for *years,*' said Nathan. 'He's made of tough stuff, that one. Shame he had to quit his police career, although I think I might just have persuaded him to see if he can go back. He's clean now, and he's definitely got the talent for it.' He shrugged. 'Mind you, he might prefer to stay as a private investigator. I've certainly never been flown to New York on a case.'

'I was going to ask you about that. Any chance that Dougie will go down for Emily's murder, too?'

'That's down to the NYPD, not us,' said Nathan. 'But this must give them reason enough to reopen her case. If the hotel security guard will testify, and can identify McKay as the man who bribed him, then it must look good for a prosecution. And if his ex-wife testifies as well he won't have a leg to stand on.'

'That's good,' I said. I took a deep breath. 'What about Caz and Ian? Where are they now?' I couldn't help feeling guilty for suspecting them, even though it was only briefly, and even though I had never wanted it to be true. I wasn't deluded enough to think that my teenage rock idol and I would ever be the best of friends, but I had liked her and I thought we'd got on. Too much to expect that we still would.

'She's back home.' Nathan took my hand and smiled gently at me. 'I told her you were the one who worked it out, so hopefully she'll still hire you to do her next dinner party.'

I laughed. 'I wasn't worried about that anyway. Where else is she going to get a caterer like me?'

# Epilogue

'Jodie, come through and have some cake.'

I was back in the kitchen of Hilltop Farm. Nathan had been wrong about me catering the Holts' next dinner party (I wasn't even sure if they'd had one), but here we were, six months later, helping her throw a belated baby shower for Rebecca and baby Leah.

Caz (I couldn't go back to calling her Carol) handed me a plate of chocolate fudge cake and a glass of champagne, as three-month-old Leah was bounced up and down on the knee of her godfather, Adam. They both seemed to be equally smitten with each other. Rebecca, with her long, dark hair and flawless pale skin, looked like something out of a Pre-Raphaelite painting. She sat next to him, watching them both intently.

'Isn't she beautiful?' said Caz. For a moment I

wondered if she meant Rebecca or the baby, but either way I had to agree. All babies are beautiful, even the ones who look uncannily like Winston Churchill (which is a higher number than you'd expect). And Rebecca, despite the dark circles under her eyes from lack of sleep, and despite the sadness and pain that had surrounded the end of her pregnancy, looked happy.

'Broody?' asked Ian, slipping an arm around his wife's waist. Caz looked at me and we both laughed.

'Oh dear God, no,' she said. 'Although I might do what Jodie did, and get a cute dog as a baby substitute.' The cute dog baby substitute pricked up her ears for a moment, farted, and then went back to sleep in front of the fire.

Nathan, who was sitting on the other side of Adam, laughed as Leah bopped her godfather on the nose with her teddy. Ian leant over to me and spoke in a low voice.

'What about *him*? Do you reckon he's broody?' He nodded towards Nathan.

I was saved from answering that by the tinkle of someone tapping on a wine glass. Neil, who was looking much better groomed and rather more sober than we'd previously seen him, stood in the manner of someone who was about to make a speech.

'Make it a quick one, drummer boy,' said Caz, and everyone laughed.

'I just wanted to say welcome to the family, Rebecca and Leah.' Neil smiled, and I was surprised to see the sudden glint of tears in his eyes. He might, in his own words, hit things and make a loud noise for a living, but he was a big softy. I got the impression he was taking his responsibilities as honorary uncle and protector of his late friend's loved ones very seriously. His wife, who was small and delicate next to him, reached for his free hand and gave it a loving squeeze. 'If you ever need anything, all you have to do is call or text or email or, I dunno, send out the bat signal, and one of us—'

'*All* of us,' corrected Caz, smiling warmly at Rebecca.

'*All* of us, yes, will be there for you. Because you're one of the band now.' At that, Leah gave a loud, gurgling giggle, and everyone laughed. 'You sound just like your dad, when we were recording our difficult third album…'

'To Lee,' said Caz, holding up her wine glass, and we all followed suit.

'Lee…'

And the baby gurgled.

# Acknowledgments

I was trying to think of a suitably musical metaphor or simile for producing this book. I was going to suggest that, like a concert (classical music, I think, rather than rock and roll), it's very much a collaborative process. I'm in the Brass section, blowing my own trumpet and playing all the right notes (but not necessarily in the right order). Over in Woodwind, (super) agent **Lina Langlee** from The North Literary Agency, and her fearless stunt double **Caro Clarke** from Portobello Literary, pipe up at regular intervals to support me. The Percussion section is made up of friends who are always happy to bang the drum about my books, and who keep the beat (and me) going when times are tough: fellow writers and all-round good eggs **Nina Kaye, Sandy Barker, Andie Newton, Carmen Radtke** and **Jade Bokhari** (I talk to these ladies pretty much every day, and I couldn't do it without them). And all the while the conductor, my lovely editor at One More Chapter, **Jennie Rothwell**, waves her baton around and keeps everyone in check.

I *was* going to use this musical metaphor, but it felt a bit tortured, so I won't.

Thank you to everyone mentioned above, plus my brother-in-law **Paul Dyer** - thank you for letting me make you a drug dealer - and to my old chum **Neil Hiller**. Sorry for turning you into a drummer; next time I promise I'll make you a bass player.

The last (and as always, biggest) thanks go to the two loves of my life, my husband **Dominic** and son **Lucas**. Thank you for listening to my mad ideas, for being guinea pigs when I'm trying out a new recipe, and most of all for not freaking out when we're out somewhere for the first time and I go, "ooh, that would be a fantastic place to hide a dead body!"

The author and One More Chapter would like to thank everyone who contributed to the publication of this story...

**Analytics**
Abigail Fryer
Maria Osa

**Audio**
Fionnuala Barrett
Ciara Briggs

**Contracts**
Sasha Duszynska
Lewis

**Design**
Lucy Bennett
Fiona Greenway
Liane Payne
Dean Russell

**Digital Sales**
Hannah Lismore
Emily Scorer

**Editorial**
Kate Elton
Arsalan Isa
Charlotte Ledger
Bonnie Macleod
Janet Marie Adkins
Jennie Rothwell
Tony Russell

**Harper360**
Emily Gerbner
Jean Marie Kelly
emma sullivan
Sophia Walker

**International Sales**
Bethan Moore

**Marketing & Publicity**
Chloe Cummings
Emma Petfield

**Operations**
Melissa Okusanya
Hannah Stamp

**Production**
Emily Chan
Denis Manson
Simon Moore
Francesca Tuzzeo

**Rights**
Rachel McCarron
Hany Sheikh
Mohamed
Zoe Shine

**The HarperCollins Distribution Team**

**The HarperCollins Finance & Royalties Team**

**The HarperCollins Legal Team**

**The HarperCollins Technology Team**

**Trade Marketing**
Ben Hurd

**UK Sales**
Laura Carpenter
Isabel Coburn
Jay Cochrane
Sabina Lewis
Holly Martin
Erin White
Harriet Williams
Leah Woods

**And every other essential link in the chain from delivery drivers to booksellers to librarians and beyond!**

## Jodies's tried and tested recipes #7

### Sausage and Leek Hand Pie

So of course the recipe this time had to be a pie! But which one…?

I was going to say 'fanfare, please!' before revealing which pie has made the cut (slice?), but the subtitle of this section has completely spoilt the surprise and you already know the result. But why did I choose this one? I did consider the Hans Gruber pie made with bratwurst and sauerkraut, as it was surprisingly tasty, but it's definitely *ein bisschen ein erworbener Geschmack**, so I thought I'd do an Anglicised version of it instead (which is kind of like a supercharged sausage roll). If you're a fan of sauerkraut (or 'Die Hard') you can swap the leeks out and use a good dollop of it, because both work just as well.

*a bit of an acquired taste. I'd hoped the German version would be fairly easy to work out in context, something along the lines of 'eine kleine acquired taste' or whatever, but - nope. But then what else do you expect from the language that came up with the 63-letter-long word *'rindfleischetikettierungsüberwachungsaufgabenübertragungsgesetz'*? (Real word, look it up!) Honestly, it's just the wurst…

In honour of my American readers (hello!) I've called it a hand pie (not to be confused with a finger pie, which has nothing to do with food and for the love of all that is holy DO NOT look that up** if you're easily shocked), but depending on where you are in the world you might know it as a pasty, an empanada, a turnover or a samosa. Or if you're Greggs (popular UK bakery chain and purveyor of the world's best cheese and bacon pastries) you'd probably call it a slice or a bake. I daren't call it a pasty, lest the ghosts of a thousand Cornishmen rise from their graves and berate me for using sausage meat and not skirt steak. Basically, it's a pie that you can eat on the move, and in this case, one you can easily shape by hand - you don't need to use a pie dish.

**really, don't look it up. It's very, *very* rude. You'll regret it. Don't say I didn't warn you.

On with the recipe! Makes four individual pies:

1. First take some good quality uncooked **sausages** and take the skins off. You can use spicy ones, herby ones, or just some plain pork bangers - I allow one per pie / per person, but it all depends on how hungry / greedy you are… Mash up the sausage meat in a bowl with a fork.

2. Finely chop **1 leek** and crush **2 cloves of garlic** (or use **1tsp garlic paste**), then fry both in a little **olive oil** and / or a **knob of butter** until soft and just starting to turn golden (but not brown). Or skip this part and just use the previously-discussed dollop of sauerkraut. Add to the sausage meat.

3. Add **1-2tsp mustard** of your choice (I prefer Dijon mustard as it's not as hot as English, but still gives the dish a good tang) and a couple of chopped **sage leaves** to the sausage meat and leek mixture. Season with **salt** and **pepper**. Stir to combine - I like to get my (clean) hands into the

mix to really squidge it all together - and form the mixture into a loose patty.

4. Take **1 sheet ready made puff pastry** and cut into four rectangles. Divide the sausage patty into four. Lay one on one end of a pastry rectangle. Brush around the edges of the pastry with **beaten egg** and then fold over to cover and seal in the sausage meat mixture. Repeat with the other patty and pastry rectangles, then brush them with the remaining beaten egg. Prick the top of each pie with a fork or cut a small hole, to let steam escape while cooking.

5. Bake in a preheated oven at **190°C/370°F** for about 30 minutes until the pastry is golden. You can either leave to cool and eat it on the go (great for a picnic!) or serve warm with mashed potato and gravy. Yum!

You could make this vegan by using vegan sausages (cooking time would probably stay the same, but do check before eating!) and brushing with plant-based milk or aquafaba instead of the egg. Most shop bought puff pastry is vegan, but do check that it's made with vegetable oil rather than butter.

All that's left to do now is pop on a (rather grubby) white vest, drop out of the nearest air vent and cry "yippee pie yay, mother fudgers!"***

***none of this will make any sense if you haven't watched 'Die Hard'. Go and watch it. Now.

Happy eating!

Have you read the other books in the Nosey Parker series?

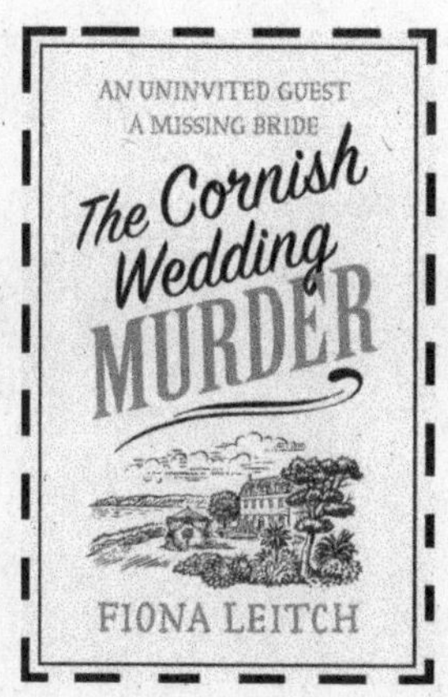


Still spinning from the hustle and bustle of city life, Jodie 'Nosey' Parker, is glad to be back in the Cornish village she calls home. But with a missing bride on her hands, murder and mayhem lurks around every corner…

Have you read the other books in the Nosey Parker series?

When a body turned up at her last catering gig it certainly put people off the hors d'oeuvres. With a reputation to salvage, Jodie's determined that her next job for the village's festival will go off without a hitch.

But when chaos breaks out, Jodie Parker somehow always finds herself caught up in the picture…

**Can she find the killer before the village faces another brush with death?**

Have you read the other books in the Nosey Parker series?

A film company is coming to the Cornish village of Penstowan, and the whole community turn up to be cast as extras, even Jodie 'Nosey' Parker.

But right on cue, the company's caterer is sabotaged and Jodie must step up. It soon becomes clear that someone is out to spoil the filming… With actors behaving out of character and the house literally being brought down, breaking a leg is the least of their worries.

**Can Jodie save the day once again, or will it be their final curtain call?**

Have you read the other books in the Nosey Parker series?

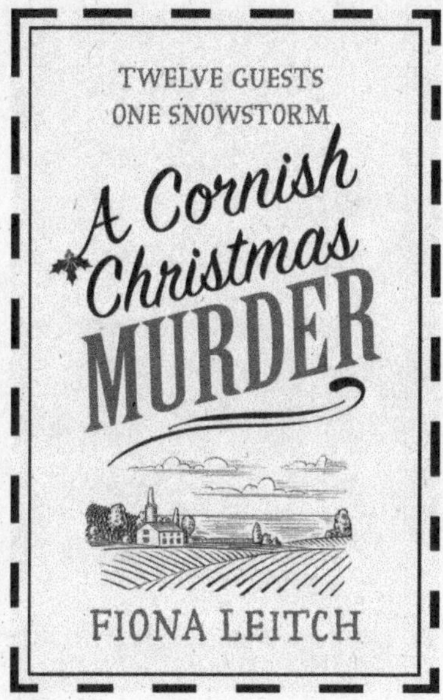


**A PINCH OF PARANOIA**

It's three days before Christmas, and detective-turned-chef Jodie 'Nosey' Parker is drafted in to cater an event run by a notorious millionaire at a 13th-century abbey.

**A DASH OF DECEPTION**

Things get more complicated when a snowstorm descends, stranding them all…

**A MURDER UNDER THE MISTLETOE**

Secrets mull in every corner – can Jodie solve the crime before the killer strikes again?

Have you read the other books in the Nosey Parker series?

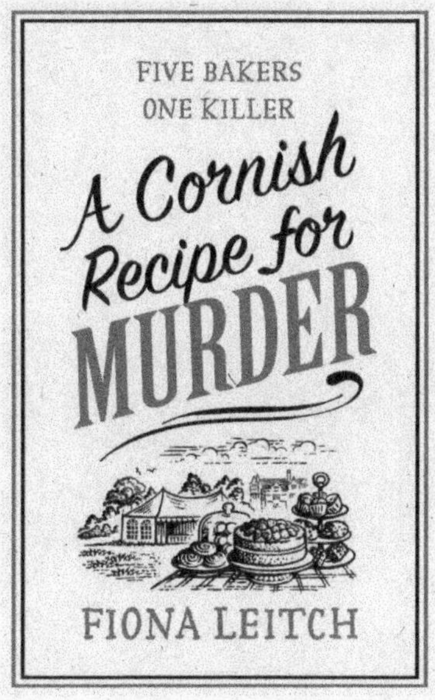


When 'The Best of British Baking Roadshow' rolls into town and sets up camp in the grounds of Boskern House, former police officer Jodie 'Nosey' Parker finds herself competing to represent Cornwall in the grand final.

But with a fellow contestant who will stop at nothing to win, Jodie discovers that the roadshow doesn't just have the ingredients for the perfect showstopper cake, but also for the perfect murder…

**Can Jodie expose the culprit? Or will the murderer become the real showstopper?**

Have you read the other books in the Nosey Parker series?

**A Siren's call... to murder**

While tourists and locals alike are falling under the spell of the annual mermaid festival with its captivating legends of Sirens luring fishermen to their deaths, Jodie and Nathan fear they may have found themselves in the middle of a very real – and very dangerous – turf war.

As the casualties start to stack up, they must face the likelihood that something sinister has been going on under their noses for some time...

One More Chapter is an award-winning global division of HarperCollins.

Subscribe to our newsletter to get our latest eBook deals and stay up to date with all our new releases!

signup.harpercollins.co.uk/join/signup-omc

Meet the team at
www.onemorechapter.com

Follow us!

@OneMoreChapter_
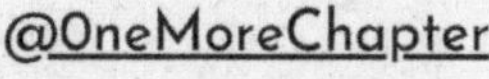
@OneMoreChapter
@onemorechapterhc

Do you write unputdownable fiction?
We love to hear from new voices.
Find out how to submit your novel at
www.onemorechapter.com/submissions

Fiona Leitch is a novelist and screenwriter with a chequered past. She's written for footballing and motoring magazines, childbirth videos and mail order catalogues; DJ'ed at illegal raves in London, been told off by a children's TV presenter during a studio debate; and was the Australasian face of a series of TV commercials for a cleaning product. All of which has given her a thorough grounding in the ridiculous, and helped her to write funny stuff.

facebook.com/fionakleitch
instagram.com/leitchfiona

## Also by Fiona Leitch

**The Nosey Parker Cozy Mysteries**

*The Cornish Wedding Murder*

*The Cornish Village Murder*

*The Perfect Cornish Murder*

*A Cornish Christmas Murder*

*A Cornish Recipe for Murder*

*A Cornish Seaside Murder*